CYANIDE

ELLA FIELDS

DEDICATION

To the man who taught me the importance of staying
true to myself.

You left this earth too soon, and before you
could see that happen.

But this one's for you, dad.

*To fall in love is to expose yourself
to the worst danger imaginable; heartbreak.*

PROLOGUE

Jared

Standing across the street from the high-rise apartments that tower over the city below, I lift my cigarette to my mouth and inhale deeply. As I exhale, I watch that same window while the smoke drifts into white tendrils that curl around my face before dissipating into the cold night air.

A car honks and a baby cries somewhere in the apartments above. Sirens blare from the slums on the south side of Rayleigh. The noise of this damn city has become the soundtrack to my life. A haunting kind of comfort that reminds me of who I am, what I've done, and what I've still yet to do. The businesses and apartments, the run-down, vandalized husks, the subway, the skyscrapers that loom threateningly above everything—all of it. Sometimes, I feel like it could suffocate me at any given moment.

But I learned a long time ago not to let this modern-day

jungle make me its bitch. Nothing can have that kind of power over you unless you allow it to.

At least, that's what I thought.

Because some months ago, I learned you're not always in control of how you feel. That particular lesson came in the form of a beautiful, blond-haired, brown-eyed woman. A woman who was married. A woman I thought I could have some harmless fun with. A woman who was forever out of reach, no matter how much I longed to change that. I knew that, so I submitted to the inevitable and backed off before it was too late.

And still, she stole something from me.

I should've learned from it. I thought I did.

It was another lesson, after all, even if I did escape with my heart in one slightly battered piece, and I'm all about not repeating stupid shit.

I thought I'd seen beautiful.

Until I met her.

I thought I'd seen all this damn city had to offer.

Until I met her.

I thought I knew the risks, the careful game of push and pull enough to not come close to falling victim to that fucking four-letter word again.

But I've never been more wrong in my life. And I've done a lot of wrong shit, let me tell you.

Though nothing of this magnitude.

And now, the poison has spread too far, too fast. Except, this time … it's so much worse. Because something wasn't just stolen from me. I didn't trip and start to stumble like an idiot who missed a step off the side of the curb.

No.

It wasn't enough to steal my heart and the very essence of who I am.

This time, it's taken over every vital part of me. Clawing and caging itself in. Slithering throughout every one of my veins until it found a home for her within the marrow of my fucking bones.

It's too late. I can't dig her out.

And the crazy thing is, I don't know if I ever want to.

She may have made me its victim, but what she doesn't know is I'm willing to let it destroy me. That I'll gladly endure the suffering if it means she'll be mine once again.

But she's about to find out.

CHAPTER ONE

T he walls are painted red. All of them. A deep, dark red that seems to pulse in an unnerving, unnatural rhythm. A rhythm beating in sync with my own heart— thundering in my chest and echoing in my ears like a gong.

"And here's the kitchen."

My gaze moves from the walls to fall on the busty blond real estate agent who keeps not-so-subtly yanking her ugly cream blouse lower over her ample chest.

"I'd stop that if I were you," I suggest. "Unless, of course, you like exposing your nipples to your clients." I let my eyes roam briefly over the kitchen, barely taking in the black and gray marble countertops and state-of-the-art appliances. Spying the back door, my feet take me to it as I mutter, "Sorry, my mistake. You probably do."

She sucks in a loud breath behind me, and Dexter quickly rushes in with apologies before saying, "Give us a moment, please."

I pause on the wooden deck outside, and he joins me, closing the glass door behind him. A pool big enough for ten Olympic swimmers to do laps in takes up residence just beyond the deck, and below it all, the bay. Water laps gently against the sand as I stare down at it.

This place is huge. It's too big. *Too much.*

Yet it's everything I always envisioned myself having one day.

"Vera," Dexter hisses. "That was uncalled for. What's wrong with you?"

The breeze stirs some of my long black hair into my face. *What's wrong with me?*

"The walls are red." I tuck my hair back behind my ear and watch a dog chase a Frisbee into the shallow water of the bay.

He breathes out a disbelieving laugh. "*What?*" He grabs my arm, turning me to face him.

"I said …" I blink, trying to focus on his handsome, clean-shaven face. But all I can seem to make out is the brown of his eyes. "That the walls are red."

He shakes his head, a few tendrils of his brown hair coming loose and falling over his forehead. He runs his hand through it, smoothing them back. "I heard you. And you know we can change that."

We can change that. The words slam into my ears with a force so different from what he intended with his soft, worried tone. They swim violently in my head, thrashing against one another until it's suddenly hard to breathe. "Can we go? I need to go." I step back, moving toward the door.

"Vera … wait."

I don't wait. Stepping inside, I walk straight past the disgruntled real estate agent until I reach Dexter's Maserati parked in the circular driveway out front.

It takes him five minutes, but he finally joins me and unlocks the car. I climb right in, my eyes closing as I sink back into the leather seat.

"You going to tell me what that was all about?" he asks, starting the car and speeding out of the driveway.

He wouldn't understand, and if I'm being honest, I don't even think I understand myself.

"It just wasn't right," I settle on saying.

He scoffs, turning out of the neighborhood. "Care to tell me why? It was perfect, and it's probably going to be snatched up any day now."

He sighs when I don't elaborate. My eyes stare unseeingly out the passenger window until we reach the turn off to the highway that'll take us back to Rayleigh. I look over at him then, studying his profile and the way his eyes narrow while he stares intently at the stretch of road ahead. His brows lower, and he chews his bottom lip in clear frustration.

"You're going to make an offer on it anyway, aren't you?" I finally find my voice.

He shrugs. "Well, if it's not what you want … but we won't find much better. Not right now."

That makes me frown. "Why the rush? And why wait until we're already on our way there to tell me anything about it?"

Where the hell was I in this decision?

"Come on, Vera. Most women would be falling over themselves at the sight of a house like that."

I snort. "Yeah, because it's not a house. It's a fucking museum."

He scowls at me briefly before returning his attention to the road. "Your father's home is even bigger."

Exactly is what I don't say.

"Isn't this something we should've talked about? You

know *together?*"

I snatch my purse from the floor and dig my nude gloss out, spreading some over my drying lips while he talks. "I wanted to surprise you. But you had to have known this was coming soon. We've been together for over six months now."

He says it like it's an astronomical amount of time. It all started when my father introduced us at a business dinner with Dexter's family. After that night, we kind of fell into this fucked-up relationship, sleeping with one another too many times in the weeks after. It's a relationship I choose to co-exist in because it's what I know. It's reliable. It's easy. And even though I knew I'd one day end up here, as he said, I just never thought it'd be this soon. And not with him. Not yet. *I'm not ready.*

"You should know by now that I'm not most women." I cap my gloss and put it back into my purse.

He laughs dryly. "You can say that again."

My teeth grit together, and I try to calm my jumbled nerves. Something vital is starting to unravel inside me that I can't quite put my finger on. And I don't think it'd be wise to do so anyway. My gut roils violently.

"You know what?" he suddenly says. "I'm not pussyfooting around it anymore. I don't see the point in putting it off. It's the natural next step for us. Couldn't you see it? Us? Raising a family there, growing old, and sharing our life together? No more of this apartment hopping crap." He scoffs. "When you even feel like seeing me, that is."

My head starts to spin. "Pull over."

"What?"

"I said, pull over." The volume of my voice rises to a harsh demand.

"You can't be fucking serious. Why?" he asks loudly.

"Just pull the fuck over. Now," I growl the words at him, tearing off my seat belt as he merges onto the shoulder of the highway.

"What the—" He's cut off when I step out and slam the car door shut. The cars barreling by have my hair wrapping around my face and my dress parachuting into the air. I quickly stuff it down and scoot precariously along the side of his car in my four-inch white wedges until I reach the guardrail. Opening my purse, I dig out my phone to call a cab.

The passenger window goes down. "Vera! What the fuck are you doing? Get back in the car. This is insane!"

I know it is, but right now, the thought of spending just one more second in that cramped car with him, the same reason my anxiety levels are shooting to the sky, makes me want to hurl on the side of the road.

"Vera, I'm not going to say it again. Get. In. The. Fucking. Car. Or I'm leaving."

Lifting my eyes from the call log of my phone, I glare at him. "So *go*. I'm not in the mood to play the doting girlfriend today, Dexter. Come to think of it; I think I'm done playing it entirely."

He leans over, trying to stick his face out the window. "You don't mean that."

"Yeah. I think I do."

He groans, his head hanging for a second before he says, "Stop being crazy. You don't want the house? Fine. We'll find another one. Can we please just go? I've got a meeting in half an hour."

When I return my attention back to my phone and ignore him, he curses. "Fuck this. Let's see where being a bitch gets you today, Vera." The window goes up, and then I'm left standing in a gust of dirt-stained wind as his car speeds off down the highway toward the city.

The words don't sting as they should. No. In fact, fighting with Dexter never stings. It's not that I don't care about him. I think some part of me does, or I wouldn't have put up with him for this long. And though I've thought about it a few times, I know I don't love him. I've never been in love and I'm pretty sure if you need to think about whether you're in love, then you're more than likely not.

Dialing the cab company, I put my phone to my ear and wait for the call to connect, but all I get is three beeps. I try again and again before realizing I have no damn signal.

Well, crap. *Nice one, Vera.*

A truck honks, causing me to fumble with my phone as I wave my hand above my head and squint at it while walking down the breakdown lane.

"Sup, sexy lady!" Some idiot yells out the window of the truck that barrels past.

Yeah, I really didn't think this one through. But in my defense, I could barely think at all just a few minutes ago. Did I expect him to leave me here? No. Though it's what I wanted, I didn't expect him to actually do it. Oh, how hard I could kick my own ass right now.

It's fine. Breathe.

I close my eyes and try to calm the rising panic. I'm still at least a fifteen-minute drive away from the turn off to Rayleigh. I glance down at my Gucci wedges. They're seriously too damn pretty to be subjected to this. But … with nothing left to do, I start walking, mentally apologizing to my shoes for the torment I'm subjecting them to.

I check my phone again.

Nothing. No signal at all. What is this shit? Aren't we living in the twenty-first century? Cell towers should be everywhere.

Giving up, I put my phone away. I need my hands free to keep my dress from blowing up my thighs every time a car zooms by anyway.

He'll come back.

But after ten minutes of walking, he's nowhere to be seen.

Loud rumbling sounds from behind me. Close. Too close. I spin around, flattening myself against the barricade when I see a motorcycle roll into the breakdown lane and come to a roaring stop. The rider is wearing a black helmet, a pair of Ray-Bans, and the most mischievous smirk I've ever seen.

God. How the hell did I get myself into this predicament?

Dexter. I'm blaming him.

The rider quirks a finger at me to come closer. Ha. *Yeah right, buddy.*

When I don't, he looks at me for a moment before wheeling his bike forward some more and coming to a stop right in front of my white wedges, which are starting to look a little cream and brown already, much to my heart's dismay. He turns the bike off and leans over the handlebars while I try to think about how fast I can run, or if there'd be any point.

"What the fuck are you doing walking down the side of a highway?" His head shifts up and down a little as he no doubt surveys my lavender Vera Wang sundress and black blazer. "Pretty thing like you is bound to cause a pileup or get yourself killed."

Okay, I'm a little scared. I've watched a few too many horror movies to be able to form a coherent reply right now. When I just continue to stare, he plucks a pack of cigarettes out of his leather jacket pocket and grabs one from the pack with his teeth. "Do you talk?" He puts the pack away and lights the cigarette. His brows furrow over his sunglasses as he continues to study me. "Wait, are you, ah … lost or some shit?"

Great. He thinks I've got a few screws loose. I guess I would look rather crazy walking down the highway in thousands of dollars' worth of clothes and four-inch heels. Let's not forget the way I was waving my phone in the air earlier as though I were at a rock concert.

Sighing, I decide to unglue my tongue from the roof of my mouth and answer him. But I suddenly do get a bit lost by the way his thin lips wrap around the cigarette and his sculpted cheekbones become more prominent when he inhales. Trying to say something, I open and close my mouth, but then my eyes zero in on the way his lips part slightly when he exhales. Smoke billows out and disappears into the dust flecked wind around us.

He smirks. Shit. "Uh-umm …" I stammer, and what the fuck? I never stammer. "If you must know, I had a fight with my boyfriend and got out of the car. Apparently, his threat to leave me behind wasn't just a threat."

He inhales deeply then says on an exhale, "Right. Why the fuck did you get out of the car?"

My shoulders tilt. "Ah, because I was pissed off." Duh.

He chuckles quietly, the sound raspy yet warm. "You should probably have held in that anger until the asshole at least got you closer to home, no?"

My face scrunches in irritation. "You don't think I know that? Now, if you'll excuse me …" I turn and keep walking, hoping like hell he fucks off and not giving a damn if he's attractive and he's got transportation. I've made enough stupid decisions today.

"Hey, where the hell do you think you're walking to, anyway?"

I choose to ignore him and keep moving. He curses, and not even a minute later, his hand is grabbing mine and pulling me back toward his bike.

"Hey! What the hell are you doing?" I try to tug my hand away, but his hold is firm. Shit, one minute ago would've been a good time to pluck my pepper spray from my purse. I'd smack myself in the head if I wasn't so preoccupied, what with some guy trying to lure me onto his death machine and all.

"I'm getting you off this damn highway before you turn into roadkill." He stops by his bike, using his other hand to tug off his helmet, and I get my first close look at him.

He's tall, but so am I; my forehead is level with his chin. Even with the sunglasses on, I know he's got the kind of face bound to have broken many hearts and shattered countless girls' dreams. Brown stubble covers his chiseled jaw; his brown hair is thick and slicked back over his head. His nose is straight and his teeth blinding white as he grins down at me while he puts the helmet on my head. My eyes stay planted on his teeth. They're all perfectly straight except for the one front tooth. It curves slightly over the one next to it, and I find it oddly endearing.

I'm snapped out of my daze when his hands brush underneath my chin while he buckles and adjusts the helmet.

I rear back. "Wait, what?" I can't get on that ... that motorcycle. "I'm not going anywhere with you." I reach up to undo the helmet, but he stops me, his eyes hardening as he stares down at me and holds my wrists in his hands. My mouth dries, and I try to decide whether I'm excited or really fucking scared by his proximity. Maybe it's both.

"Don't. You're getting on that bike whether you like it or not."

Who the hell does he think he is? I ask him as much.

"Someone who's trying to save your clueless ass. Get on the bike."

He pulls me over to it, and I scowl at him. "I don't even know you. This is …"

"Zip those sexy lips and let's go." He releases me and climbs on to start it up.

This guy could possibly still kill me. Horrific images of warehouses or woods and torture dungeons flash through my mind. But with no cell service and Dexter probably back in the city, arriving at his meeting, do I really have another choice?

God. I'm *totally* going to kick my own ass back to whatever hellhole I crawled out from. That is if I survive this shit.

Once the bike is finally started, which has a Harley-Davidson badge, he grabs my hand again and directs me to sit behind him. It's awkward, trying to get the skirt of my dress under my ass and between my thighs so I'm not displaying the goods to everyone.

"Where're you going?" he asks loudly over the noise of the engine, taking my purse and shoving it in a bag on the side of the bike.

I've gone this far, so I may as well see if he'll take me home. "Rayleigh. Oceanside apartments."

I swear his head shakes, but he simply says, "Put your arms around me and hold on tight."

I reluctantly do, in barely enough time to stop myself from flying off the back of the damn thing.

The helmet and the direction of the wind thankfully keep my hair from slapping me in the face, but my stomach still lurches harshly when he kicks it up a gear, and then we're flying down the highway. My arms wrap around him in a death grip, and I bite my lip, clenching my eyes closed. I must look all kinds of stupid, but I guess it's better than walking down the side of the road.

His scent travels into my nose. He smells like clean linen

and tobacco with a slight undertone of grease. Though that could be the bike. Do serial killers usually smell like they use good laundry detergent? I'm going to make myself feel better by saying no. They probably wouldn't bother.

We're soon slowing down for him to take the turn off into Rayleigh and then we're weaving in and out of traffic as he takes the back streets to my apartment.

My heart finally stops racing when I think I'll live to see another day.

He pulls up to the curb outside my black gated apartment complex and leaves the bike running. I take my purse from him and unclip the helmet, fumbling with it for a second before handing it over.

He dumps it on his head and holds a hand out. My brows lower as I look at it, which makes him laugh and causes my stomach to lurch in a whole different kind of way.

"Take it. If you've never been on a bike, your legs are bound to feel like jelly."

Jelly? I snort and swing my leg over, standing before my legs indeed wobble slightly, and his hand is grabbing my arm to steady me.

He chuckles, and I glower at him, which just makes him laugh even more.

"Thanks … for not being a serial killer," I mutter before turning to walk up the sidewalk to the gates while he continues to laugh.

"No problem," he calls out. "Stay off those highways, yeah? Or better yet, dump that boyfriend."

I wave him off, resisting the urge to turn around and look at him one more time.

CHAPTER TWO

Walking out of the lobby of Bramston Inc., I turn left and head straight for the café on the corner where Cleo and Isla said they'd meet me. Neither of them work, so they're always available for an emergency meeting when I need to call one. And my anxiety levels have finally gotten to the point where I need to vent or I'm not going to be held accountable for my actions.

The usual midday percussion of traffic, voices, and seagulls circling overhead from Rayleigh beach hums throughout the city. Opening the door, I walk in to find the girls seated in the back.

"Hey," Isla says then frowns when she sees my expression, which is probably more glacial than usual.

"What's up?" Cleo glances from Isla to me before bringing her mug to her pink painted lips.

Sighing theatrically, I plonk myself down on the chair opposite them and order a coffee when the waitress comes by.

"What, you couldn't order for me?" I raise an irritated brow at them.

Isla smiles sweetly while Cleo just snorts. "Um, the last time we ordered for you was exactly seven months ago," Cleo says. "I remember it like it was yesterday because you looked like you were about to throw your coffee at our faces after taking one sip."

Isla nods, her brown hair shifting over her shoulder with the movement. "Yep. What did she call it again?" she asks Cleo.

I drop my purse on the table while Cleo squints one eye as she thinks. "Oh!" she finally says. "A cup of scalding hot shit."

They both laugh while I roll my eyes. "Why the hell do I put up with you two?" I grumble, but not very quietly for they both laugh again.

But I know why. I've known them since we were in kindergarten. My father is close friends with both of their parents, and we're just lucky we like each other enough to still be friends. Because growing up is never easy, but growing up with rich catty girls? Yeah, try almost impossible. Over the years, we weeded out the worst of them and survived with our friendship intact, thankfully.

"So ..." Isla puts her mug down, crossing her legs. "What's happened?"

"What do you think?"

Cleo frowns down at the table and then gasps, "They're bringing back fur?"

"Seriously?" I pause. "No, wait, I don't think so ... Ugh, Christ, no. Fur is not the problem."

Cleo's blue eyes harden. "Oh, but it so is."

Isla giggles and turns to me. "Dexter?"

Inhaling a deep breath, I nod. "He dragged me to Bonnets Bay to look at some castle of a house yesterday. No warning, nothing. Completely blindsided me and expected me to be over the moon about it all. We argued on the way back. I'm an ungrateful bitch, etcetera, etcetera."

They don't look surprised, not even Cleo. They don't even bat a mascara-coated lash.

I groan. "Well? Where's the outrage? The name-calling? Come on, give it to me …"

I mutter a crisp thank you when the waitress places my coffee down in front of me.

"Asshole."

"Dickhead." Isla nods.

"Total douchebag," Cleo declares.

"Waste of time."

"Smelly bum head," Cleo says loudly, causing people seated nearby to look over at us. I glare at them, and they quickly turn away.

"Bum head? What are we, in fifth grade?" Isla laughs.

Cleo shrugs, picking up her coffee and swallowing a large mouthful before saying, "Well, he is."

She has a point there. We sip our drinks quietly for a minute, and I feel the anger start to abate.

"It's frustrating. I don't even know if I'm angry with him or me …" I trail off, wrapping my hands around my mug to warm them.

"Him. Definitely be mad at him. Total dick move." Cleo nods firmly.

Smiling thinly, I continue, "I think I'm mad at me. This whole stupid charade was doomed from the start."

"Yeah, but looking at it objectively, he's quite a catch. And nobody wants to be broke." Isla winks, trying to lighten the moment.

"Right?" Cleo agrees. "Dexter definitely isn't hard to look

at, honey."

He's not. He's tall, lean, dark-haired, and handsome in a way that resembles a Greek Adonis.

"So it's over?" Isla asks quietly.

"I haven't answered his calls, but yes, I think I'm finally done."

They're both quiet for a moment. "What?" I snap.

Isla looks up at me. "You deserve better; he can be a total sleaze ball. But you know your dad won't be impressed if you two end things. He's one of your father's most prized employees."

I deserve better. The words hit me straight in the gut. Better than everything I already have? I don't know how that's possible. My head shakes. "What's he going to do? It's my life."

They both stay quiet, drinking more of their coffee.

"Anyway, what happened? You totally carved him a new asshole, right?" Cleo leans forward, placing her elbows on the table.

Isla's face screws up in disgust, and she rears her head away from Cleo. "Eww, what the fuck, Cleo?"

Cleo merely shrugs and waves her hand at me. "Details."

I sit back in my chair and mull over how much I should tell them before deciding to just tell them everything.

They gasp and scowl at me as if I'm the one who drove away and left me stranded.

"What the hell were you thinking?" Isla asks. "You could've been run over."

Cleo's eyes bug out. "What a dick. He just left you there?"

I wait for them to get over their outrage, which takes a minute, and finish my coffee before checking the time. I need to get back to work in ten minutes. I might only work part time, and even though I have enough money that I don't need to work at all, I'm still no flake.

My father's a real estate tycoon, and I'm just one of his many minions. Going to college and studying literature wasn't enough, nor was it okay. No, I had to make sure I majored in something that would help the family business. So to be the bitch that people say I am, I became an accountant. I know, totally boring. But my father sucked it up, and I now work part time as one of the accounting assistants for his company. Not very glamorous, but having lots of money is, so I do what I must to keep it that way.

"How'd you get home?" Isla finally asks.

I chew on my lip for a moment then scold myself when I remember I put on my favorite shade of Chanel earlier. I quickly dig out my compact mirror to check it while saying, "Some guy on a Harley pulled over and demanded I get on his bike. He didn't kill me, thankfully, just drove me home."

Satisfied with my lips, I snap the compact closed and tuck it away then look up to find their wide eyes fixed on me. "Yeah, I know. I could've been one of those stupid victims you see in a horror movie, but I kind of had no other choice. My phone had no reception, which, oh my, God, how is that even possible these days?"

"Wow," Cleo breathes. "Was he hot? Some grizzly looking biker dude?"

Isla's brown eyes narrow at her. "Not important." She then twists her lips to the side and changes her mind. "No wait, was he?"

I smirk at them, tapping my nails against the table as nameless guy flashes through my mind. His scent remains imbedded in my nose, and despite not being my type at all, I will admit to being curious. "He was. Well, from what I could see. He didn't take his sunglasses off, and he wasn't old." *Not at all*, I think to myself, remembering the feel of his firm body that I'd wrapped my arms and hands around.

"Did you get his name? Number?" Cleo asks.

"Nothing. He's not my type anyway." I run my finger over a crack in the wood of the table.

Isla lowers her voice. "Who cares? It'd be so much fun."

Cleo nods frantically. "You're an idiot for not getting more info."

I decide to steer the conversation away from my nameless hero. "Halloween ball this weekend—you ladies ready?"

Isla's brows pull in at the subject change, but she lets it slide. "Yeah, I just need to book my hair and makeup appointment."

We finish talking about our dresses and what time we'll meet before I realize I'm about to be late. "Gotta run. I'm due back in a few minutes," I say as I get up, adjusting my black pencil skirt and grabbing my purse.

I blow a kiss and wave goodbye before walking out onto the street. Weaving and dodging busy lunch goers, I walk as fast as I can back to work in my four-inch black pumps.

The smell of garlic and rosemary drifts down the long hallway from the kitchen. I clutch my book tighter to my chest. Rapunzel is what I've picked to have Gloria read to me this afternoon. I wonder if she'll braid my hair just like Rapunzel's after she's done. Of course, she will. Gloria always does exactly what I ask her to.

"What's got you in such a bad mood?" our cook, Paul, asks from the kitchen. My sock-covered feet stop moving on the marble floor so fast that I almost slip. "What else? That child," comes Gloria's answer. I lean back against the wall just outside the

kitchen entry. *That child? Only one child lives in this big house. I might only be seven years old, but I know instantly that that child is me.*

"What's she done now?" he asks her. The tap turns on, but Gloria's honeyed voice rises above the noise of the water splashing against the metal sink. "What hasn't she done is the question. Lord, if my Tabitha were anywhere near as demanding as Vera, I'd likely have put her up for adoption."

Paul laughs, and my stomach clenches at the same time my fingers grasp the thick binding of my book held tightly against my chest.

"Oh, stop it. You know I'm joking. But I swear, sometimes I wonder if her mother knew exactly what kind of child her daughter would grow up to be before she decided to skip town with her lover."

Paul hums. "Maybe. Though Vera is very different from her mother." The tap turns off.

"How so?" Gloria asks.

"Well." Paul pauses. "Erica was always bursting with energy and couldn't sit still for a minute. Always looking for her next adventure. I think becoming a mother just wasn't the adventure she thought it might be."

My eyes squeeze closed. My heart slams shut. I don't want to hear this. But I do. Daddy never talks about my mother. My hungry heart and curious brain keep my feet planted firmly outside the kitchen.

"No kidding. Though it doesn't take a genius to see she's exactly like her father."

Paul simply hums again in response.

Gloria continues, "The way he spoils that child makes me sick. I can't blame him for not wanting to spend a lot of time with her." She laughs lightly. "I'd have quit a long time ago if he didn't *pay me so damn well. But shit, he's just creating a monster, you know? She's always asking, demanding, and expecting the world to be handed to her when she wants it and how she wants it. And don't even get me started on those stupid stories she loves so much."*

My eyes open wide. A tear leaks out and runs down my cheek, landing on my bottom lip.

"What about them?" Paul replies distractedly. Something clangs, one of his wooden spoons against a pot maybe.

Gloria snorts. "You're joking, aren't you? Her fascination with those princesses, those fairy-tale worlds is so ironic that I have to bite my tongue in an effort not to laugh every time I read them to her. She's nothing like the girls in those stories. If anything, she's like the nasty stepsisters or the wicked queens."

The sound of their laughter chases me down the hall as I run, run as I've never run before around the corner, up the winding staircase, and into my room. Tears spill onto my cheeks and into my hair while I lock the door then throw myself face down onto my white, four-poster bed. Silently, I let the tears run free while those hurtful words squirm around in my head.

After a while, I sit up, wipe underneath my eyes, and stare out the window. A knock sounds on my bedroom door. "Vera?" Gloria asks. The door knob turns. "Vera, what are you doing? Let me in, please."

Swiping my hair back off my face and tucking it behind my ears, I rise from the bed, checking my blotchy face in the mirror on my way to the door.

I don't see a monster, a nasty stepsister, or a wicked queen. But perhaps I am spoiled rotten. Besides a pony, I've gotten everything I've ever asked for.

But I still don't understand. If I'm so rotten, why doesn't it feel that way to me? Except that I must be, I think to myself as I *study my blue eyes in the mirror. Because if I wasn't, then maybe she'd still be here. Maybe my father would play with me. And maybe Gloria would only have nice things to say about me after caring for me for all these years.*

"Vera?" Gloria bangs on the wood of the door. "This isn't funny, dear. Let me in. I'm starting to get worried."

Worried. A lie.

Taking a deep breath, I move to the door and open it to let her in.

Her brown eyes narrow when she looks down at my face. "What on earth is the matter? Are you feeling unwell?" She takes a step closer, and I tell myself to stand still. I tell myself that letting her know what I heard earlier might only result in her leaving or being fired and then Father will get me a new nanny. And then would she barely tolerate me, too?

No. What's that saying I've heard my father use? Better to stick with the devil you know.

"Nothing. I was just waiting for you to read to me and fell asleep. Will you read to me now?"

She smiles, and I see it. The way her eyes don't light up the way they should if she were truly happy about something.

"Of course, dear. Come on." She takes my hand, and I let her lead me over to the bench seat by the window in my room.

My phone buzzes on the coffee table in front of me, snatching me from my head. I pick it up and stare at her name on the screen. God, I wish I could just ignore her calls, but she'd keep at it or, instead, try to make my father's life hell until she gets what she wants. She's relentless.

I put the phone down beside me, yawn and sit up. She can wait five minutes because I need coffee for this shit.

After yesterday's episode of "Dexter makes me do insane things: part three" and explaining everything to the girls today, followed by a shitty afternoon at work, I'm more than ready to just go to bed. But visions of two kids chasing me through red painted halls and a nameless stranger with a crooked grin plagued my thoughts last night until I finally passed out, and I don't want a repeat.

To be honest, I don't even know why I reacted the way I did when I know exactly what Dexter is like. He does whatever he wants. I'm more pissed off at myself. I'm usually able to brush off the predictability of my future, but yesterday, those revelations about why he insisted I go look at that giant home with him have rattled me. They've made me creep out from this perfect fog of ignorance I'd placed myself in long ago. Realizing that I have no desire to be trapped with a man like him has left me feeling oddly lost.

I grab a mug and flick the coffee machine on, getting the milk from the fridge as the godly aroma of coffee fills my kitchen. It's my one true love, I've decided. Who needs a good man when you have good coffee? And good wine. Can't forget about that.

I froth the milk and traipse back to my leather couch, curling my legs under me and picking up my phone again. I pull up her number and hit dial then place the phone between my ear and shoulder while it rings so I can blow on the hot liquid. She picks up after only the second ring as predicted. When she wants something, she doesn't try to hide her desperation.

"Darling!" she hollers into my ear.

"Mother, what can I do for you on this fine day?" I take a small sip of my coffee, wishing I hadn't as it burns its way down my throat.

"Oh, good Lord, lighten up, would you? I just called to say hi and to see how my baby girl is doing."

"I'm fine. What do you want?" Patience and I aren't really friends. But talking with her? It's virtually laughable to think patience will ever exist. I don't need useless chitchat with the woman who took off to be with a younger man when I was barely out of diapers. She never once looked back or bothered to check in. I've grown up with a nanny my whole life. But these past twelve months, she's made it a habit to call and "check in." Which means she knows I'm receiving my inheritance on my twenty-fifth birthday in a few months' time.

My grandmother was a crafty woman who knew exactly what her son was like. Needless to say, when she died years ago and my father discovered she left most of her remaining fortune to me, he wasn't very happy.

Which also means that instead of getting a measly few thousand of my father's money from me, Mother dearest can hit me up for more. *Good luck with that, sweetheart.*

I don't know why I bother with this stupid dance. I blame it on that traitorous piece of my heart that still cares about my ruthless businessman of a father. Because if she didn't call me, she'd call him. And though he may appear an asshole to the rest of the world—and let's face it, he totally is—Erica has always been his weakness. He'd turn quiet for days after she'd call when I was a child. I know I'm trying to protect him in some way. Even though he doesn't deserve it, I just can't help it. Knowing his weakness is a painful reminder that you can have everything you've ever wished for, but nothing your heart really desires.

You simply can't have both.

She sighs dramatically before finally getting to the point.

"Well, I just need a small bit of help, you see. My car is having issues, and Eduardo forgot to pay our rent last month and this month, so …" She trails off on a giggle. "Stop, Eduardo, I'm on the phone. Wait until I'm done."

Jesus fucking Christ. I think this is boyfriend number three since she started calling me.

"Okay, let's wrap up this lovely little chat now, shall we? How much? And for the love of all that's holy, don't beat around the fucking bush."

"Vera! What does your father say about that mouth of yours? So crass." She tsks into my ear.

I set a cackle free. "He says that in a world swimming with sharks, it pays to sharpen your teeth. Give me a number or I'm hanging up."

"Okay, okay, yeeesh. Two thousand," she says quickly.

Huh. That's actually kind of small. I'm not about to argue or point that out, though.

"Done. Bye."

"Thank you, wait—" I hang up, set a reminder to wire the money through later tonight, and toss my phone down beside me on the couch.

I spend a few moments just staring out of my floor-to-ceiling living room window while I drink my coffee.

The city of Rayleigh isn't a huge one, but it's weirdly alluring. A mixture of old charming brick buildings competing against new steel and glass architecture and an occasional skyscraper here and there. There are rough parts of it, which I try to avoid. But this manmade jungle by the beach has been home since I left my father's fortress after high school, even if most days I feel like it might trap me in this constant spin of repetition.

My phone rings again, and I drag my gaze back to it,

finding Dexter's name lighting up the screen. He's been calling since yesterday but has yet to make an appearance. After I'd long gotten home, he sent me a text asking me to at least tell him I was okay; otherwise, he'd be coming over to check for himself.

That was the last thing I wanted, so I grudgingly replied and told him I was fine before turning my phone off. I might not be an expert, but I'm pretty sure if your boyfriend has fucked up in a colossal way, then they should probably be at your door, banging it down and asking for forgiveness. Not Dexter apparently. He has better things to do. Like maybe trying to wedge his dick between Lisa's double Ds. Yes, I caught him fucking another woman on his kitchen counter once. That woman would be Lisa. The fact I didn't care should've made me get my head examined. I cared more about him having never fucked me from behind than the fact he betrayed me. I simply told him if he does it again, I'll be gone. And that he's never to fuck me without a condom. Ever.

I hit ignore and take my phone to my room to charge it. This weird funk doesn't seem to want to go away anytime soon, so I turn the water on in the tub and walk into my spare room, also known as my library, to grab one of my favorites.

I may have a wee bit of an addiction to my vintage book collection or just an addiction to books in general. Reading always seems to calm me as only getting lost in a good book can do. And what's better than going back to a guaranteed favorite? It's trustworthy.

Dependable.

A promise that can't be broken.

Something you know will leave you satisfied once you turn that last page.

Over and over again.

CHAPTER THREE

"**B**ut this is getting close to the bad side of town, Gloria." My feet still follow her, though. She waves her hand around. "Nonsense. It's on the outskirts. And I happen to live on that bad side of town, you know?" She raises a brow at me, and I stare blankly back at her as we stop outside what looks to be a bookstore. I tear my gaze from her offended face and look up at the sign. Always Booked. Oh yeah, real original.

"Come on then. Some of us can't afford to shop at the bookstores in the mall all the time, so if you want to go book shopping, it's going to be here today."

I reluctantly follow her inside, my nose scrunching at the musty smell of used books.

A bell jingles behind us, causing a man's head to appear from behind a stack of books at the front counter. He stares at me for a beat then snaps into action. "Good morning. How can I help you lovely ladies today?"

"Do you have that new one by Danielle Steel?" Gloria asks

while I move farther into the store. I keep my hands clasped together in front of me, eyeing the rows upon rows of books. There seems to be no distinguishing the old from the new; it appears they've just been mashed together in whatever genres necessary.

"Maybe. Give me a moment and I'll take a look." I hear the man finally answer her.

When I reach the children's books, my eyes zero in on an old copy of Anne of Green Gables. *I move quicker than lightning for it, plucking it off the shelf. The pages have yellowed a little, but otherwise, it's in perfect condition. My fingers trail over the blue cover, dipping in and over the bronze border then tracing each letter of the title.*

"A Gables fan?" a deep voice says from behind me. I turn around, finding the man who works here. I must've been standing here a while. Nodding my head, I turn back around and peruse the shelf.

"Quite a story, that one is. How old are you?"

My finger runs along the spines, pausing on an old edition of Snow White. *"Isn't it rude to ask strangers how old they are?"*

His shocked laugh is loud and gruff and has me spinning around to glare at him. "What's so funny?"

He shakes his head, and my eyes take in his hair. Dark brown, almost black, with a streak of silver on either side of his head.

His blue eyes sparkle with mirth. "Nothing. I was just curious. You can't be much older than eleven, and we, I mean I"—his eyes close for a second—"don't get a lot of young kids stopping by for books like that."

"Well, they're missing out then, aren't they? And I'm ten." I tuck the book close to my chest. "Now, if you'll excuse me, I need to find my nanny."

He stares at me curiously for a moment before stepping aside and allowing me to pass. I find Gloria near the front, reading the blurb on the back of a romance novel.

"Ready?" I ask, placing my book on the counter.

I try not to smile at the way her eyes widen. "You picked a book? From here?"

If she was hoping to make me go home without a book for once, she's going to be sorely disappointed. And I always aim to please Gloria these days. "Of course. That's why we came here, isn't it?" It's my turn to raise a brow at her. She scowls, shoving the book she was looking at back into the bargain bin while the man rounds the counter.

"It's a crime to treat books like that, Gloria. You should know better."

She shoots daggers at me, cursing under her breath about other things that would be considered a crime.

"Problem?" the man asks, his eyes darting back and forth between my flustered nanny and me.

"Not at all." My smile is full of glee as I fish out my wallet. "How much do I owe you?"

"Nothing. It's yours." He smiles back at me.

My hands freeze. "What do you mean nothing?"

He shrugs. "Exactly as I said. It's free."

I start to stutter. Not understanding. "B-but nothing is free. Don't be stupid." I dig a fifty out. "Here, it's a rare edition. At least take this."

"Vera Marie Bramston, you watch your mouth," Gloria hisses at me.

The man's eyes widen again while he stares at me. I grab the book, drop the fifty on the counter, and then head for the door, not in the mood for mind games.

I hear Gloria mutter to him as I go, "I'm so sorry. She can be a real piece of work, that one." She laughs nervously. "As you just saw, I've definitely had my work cut out for me ..."

I wait outside, cringing at the sound of her voice and her blatant disregard for my feelings. She stopped with the pretenses years ago. But sometimes ...

Sometimes, I wish she'd just fake it again.

The same bell jingles when I step inside, the scent of old books filling my nose and travelling straight to my heart. This place now soothes me in a way that has me seeking out the old, dilapidated store whenever I feel unsettled. And I've never felt this unsettled before in my life.

"Vera." Badger greets me, walking down the aisle with a couple of hardbacks in his hands. I've never asked his real name. I dubbed him Badger when I was eleven years old. The odd streaks of gray that gave him the nickname in the first place have now taken over his whole head. He's old, probably early seventies at least. I've often asked when he's going to retire, but I'm always given the same answer. "When it's time, my dear Vera, when it's time."

"Hi, Badger." I move past him to the far aisle in search of something a little different. Romance? Suspense? The two always go well together. But no, I think I need an added dose of intrigue today. My eyes land on a fantasy novel, and I pick it up to read the blurb.

"It's been a little while. Where've you been?" Badger places some books on the shelf beside me.

I put the book back and peruse a few more before deciding to answer with, "Nowhere important."

He hums, and I turn to face him when he takes a seat on an

armchair in the seating area at the end of the aisle.

"Your hip bothering you again, old man?" I grab a few books to look at and take a seat on the armchair beside him.

He chuckles, and the sound, as it always does, brings a tiny smile to my face. "You needn't worry, my dear. I'm fine. Just tired." My brows lower as I stare at him. He smiles at me. "I'm okay. What's troubling you?"

He always seems to know when I'm in a bit of a funk. But I don't know if *funk* is the right word to describe this. I flip one of the books over, running my fingers over the worn edging of the back cover. "Nothing. I'm being stupid."

"Define stupid. Everyone always has different opinions on that one."

I shake my head. "I don't know …" My teeth tug my lower lip into my mouth then release it as I heave out a weary sigh. "Dexter took me to look at a house last weekend."

I glance over at him when he doesn't say anything, finding his blue eyes on me. "You didn't like the house?"

"It was huge. Beautiful. Everything I always thought I'd have. But no, I fucking hated it."

He smirks, and I scowl. "Oh, don't even start. I know, poor me, right? What a hardship. To have such a stunning monstrosity bought for me. How will I ever survive?" My tone is dry and mocking.

He doesn't care, though. Nothing I say ever seems to faze him. "Did you tell him you didn't like the house?"

I shake my head again, scuffing my Louboutins on the old wood flooring. "I don't think I needed to."

Badger's quiet for a minute, and I stare off at the rows of shelves. Some are brown, some are white, and some are metal. None of it matches. All of it clashes yet it all fits together to make this store exactly what it is. What I've grown to need it to be.

A place where I can be myself.

"Vera, you know you're the only one who gets to decide what you want for your future."

I grab my purse and dig a hundred-dollar bill out. "That's enough of the shrink talk for today. I need coffee."

As usual, he shakes his head at my money. But I place it on the little table between us anyway and stand, righting my long, cream knit cardigan before heading for the door.

"Oh, and Vera?" I hear his voice and footsteps behind me. I turn around, stepping out of the way for someone to walk in the door. Badger jerks his thumb to the left. "Try that little coffee shop on the end of the street already. It'll change your life." He winks and turns to greet the new customer.

I don't know why, when he's been telling me for years to try their coffee, that I pick today of all days to actually listen to him. Maybe it's my scattered thoughts and all these doubts swimming through my head. I don't know, but two minutes later, I find myself standing inside the small coffee shop.

It's even more run-down than Badger's bookstore, but I try not to let it unnerve me and move toward the counter to order a skinny latte.

"I'm sorry, a what?" answers the lady behind the counter, whose name tag reads Tori. Exasperation coats every word that just left her pinched lips.

Ugh, really? "A latte. You know, coffee? Want me to spell it out for you? L-a-t—"

She halts me with a hand, annoyance marring her kind of pretty face. "Got it, thanks."

I shrug and move over to the side to wait when I spot some empty booths in the back near the windows. Glancing down at my books, I decide to grab my to-go cup and make my way over to one of them. Placing the books, coffee, and my purse down on the table, I sink into the old bench seat and take my first sip of coffee, hoping like hell she didn't spit in it.

Well, I'll be damned. Badger is right again. I laugh quietly, knowing he's going to get a kick out of saying *I told you so* next time I see him. My phone rings in my purse, so I put my coffee down and check to see who it is. Dexter. I let it go to voicemail and tuck it away. Seeing his name has my hand snagging one of the books and opening to chapter one.

I make it to chapter two before I'm rudely interrupted by someone taking a seat opposite me. Sighing, I glance around. "There are plenty of other free tables. Give me my personal space and …"

I trail off when I see who it is.

He gives me a crooked grin. "Well, well. If it isn't little Miss Hitchhiker."

"You." The word is a breath, one that escapes my lips without my brain telling it to do so.

"Me. Jared, if you're fishing for my name. No need, I'll happily supply it." He winks, and my eyes get stuck on his. Green. Quite possibly the greenest eyes I've ever seen. A pair of emeralds framed in dark lashes that would make him seem too pretty if it weren't for the square, stubble-covered jaw and harsh planes of his sculpted cheekbones.

He leans forward, his arms folding to rest on the table. "Cat got your tongue, beauty?"

I blink rapidly. "No. And I wasn't hitchhiking." When he continues to stare at me, I snap, "Can I help you with something? As you can obviously see, I'm quite happy here, minding my own damn business. Maybe you should do the same." I look back down at my book. "Elsewhere."

He chuckles, and if I wasn't so caught off guard by the

sound, by *him,* then maybe I'd have been able to stop him from plucking the book from my hand.

"*Magic Bites.*" He eyes the title and flips it over. "Interesting. Never would've pictured you to be the type for stories."

A growl crawls steadily up my throat. I keep it in, just, and snatch the book back from him. "You don't know anything about me."

He sits back and lowers his brows as he studies me. The same waitress who hopefully didn't spit in my latte places a mug down in front of him, smiling at him then walking off. Of course, she's pleasant to him, and of course, he's going to now sit here and drink the damn thing. I don't know why that bothers me so much. Oh, wait. Yes, I do. I like to be alone. And I don't like the way this weird feeling uncurls in my stomach at his nearness.

"Oh, I think I know some. How's that boyfriend of yours treating you?"

"None of your damn business. Now kindly get lost, please and thanks." I open my book back up, well aware that I won't be able to read a damn thing with him here, but he doesn't know that.

"Now, is this any way to treat your savior?"

Glancing up, I find his head tilted, lips pursed mockingly, and his hand on his chest.

I have to bite my tongue to stop from smiling. "Whatever. You're a real hero."

"I'll say." He pauses, brows lowering. "I'll also say that you're fucking stunning, frosty one."

That startles me. My eyes flit over his face, noticing a tiny scar under his bottom lip.

He smiles at my expression. "Wow, it's kind of fascinating

the way a few words can get a whole different reaction from you."

"Look, I don't know what game you're playing here, but thanks for the ride home, and no, I'm not sleeping with you," I blurt then force myself to resist slapping a hand over my mouth.

He laughs, loud and deep with his head thrown back. His Adam's apple draws my gaze like a magnet. Jesus, it's getting warm in here.

He straightens but keeps the smile plastered on his annoyingly handsome face. "You're a real ballbuster, aren't you? But don't worry." He pulls his mug closer. "When I want between those creamy thighs of yours, you'll be more than ready."

I almost choke on a sip of coffee, lowering my cup and glaring at him. His heated gaze sets my nerves free-falling into chaos. So much so that my mouth opens and closes, but I can't get any words to come out. What's with this guy having the ability to do that?

I then watch in amused shock as he adds about six packets of sugar into his mug.

My tongue finally lowers from the roof of my mouth. "Did you want diabetes or a coffee?"

"Worried about me, are you, Frost?"

I scoff loudly, ignoring the weird nickname. "Hardly. I don't even know you. Give yourself all the diseases you please." Picking my cup back up, I take a huge mouthful.

We sit in silence for a few minutes, drinking and not talking. His eyes don't leave mine. Like some silent challenge has been initiated, and we're both waiting to see who'll be the first to back down.

And with my stomach starting to tingle, I decide that it

may as well be me.

"Well, thanks for not listening and ruining my coffee break." I stand, grabbing my purse and books. "I'll be going now." I walk out the door to the sound of his laughter and shiver even though the late afternoon sunlight is enveloping me from head to toe.

CHAPTER FOUR

Blinking and walking unsteadily down the hall, I try to remember if I'd even fallen asleep or not. But more pounding on the door of my apartment has my eyes opening wider.

"Vera! Open up, already!"

It would seem that I can only dodge Dexter's calls for so long, and he's now taken it upon himself to bang down my door at ten thirty at night. What a catch. I really know how to pick them.

"Dexter, you do know it's been a few days, right? No point showing up now and at this hour." I swing open the door and hiss at him.

He stumbles back a step. "Why haven't you answered my calls?"

Leaning a hip against the doorframe, I pretend to think about it. "Hmmm … let's see; maybe it's because you left me stranded on the side of the highway. Though I could be wrong."

I glare at him. "Nope, actually, I think I'm absolutely right."

He scowls, taking a step closer to me. "I came back for you, and you weren't there. What the fuck was I supposed to do?"

A disbelieving laugh escapes me before I can stop it. "Oh, I don't know. Maybe *not* leave your girlfriend stranded somewhere dangerous by herself? Or maybe, check in on her well-being well before now?"

He ignores me and changes the subject. "If this is about the house, we can discuss it. I'll find us something different, something smaller. If you want." His hands reach for my waist, and I step back inside my apartment. "I don't want to." I sigh, knowing that I need to do something about this. Badger's right. And even though I'm slightly terrified because I don't know what might happen after, it doesn't change the fact I need to end this. "Look, I don't want to do this anymore. Like I told you, I'm done, Dex."

He rears back like I've just punched him. "Done? What the fuck do you mean *done?* I thought you were just pissed."

The volume of his voice startles me, but I don't let it show. "Exactly what I said."

His brown eyes narrow to thin slits as he stares at me. His jaw clenches tightly. "Un-fucking-believable," he mutters. "You can't just do this. Who are you to say that we're over?"

My brows rise. "And who are you to make all these life-changing decisions for me?"

He shakes his head, rubbing a hand over his mouth. "That's bullshit, Vera. You've known your whole life, just as I have, what's in the cards for people like us. And you and me, we make a good team. You can't just decide to opt out now."

"Oh, can't I? I'm sorry, but I just have. Why don't you give Lisa a call? Goodbye, Dexter." I slam the door closed and lock it before marching back down the hall to bed. He knocks again then calls my phone until I switch it off.

And for the first time in my entire life, even with the fear accompanying it, I feel an odd sense of freedom. It might only be small, but it's enough to have my eyes closing and sleep finding me without any trouble at all.

It's Wednesday morning, and I'm busy pounding away at the keyboard; just another slave to the clock who's counting down the hours until I can go home.

Just kidding. I'm doing some online shopping at Nordstrom, seeing as these idiots don't think I can handle a real part-time workload. I've lost count of how many times I've told them otherwise. I think it has to do with my father, to be honest, but he wanted me to be a part of the family business in some way, so he's going to have to learn to trust me. As it is, I've already finished my work for the week.

Oh, that red one's nice. I zoom in on my computer screen for a closer look at the intricate beading around the neckline. I'm not normally one for too many eccentricities on my clothing, but I must admit this little number is quite pretty. I'm about to add it to my cart when Sally, one of my father's lead accounting minions, rounds the corner of my cubicle, looking a little harried. She stops right freaking next to me. My eye twitches. Has no one heard of personal space these days?

I slowly swing my chair back a bit to face her, not liking the disadvantage of sitting when she's standing over me. Especially when she's looking like an enraged pit bull who's wearing a shade of mauve lipstick that totally clashes with her maroon sweater dress.

"Vera," she says nasally.

"Hi, Sal. Still got that cold?" I try not to smirk, though it's really hard.

She shakes her head, exasperated with me already it seems. "For the love of God, I don't have a—you know what? No, just no." My eyes widen with my smile. "You're not going to distract me today." She points a finger at me, and I admire the shade of cream she's painted her nails.

"Where'd you get your nail polish?" I ask.

I swear she growls before throwing her hands up in the air. "I don't even know why I bother. Seriously."

I laugh; she's always so amusing. "Seriously, indeed. Now, what do you need to chew my ear off for today, Sal?"

"My name's not *Sal*. It's Sally."

"Semantics. Come on, spit it out already." I briefly admire my own brown painted nails. "Lots of work to be done and only so many hours in a workday."

I glance up in time to see her roll her eyes. "Yeah, because your client list is a mile long."

The smile wilts off my face, but I shrug. "Again, why are you here?"

"My parking spot. You know parking spots by the elevator are reserved for full-time employees only. Move your beast of a car someplace else."

I sigh dramatically. "Really? When are you going to get over this? You and I both know that that's not actually a rule." She's a stickler for them, this one. So much so that I swear she makes some of her own up just to have more to follow.

My cubicle phone rings, which is a rarity, but I'm thankful for the out. "Oh, would you look at that? Duty calls. We can continue this enlightening debate later, yes?" Not waiting for an answer, I scoot my chair back toward the phone, watching as smoke practically leaves her nose and ears before she huffs loudly and storms off.

I spend the next half hour on the phone with a client then spend the following few hours trying to sort out a bunch of butchered returns of theirs that someone other than me did. And my father thinks I'll screw things up. Jesus.

I grab some lunch from the café downstairs and return to my cubicle to continue my hunt for winter clothes. Summer's well and truly come to an end, and a girl needs to be well prepared. My phone vibrates on the desk next to my half empty to-go cup. Damn, I forgot about that. I take a quick sip of the now lukewarm drink and pick up my phone.

"Vera." Shit. Why didn't I check caller ID? Not that I'd ever ignore his calls. Few things scare me in this life. But my father is, unfortunately, one of them.

"Hi, Daddy." I try to put some sugar into my tone and fail, even to my own ears.

"You'll be attending the Halloween ball this weekend, won't you?" That's his way of asking how I am.

I take a deep breath and let it out as silently as possible. He, of course, won't be attending. He doesn't lower himself to such standards anymore, but that doesn't mean I'm allowed to be a no-show, though. Lucky for him, and for me, shopping and dressing up are two of my favorite things to do. "Of course, I will be."

He grunts into the phone, and I wait with bated breath to see if he'll mention Dexter. It was only last night. Surely, he hasn't found out yet. Not that he can do much about it, but it still worries me some.

"Good. I'll be out of town for the coming week, so if you need me, call Clyde and he'll forward me a message."

He's always going out of town. I sometimes wonder if that's

code for getting laid somewhere without prying eyes and gossip. Hmm, yeah. On second thought, I don't need to know anything about that. "Will do. Have a safe trip."

He grumbles something to someone in the background before responding with, "We'll talk when I get back. Don't show up late to the ball, and don't leave too early."

He needn't bother to tell me this. He's told me the same thing a thousand times. Ever since he decided to have me make an appearance at any events he didn't deem important enough to attend himself.

"Of course, talk soon."

He gives me a short, gruff goodbye in response then hangs up.

I drop my phone onto the desk, my head following it as I groan. I suddenly know how he must have felt after dealing with my mother's phone calls over the years.

Because one phone call, just one miserable excuse for a conversation, is all it takes to burn any crumb of happiness from my body for the remaining hours of the day.

CHAPTER FIVE

I turn the car off, glancing up in time to see a woman on the sidewalk drop her purse. Her belongings scatter over the concrete, and she bends down, frantically trying to pick them all up. But she's not alone. A stranger has stopped to help her. A cute guy in a pair of glasses who makes her head duck and her cheeks no doubt flame when she notices him. He puts what looks like a set of keys and a tube of cream into her purse then helps her to stand. My eyes stay fixed on the way she smiles as if she's giggling nervously while he grins down at her.

Men have always confused me. Almost as much as the concept of love. Just when I thought I could lump them all into one category, something always happened to change that.

It's frustrating. I need to make sense of things. Order and predictability are how I navigate this precarious world of mine. Which is probably why I gave up trying and decided that the only way to stay on the path of least resistance was to be with someone like Dexter. He felt safe. Our relationship felt predictable. Easy. And a certain amount of comfort comes with sticking to what you know.

Until you suddenly can't make sense of what is comforting you or slowly destroying you anymore.

My ringing phone has me tearing my gaze away and climbing out of the car. I answer it as I step up onto the sidewalk. "What's up?"

"Hey, I just sent you a picture of my dress, but I think I need something else."

My feet halt. "What? Why?"

"Cleo said blue washes me out, and that I should return it," Isla says. "Should I?"

I continue walking, pushing the door open to the little coffee shop I visited a few days ago. I've been craving one of their coffees, but I've been stubborn. Now I'm giving in.

Waiting behind a woman and her toddler in line, I readjust my hold on my phone. "Hang on; I'll look." I open the picture Isla sent me of her in the shimmering blue gown she's bought for this weekend's Halloween ball. I don't know what Cleo's talking about. She looks stunning, like a real-life Cinderella.

I put the phone back to my ear. "Okay, I'm only going to say this once, so listen and listen carefully." The woman moves aside and the same barista who served me the other day frowns. "One sec, Isla."

I order, thankfully without any hassle, and move to a booth in the back.

"Sorry, coffee calls. Anyway, Cleo's never looked good in blue, and ever since we told her as much, she's resentful of anyone who does. Don't listen to her. You look amazing."

She knows me well enough to know I'm being honest. Her sigh of relief is loud. "Thank *God*. It cost me a fortune, and it was love at first sight."

I rummage through my purse for my lip gloss and book. Placing my book on the table, I swipe some gloss on. "I still can't believe you're going as Cinderella."

She laughs softly into my ear. "Well, duh. If you're going as the wicked queen, I'm totally not about to let you show me up."

She doesn't know how much her costume choice strikes a chord within me. I wouldn't be caught dead going as a princess. I'd be the laughing stock of the room. But Isla? She's got an aura about her that screams sweet. A little sassy, but very sweet.

"Oh, can you look at my shoes? I'll send a picture."

I open my book. "If you must, but I'm kind of busy now. I'm sure they're fine."

"Please, Vera." I can almost see her pouting that bottom lip of hers.

"Ugh, fine. Send it. I'll text you when I get home. Bye."

The waitress delivers my coffee, and I nod grudgingly in thanks to her.

"You're the best, bye!" She hangs up, and I drop my phone to the table, glaring at it. Just daring it to ring when I finally have my coffee and book open.

"Yeah, that's what I thought," I mumble and direct my gaze to chapter twenty.

"You know, talking to inanimate objects would make some people think you're a bit crazy."

My stomach jolts. That voice.

Lifting my head, I see a worn, dog-eared copy of *It* by Stephen King hiding a man's face in the booth directly across from me. But I don't need to see his face to know who it is.

"Greetings, Hero, and I wouldn't concern yourself with my welfare. You're the one who needs your head examined if you think it's okay to allow a book to fall apart like that." I take a sip of my coffee, warmth filling my stomach when he lowers the book to reveal a huge grin. "I should've known."

Gritting my teeth, I cave and ask, "Known what?"

"That you'd be a mother hen with the things you do like."

Like isn't a strong enough word, but I don't tell him that. "Why are you here?"

He chuckles, swiping a hand over that perfect amount of scruff on his jaw. "I come here almost every day. I think the better question is, why are you here?"

Frowning, I ask, "Why wouldn't I be?"

He shrugs as he folds the corner of a page in his book, watching me visibly cringe as he closes it. He smiles. "Chill. The book's older than I am. And because this place isn't exactly across the road from your sky-high apartment building."

My back straightens. I grab my bookmark and close my book, raising a brow at him as I do. Which only makes that smile turn into another full-blown grin. My chest rises and falls faster with a weird sense of satisfaction at the knowledge I put it there. "I heard the coffee is good." I take another sip from my mug, eyeing him over the rim. "I'd do anything for good coffee."

"Anything?" He raises a brow and leans forward over the table on his elbows.

Rolling my eyes, I place my mug down. "And the age of that book makes it even worse, you know." I dodge his question and nod at his closed book. "You should always respect rare editions."

"Rare? I don't know about that. I found it on the subway when I was twelve." He gets up, grabbing his coffee and book. My brows shoot up as I watch him take a seat across from me.

"What are you doing?"

"Sitting down." He reclines back in the booth seat, and I feel his boot touch the top of my ballet flat. I move it away, and his eyes twinkle knowingly at me.

"I never invited you."

He stretches his arms up and over his head, and my own eyes involuntarily roam over his chest, his dirty blue shirt pulling taut with the movement. He yawns, dropping his arms. "Well, considering half the customers in here were probably privy to our conversation just now, I thought it a wise move."

"Privy?" I shake my head. This guy is nothing like I expected. "Wouldn't it be wise to ask first?"

He shrugs again and places his elbow on the table, tilting his head to rest in his big palm.

"Let's quit wasting time with pretenses, shall we?" He lowers his voice. "You're out of this world hot, and I've got a big cock I know how to use. And I'd really like to use it on you, in you, all over you."

Flinching as if I've been slapped, I try to wrap my head around the crass words that just vacated those sexy lips. But it's hard to do when my thighs squeeze together, suddenly in search of friction, and breathing becomes foreign.

His teeth scrape over his bottom lip while he stares at mine. I try to swallow so I can talk. His green eyes flit to my blue when I finally clear my throat. "While that sounds … um, nice, I think I'll have to pass."

He leans forward, narrowing his eyes playfully. "I can see I've ruffled those feathers again, which I'm assuming is not an easy feat. I'm also guessing you don't let yourself have a little fun very often, do you?"

What in the ever loving … "I'm charmed, really. But you're looking for fun in the wrong place, Hero." I pick my coffee up and drain the rest, trying to douse the inferno taking my stomach hostage.

"Worth a shot, right?" He grins and grabs my phone.

"Hey! Paws off." I try to grab it, but he holds it above his head, and I give up.

He places it back near my purse, completely disregarding the scowl on my face. "Don't you have somewhere to be? A job maybe?"

He downs the rest of his coffee. "Yep, I do. But even us lowly citizens need a lunch break." He winks and stands, causing my eyes to travel over his Dickies, and his stained, long sleeve blue shirt. Right.

"Whatever. Bye now." I reopen my book, almost jumping out of my seat when his warm breath washes over my ear. "My number's in your phone, in case you ever feel like letting that hair down for me to wrap around my fist."

Then he's walking out the door.

My hand drifts up to touch my messy bun as a violent shiver assaults my shocked body.

CHAPTER SIX

The Hedgington hotel is a mass of old world brick and ce-
ment architecture in the center of Rayleigh. Even with
countless renovations, it's still managed to keep that clas-
sic edge to it. Isla's driver pulls the Town Car up outside the
drop-off zone, and he comes to open my door for me. I grab
the black silky material of my gown and my clutch in one hand,
allowing him to take my other hand and help me out. He runs
over to the other side to assist Isla and Cleo while I step up onto
the curb, smoothing down the layers of my dress and surveying the line of cars behind Isla's.

I opted for a midnight black gown with tiny crystals imbedded across the bodice, which wraps tightly around my
chest in a corset. The skirts billow out to the floor with feathers
draped over my chest and shoulders. My own rendition of the
wicked queen from *Snow White*. And, if I must say, much better designed. Once the girls join me—Isla dressed as Cinderella
and Cleo as Dorothy from the *Wizard of Oz*—we link arms

and walk inside. The upholstery, carpet, and furniture have remained its signature cream and red; the Halloween decorations are sparse, no doubt to keep from looking tacky.

We make our way to the ballroom and immediately grab a glass of champagne from a passing waiter's tray before finding a corner where we people watch while the last of the stragglers arrive. We discuss the usual culprits who take the liberties of Halloween too far with outfits that would have gotten them turned away from this establishment if it weren't for the money exchanging hands. That's when my eyes find Dexter. Dexter and Lisa. The champagne bubbles strangely in my stomach when his gaze falls on me, a malicious glint in those brown depths. I don't give a damn if he's with her. I really don't. But I do care about being made to look a fool, and he probably knows that. Scoffing, I tip my champagne flute back in a rather unladylike manner and down the rest of its contents.

"God, what a prick." Isla stares over at Dexter, who's now smiling down at Lisa's chest and likely ignoring whatever she's babbling about.

"Don't spend another minute of your time worrying about that moron," Cleo declares, grabbing another glass of champagne when a waiter stops by to take our empty glasses.

"I can totally see why you would waste your time, though," Isla interjects with a sigh. "The asshole is too good looking for his own good." She tips her champagne into her mouth and eyes them over the rim of the glass.

I'm just glad my father isn't here. I also wish I hadn't shown up, my father's temper be damned. But this dress ... I glance down at it. It'd be such a waste not to show it off.

Even if my boobs feel as if they're about to burst out of the bodice.

Dexter's gaze returns to me, so, like the true lady I am, I

lift my middle finger to my cheek and pretend to scratch something off it, effectively flipping him off before turning away.

Isla giggles. "You're lucky your father isn't here."

I really am. "I'm going to the ladies' room. You two coming?"

They shake their heads. "No, the food is starting to circulate, and I'm starved." Cleo looks over at the waiters who are starting to circle with trays of finger food.

Leaving them to it, I weave my way through the crowd, smiling thinly at anyone who says hello but not stopping. That champagne went right through me, and I need in that bathroom, now.

Once I'm done, I spend a good few minutes righting my dress and then applying another coat of red in the mirror. I move my head side to side, pleased that my braided updo is holding. Not bad, considering I did it myself. I grab my clutch and head for the door. As soon as I step outside, my hand is grabbed, and I'm being tugged farther down the hallway.

"Dexter," I growl. "Let go of me."

"We need to talk; this is getting ridiculous."

"I've said all I need to say." I turn to go when he releases me, but he steps closer, placing a hand on my waist. Bristling, I stare glacially at him. "Remove your hand, now."

He shakes his head. "I don't think you quite understand, darling. But ..." His hand lifts, fingers trailing softly down the side of my cheek. I recoil from the touch, feeling my blood ignite to a steady simmer with anger. "You're mine. You and I both know that. No matter what I do or who I do, you're always going to belong to me."

"Is that so?" My tone is laced thick with biting sarcasm.

"You're damn right it is."

"Look, it's bad enough you've embarrassed us by showing

up with the biggest airhead in Rayleigh. Don't make it worse by causing a scene after I've already dumped you."

He laughs, the sound rich and dark, but it does nothing for me. It stopped doing things for me months ago, which only reaffirms I've made the right decision.

"Appearances, appearances. God, your shallow heart knows no bounds, does it?"

I inwardly flinch from his words, but outwardly, I keep the bored mask plastered to my face. "In all honesty, you're making a grave mistake. Daddy dearest isn't always going to want to pay your way. I'll take care of you; you know I will."

"I don't need taking care of." I spit the words at him.

"Really?" He gestures down the hallway. "Then tell me, my cold, beautiful, temptress, what are you without all this?" He laughs again when I don't answer, curling his arm around my waist. "Exactly. You need me, and I want you. So stop with the games and—"

I shove his chest. "Shut up and let go of me."

He ignores me. "Don't make me—"

He's interrupted again but not by me. "I believe the lady asked you to kindly fuck off."

Him. *Here?* A shiver rolls down my spine, and Dexter finally steps back, revealing Jared, who appears to be wearing a valet uniform.

"Who the hell are you? We're having a private conversation here. Now scamper off and go attend to somebody's car," Dexter sneers.

Jared steps forward. "I'm sorry for the confusion, but you seem to have mistaken me for someone who gives a fuck about your privacy." He takes another step forward. He's a bit taller than Dexter is and more muscular. His mere presence, in general, is just *more*. "Now, quit hassling the lady and beat it before

I tell management that some suspicious character is hanging around outside the bathrooms."

Dexter's nostrils flare as he stares hatefully at Jared, but then he finally tears his gaze away and glares at me. "This isn't over, Vera, and you know it." He stabs a finger at me then stalks off down the hallway, heading back to the ballroom.

"Boyfriend who left you on the side of the road?" Jared stares at his retreating back before his eyes fall on me. They then stalk up and down my body in a way that makes my blood heat for a whole different reason. The way he looks at me is almost feline with its laziness, as if he's found something he wants to take his time devouring.

I clear my throat. "Ex and yes."

"Vera." His eyes attach themselves to mine, my name leaving his mouth in a husky rasp like he's sampling the sound of it. My gaze stays glued to his for a heartbeat too long. What the hell is wrong with me? He's the valet, for Christ's sake. Not to mention a foul-mouthed flirt. I should go. I need to go. But my feet don't move, and I can't stop staring. "You seem to be in the habit of rescuing me."

His teeth sink into his bottom lip. He drags them over it before releasing it and saying, "I can be in the habit of doing anything you need, beauty. Say the word, and I'll put you on the back of my chariot and whisk you away."

"You're persistent."

"You're probably more than worth the effort," he fires back.

My brows rise, but my heart kicks forcefully at my ribcage at his words. "For what?" I ask. "A quick fuck?"

His eyes narrow. "Well, I wouldn't say quick. In fact"— he holds up a finger and steps forward, crowding me into the wall—"I can make it last. All. Night. Long." His finger drops to the exposed skin of my chest, his gaze following and no doubt catching the way my breathing escalates. He trails it over the swells of my breasts, lifting his gaze to fix itself to mine. He's barely touching me, but I feel it in every part of my body. Zapping every one of my nerve endings to life like an electrical current.

"And then what?" I manage to breathe out.

His brows lower over those captivating eyes. "What do you mean?"

"What happens after?"

He shakes his head. Disappointment washes over me when his hand leaves my chest to drop down to his side. "You've never had a one-night stand?"

I just stare at him in response. He blows out a heavy breath. "Well, it goes a little something like this ..." His lips tug to the side. "I take you home, or anywhere you want, strip you naked, and lick every inch of you. Then, if I should be so fucking lucky, you might wrap those perfect bee stung lips of yours around my cock so I can fuck your mouth. Then ..."

Feeling so turned on that my panties are now wet, I almost scream, "Stop." I take a deep breath. "Please, I get it."

He tilts his head. "Oh, I think you're starting to. But as to what happens after?" He shrugs, placing his hands in his pockets. Like he's teasing me. Like he knows I need them on me and is taunting me. "We both go our separate ways. And if I've done my job right, which I always do, then you're officially ruined for anyone else."

I squeeze my eyes closed then open them and direct them to the wall behind his head, scared he'll see my crumbling willpower.

I quickly search for some bravado. "Why would I want to do that? If it's a one-time thing, I mean. A girl can't go through life having mediocre sex, now can she?"

He frowns. "I'm not looking for anything serious."

He says it like it's a disease he doesn't want to catch. It makes me laugh.

"Right. Just fun?" I straighten from the wall and adjust my dress.

"Right. I'm not in the market for anything more than that."

"You're making a really convincing argument; you know that?" I huff out another disbelieving laugh.

That mischievous smile returns. "Women know what they're signing up for with me. No reason you shouldn't be aware, too."

I stare at him for a minute, wondering what it'd be like to let go. To allow this man—who's nothing like what I'm used to—to have his way with me. My panties grow wetter, but my head says to walk away. "Good night, Jared."

I leave him without a backward glance, heading straight for the bar to try to wash away the heat coursing through my veins.

"Vera, darling. How are you? How is your father?" Margaret Collins, wife of one of my father's colleagues, asks as she sidles up next to me. Fantastic. I've barely had a sip of my champagne, and someone has already found an opening.

"He's good. Busy, as usual." I don't offer up any questions about her well-being in return. Because, to put it mildly, I don't really care. Margaret smiles thinly then purses her lips as her eyes skim over my outfit. Whatever. Many of the older crowd usually choose not to dress up. Well, not to dress up as anything other than their soulless selves. "Good to know. Have you tried the crab cakes? *Divine.* Anyway, I really should be getting back to Richard. Have a good night, dear."

I nod my head and give her a forced smile before taking a huge swig of my champagne. The girls finally find me a few minutes later, thankfully distracting me from searching the crowd for Jared. Not that he should be out here anyway, being the hired help and all.

"We thought you might've fallen in and were about to come see if you needed rescuing," Isla remarks while frowning at my still flushed cheeks.

Tipping my glass back, I relish in the feel of the icy liquid sliding down my dry throat. I place it down and gesture for another one. "Someone else rescued me," I tell them. "From Dexter."

Their brows rise as they turn to face me fully. "What happened?" Cleo whispers.

"The guy who took me home earlier this week? When Dexter left me on the highway?" They both nod. "He's here, a valet, and told Dexter to leave me alone when he found him harassing me in the hallway."

They both smile. "Oh, my God." Cleo claps her hands together. "What are the odds? Wait, valet?"

I nod. "Oh …" she says.

Isla elbows her. "Who cares. He's hot, right?"

Hot isn't really a term I'd use to describe Jared. *Too much* is what comes to mind, instead.

"He's a cunning bastard who offered to whisk me away." I laugh hoarsely.

Their faces morph with eager excitement when I whisper what he said to me.

"Holy shit, Vera." Isla starts fanning herself.

"You should totally hit that," Cleo says firmly.

"He's not for me." I take a sip of my champagne.

"So?" Cleo says. "He doesn't have to be your type to rock your world." She winks, but it looks more like she has Tourette's.

Isla laughs. "Lord, give up trying to wink already."

Cleo huffs and sips some of her cocktail. We move into the room and grab some food, dodging our family's business associates and their wives with expert precision. Dexter doesn't move from his spot by the wall, his hawk eyes watching my every move as Lisa vies for his attention.

When it nears eleven o'clock, I find a secluded table on the outskirts of the room while Isla and Cleo dance and laugh with the Devon brothers. My feet are killing me, and I'm tired, but I'll wait until they're done to tell them I'm going home.

Resting my head on my hand, I watch them, observing the casual joy that radiates from them as they do something so simple. And in doing so, I can't help but wonder where I went so wrong. Why I can't stumble across something—feel something—other people take for granted just as easily?

It doesn't seem fair.

Then again. Life is never fair. There always needs to be balance.

The organ that beats in their chests is good. Pure. It makes sense that they get to tip the scales when they should feel like it.

My peripheral vision locks on a figure in the doorway to the ballroom, and my gaze shifts to take in Jared. Who's watching me. Nothing about his playful expression gives anything away, but I know he's giving me one last chance to take him up on his offer.

Maybe it's the champagne. Maybe it's sitting here feeling disgustingly sorry for myself ... but indecision wars within, making my stomach coil into a tight knot.

Looking back at the girls and taking in their laughing faces once more, I decide to do something I know I'll likely regret. But my feet carry me across the room anyway to say goodbye. They both giggle and demand I call them tomorrow with every last detail, but I hardly hear them. My ears are ringing with the sound of my stampeding heart beat as I turn and walk over to the exit. To Jared.

"My place or yours?" I ask once I've reached him.

His eyes widen a bit, but he replies instantly. "Yours."

I nod and let him grab my hand, reveling in the rough warmth of it as he leads me toward the back of the hotel. "How're you planning on getting us there?"

"My bike's out the back." I stop and glance down at my dress then raise my eyes and brows pointedly at him.

"Right." He scrubs a palm over his mouth. "Never mind. We'll make it work." He starts walking again.

"Hey," I hiss. "Stop. I'm not getting on that thing in this dress."

He doesn't answer me, just turns us down a bunch of hallways before finding an exit. He pushes the door open to an alleyway, and the late October chill instantly assaults my bare arms. We stop at his bike, tendrils of fog drifting in the night air as I glance around at other employees' cars, dumpsters, and garbage cans. Lovely.

His hand gently tips my chin around to face him; he removes his hold on my hand to tuck the helmet gently over my head. His gaze roams up and down my body while he buckles it. "Wank bank material for months."

"Excuse me?" I ask.

"Nothing." He grins, turning and throwing a leg over his bike then taking a few minutes to start it up while I just stand here. Trying to think about what to do with my clutch, I start to wonder how the hell I even ended up in this situation. This isn't me. I don't do this kind of thing. Why the hell am I inviting this valet into my bed?

A steady rumble follows the roar of his bike, echoing off the brick walls in the deserted alley. Then he's taking my clutch and tucking it away in a bag attached to his bike.

"Come on." He revs the bike and gestures with his head for me to climb on.

Despite hating everything about myself right now and my confusion, I can't help but feel a little excited as I climb back on this death machine. I know, I need to make an appointment with a psychiatrist or something. Stat. I place a hand on his firm shoulder and use my other to lift the skirt of my gown into a bunch of material as I climb on behind him. I stuff it all down between my legs as best as I can, my bare legs protesting the chill. Jared reaches into the bag on the side of the bike and passes me a jacket. I stare at it dumbly for a moment before he says, "It won't bite, Frost. Put it on."

"Frost? What is with that?" I ask, taking it from him and reluctantly pushing my arms through the leather sleeves.

"You're a little frosty, sweetheart. But that's okay; I'm not looking for nice tonight. Wrap your arms around me."

Dumbfounded by his statement, I do as I'm told and wrap them tightly around him. Then we're moving down the alley and turning onto the busy city street. The lights and sounds all blur into one sensation that wrap around me like a bubble. Some of my dress escapes and flutters into the air behind us, but my thoughts have flown away in the wind, so I can't find it within myself to care.

CHAPTER SEVEN

I grab my clutch from Jared, hopping off the bike to open the gates for him to drive through. While I wait, I throw a wave to Frank, one of the security guards. Jared parks in the visitor parking, and I start walking up the sidewalk to the glass doors while he follows behind.

My mind free-falls into returning confusion and doubt when the elevator finally dings and we step inside. But the second the doors close and I press the button to my floor, I'm against the wall, and Jared's hands are running down the bodice of my gown, trying to find a way to get it off.

His lips touch my throat, and that's all it takes to make me melt into him.

"You smell amazing ... What is that?" His nose runs up my jaw, and he inhales deeply. Fingers tug, finally finding the clasps at the back of my dress, and he starts undoing them one by one. The elevator dings, and he slowly steps back. Holding my dress up with one hand, I step out and move down the hall to unlock my door. I drop my purse on the entry table, and in an effort to stop myself from second-guessing what I'm about to do any longer, I let go of my dress. It pools to the floor in a mess of black material, feathers, and shimmering crystal. Standing in my black pumps and matching lace black bra and panties, I take a deep breath and lift my gaze to Jared.

He's leaning against the closed door, a hand rubbing over his mouth and the scruff on his jaw. Swallowing hard, I steel my spine and lift my chin. I've never been self-conscious about my looks. But suddenly, with the way he's looking at me, nerves set my blood on fire. My chest heaves up and down, and his eyes lower to it, roving over my c-cup breasts. I tell myself to stop it, to calm down, but then he moves. I blink, and he's right in front of me, his green eyes vibrant and hooded while he murmurs, "Well, shit. Just when I thought I'd seen the best …"

My brows lower, my lips pursing while I try to wrap my head around his words. He doesn't give me a chance, though. With his fingers tilting my chin, his warm breath ghosts over my lips. His eyes flit back and forth between mine. "I wanted to take my time savoring you. Every fucking beautiful inch." He swallows audibly. "But seeing you like this has me so fucking hard I can barely see straight."

That makes me smile, and seeing it, he chuckles. The sound evokes a shiver. His other hand wraps around my waist, and my palms plant themselves on his hard chest. I tentatively move them up to his shoulders, trying to resist the urge to pull his mouth to mine.

My lashes flutter and breathing becomes insignificant. The only thing I need is those lips touching mine. His head lowers even more, his mouth hovering a hairsbreadth out of reach. The anticipation is killing me in the sweetest possible way. Can you die from too much of it? I have an alarming thought that if you can, it'd be a beautiful yet horrifying way to go.

Breathing the same air, I taste the hint of tobacco and mint on his breath; my restraint snaps, and I close the tiny gap, melding my lips to his. My eyes close, and I'm lost in the unexpected softness of his lips. He groans, and I rejoice at the sound, my heart skipping unevenly and my stomach rioting with flutters. Parting my lips, he skims his tongue between them. My hands move up his neck, sinking into his thick hair. I tilt my head more, inviting the warmth of his soft tongue inside my mouth when I open even farther. At the first touch of our tongues, I whimper, and any thread of self-control he was holding disappears into the charged air of my apartment.

He picks me up, lifting me out of my dress on the floor. My legs wrap around his waist, my heels digging into his ass. Reluctantly tearing my lips from his—my breathing uneven and my vision slightly blurry—I growl, "Off," and tug at his vest and white dress shirt. He smirks and stops in the hallway then turns for the kitchen. He lowers me to the counter, my ass resting on the cool marble countertop, and I pull the vest open, shoving it down his arms. I let go for him to tug the white shirt over his head. His arms are lean but still thick, and his chest broad. Both muscular. My mouth hangs open at the sight of his tattooed arms, roses and tombstones shaded in black and gray cover them.

He moves to unzip his fly, and I snap into action, stopping him. Biting my lip, I reach down between us and do it myself then tuck my hand inside his black boxer briefs. My eyes never leave his, so I catch every reaction my touch elicits. His nostrils and eyes both flare when my hand finds his velvety length. Rock hard with pre-cum resting at the tip. I swipe my thumb over it, and he visibly shivers. Grinning, I squeeze him gently and start to move my hand up and down, loving the way his breathing turns ragged until he stops me. "Shit, you gotta stop, or this will be over real quick."

"Oh? What happened to all night?" I taunt.

He leans in to nip my bottom lip, and my panties grow even wetter. "Frost"—he tsks—"this is only round one."

My breath hitches, but I try not to let any more surprise show and lift my thumb between us to my mouth, sucking his excitement from it and fluttering my lashes.

"Jesus fucking …" His mouth crashes into mine, rough hands tangle into my hair, and I hear the *ting* of my hair pins as they fall to the counter and floor. Teeth biting and tongues tangling in a violent war of heat and all-consuming lust have me wishing these minutes will never end.

Fumbling with his pants, he removes his lips from mine to tear open a condom wrapper with his teeth. I almost explode right then and there, just watching his animal-like expression, his eagerness to get inside me. Taking the condom from his mouth, he hisses when I toss the wrapper to the floor and roll it onto him. I scoot forward to the edge and move my panties to the side, but his fingers shove mine away. His eyes probe mine when his thick, calloused finger trails through my folds. "Fuck me; you're soaked."

"Uh-huh." It's all I can say, and I'm surprised I can even say that much. My head rolls back when his finger finally fills me. He hooks and drags it exactly where I need it, and my need to come builds so rapidly that for the first time in my life, I'm not above begging.

"Please."

Teeth scrape over the mounds of my breasts, and he tugs the cups down. "Please what?" His voice is throaty, only fueling this inferno blazing inside me.

"Fuck me."

He chuckles. "I've never heard two words sound so good."

His hot mouth wraps around my nipple, and I start rocking into his hand. "God damn, these tits." He releases my nipple and removes his hand. I almost growl at the loss until he squeezes both my breasts roughly and stares at them in awe. "Most perfect tits I've ever seen."

Despite my frustration, I can't help but laugh at the boyish wonder plastered all over his beautiful face.

He rears back, tilting his mouth up on one side. "Something funny, Frost?"

I nod. "You. They're only boobs."

He shakes his head. "You wouldn't understand." He exhales loudly. "Christ, I'll never forget these tits." He squeezes them hard then circles his thumbs over my hard nipples. "But can I take a picture? Just in case?"

Laughing again, I grab both sides of his face and bring his forehead to mine. "One-time deal means no pictures, Hero." He pouts, and I almost cave. Almost. "If I don't come soon, I'm liable to throw you on the floor and have my way with you until I do."

"Holy … okay. Later. You can totally do that later. Right now, though?" He presses his lips to my ear and rips my panties clean off before aligning himself at my entrance. "It's my turn, so I hope you like it rough."

I frown in dismay. "Those were a limited edition Victoria's—" My mouth slams shut, thanks to his cock sliding inside me. He doesn't stop, and he doesn't allow me to catch my breath until he's all the way in. "You were saying?" His hand wraps around the back of my head, tangling into the strands of hair at the nape of my neck.

"I w-was … oh, fuck …" He swivels his hips, and my eyes squeeze closed. I can hardly think, let alone talk. I've never felt so full. Not just of him, but of everything this moment is causing me to feel.

He chuckles again. "Hold on, beauty."

I moan loudly when he pulls out and slams back home. Over and over until I'm clawing at his chest and biceps. His hands move to my thighs, opening me wider, allowing him to sink inside even more. He holds them in a grip so tight it's bound to leave bruises, but I don't care. I climb higher, faster, with every single thing he's doing to me. My eyes open and stay locked on his, our mouths touching yet unable to do anything more than that. It's already too much.

His thrusts slow, and he looks down, watching his length drag out of me before slamming home so hard the meeting of our flesh creates an audible slap that makes us both groan. "Shit, you feel so good. I'm not going to last much longer."

I don't respond; I'm so close I'm lost to it, almost delirious.

"Gonna come, are you?" His voice almost undoes me, and all I can do is nod.

"Yeah?" he asks. "I can feel you." He keeps torturing us—both with his thrusts and his talking between them. "Squeezing me. So damn tight." He grunts then releases my thigh to move his hand between our panting mouths. He sucks on his thumb, and if that wasn't enough to make me fall apart, the way he lowers it to where we're connected and uses it to softly circle my clit definitely does it. My hips buck as my walls clench tight.

Utter bliss rolls through me from my spinning head to my curling toes. I moan so loudly that his lips crush themselves to mine, his hips circling and grinding into me draw out the pleasure. He pulls out, thrusting twice more, then grunts loudly and groans. The gruff sound vibrates deliciously against my kiss swollen lips.

We breathe heavily into each other's mouths, and a laugh

escapes me. "Well, fuck."

He laughs, too. "You got that right."

After kissing me softly, he hooks his arms behind me, grabbing my ass to carry me out of the kitchen and down the hall. "Bedroom down here?"

I nod, wrapping my arms tighter around his neck. "Yep."

He whistles as he steps inside, moving over to the bed. "Quite the palace you've got here, beauty."

He takes a seat on the bed, and I pull back to stare down at him, wiping some of my red lipstick from his mouth. "Yeah. You do realize you're still inside me?"

Reaching up to tuck some hair behind my ear, he bites my bottom lip, dragging it into his mouth and rolling it between his teeth. I feel him twitch inside me. "Get used to it. It's where I'm staying all night."

His words both scare and excite me. I run my nails over the back of his neck, and I swear he purrs. "Sounds good to me."

CHAPTER EIGHT

Waking up alone has never bothered me before. In fact, I rather like having the bed to myself and used to loathe the nights when Dexter stayed over. Waking up this morning felt different. When I opened my eyes and rolled over to pat the empty side of the bed, it was already cold. I'd almost believe last night never happened at all if it weren't for the note on the nightstand, the slight ache between my legs, and his scent still on my pillow.

Best I've ever had.
You've got my number,
Frost. ;)

P.S. You should
definitely use it to
send me a picture of
your tits. K? Thanks.
xo

I sit back on the couch, trailing my fingers over his messy scrawl as memories of last night flash through my mind with such vivid detail that I fear they'll haunt me forever.

Ruin me, indeed.

He gave me two more orgasms before we finally fell asleep in a sweaty, sated tangle of limbs in the early hours of the morning. One with me riding him, his hands and mouth all over my breasts. The third from him spooning me. It was sleepy, lazy, and so fucking good that I feel flushed just thinking about it.

My phone rings, and I stare at it for a moment then lean forward to finally answer it before it hits voicemail again. "Vera! Oh, my God. Spill. I've been trying to call you all morning." Isla's preppy, excited voice does nothing to move me out of my tired, post-orgasmic haze.

"Hey." I clear my throat. "Yeah, I slept in."

Which isn't a lie. By the time I woke up to discover that Jared was gone, it was midmorning.

"Whatever. So? Tell me already! How was it?"

My sigh is so big that my whole body seems to heave with it. But I go ahead and tell her. Not every detail but enough.

"Oh. My. God." She groans. "I'm not going to lie; I'm actually a little turned on right now. In the kitchen? Shit." I sputter out a laugh, and she continues, "But wait, why do you sound like someone ran over your nonexistent dog? You've just had the greatest sex of your life."

And that's what I don't understand myself. "I don't know."

Regret. I should regret it because I know he's right. There's no way I'll have sex again in the next decade without comparing it to last night. But I can't. It felt too good.

This might sound dumb, but doing that with him, during those mere hours … I felt free. Like I could step outside myself. Out of my life. Be somebody else for a little while.

"What do you mean you don't know? Oh," she says. "Do you like *like* him or something?"

Like him? "We're not in high school anymore, Isla. And no, I don't like *like* him."

But I kind of do. Something about him calls to that small, restless part of me, and despite his bad-boy exterior, I know there's more behind those emerald eyes than he allows the world to see. He's intriguing and captivating, capable of drawing you in against your better judgment.

"Okay, if you say so. Anyway, Cleo totally got out of her mind drunk and went home with Cameron Devon."

Oh, hell. "Again? Didn't she sleep with him in our senior year?"

Isla hums. "Yup. He took her virginity, remember?"

My hand meets my forehead. "Oh, dear God. He did too! She said she's always regretted that."

"Uh-huh. Well, gotta go. Just wanted the deets. And hey, you should totally get in touch with him again if he was as good as you say. Especially seeing as Dexter took Lisa home." She yawns. "You're a free agent again, so go get 'em, tiger."

Laughing, I hang up the phone feeling slightly better. Isla mentioning Dexter leaving with Lisa doesn't bother me. It also doesn't surprise me. I knew it'd probably happen, and who knows how many times they've slept together behind my back anyway. A quiet snort escapes me because it was probably more times than he fucked me. Again, I thank God I made sure he wore a condom.

My thoughts move back to Jared, and Isla's parting advice to call him has me chewing my bottom lip. But I know I can't do that. He said one night, that he wasn't looking for anything more. And even if he was, I can't have him. Not only is he not my type, but he's also not part of this fucked-up world I live in. There'd be no future there.

The thought has my heart sinking.

So, no, I won't be calling him. If he's ruined me after one night, I'd hate to see what he could do after two. And I know—even if he loves my boobs—he's had a taste and is probably satisfied now anyway.

The following week brings the start of November. It also passes by at an unbearably slow pace, only to be made worse when my father calls on Thursday morning to ask—though it's never a question—me to be at his place for dinner by seven p.m. Way to ruin my first day off for the week.

I order some groceries and spend the day trying to get lost in a book, but every time I read about a character with green eyes, a certain pair comes to mind. I get so flustered that I almost whip my vibrator out. But I'm too unsettled. Even for that.

Once it hits six o'clock, I get ready and make the half-hour drive from Rayleigh to my father's castle-like home in Bonnets Bay. I'm not even exaggerating. Much.

The cream exterior and sweeping balconies on each of the eight bedrooms upstairs, the vines crawling across it all … It's a fairy tale kind of home. But it's allure is deceptive. And when I step inside, my feet landing on the same marble floor I used to slip and slide on in my socks, much to Gloria's annoyance, I instantly wish I could turn around and walk back out to my car.

It's cold. Too clean. Sterile. The picturesque staircases, expensive paintings, plants, and statues only make it worse. It's more of a museum. And despite what my father says to me tonight, I know there's no way I could've gone ahead and played house with Dexter. I may be stuck, and I know exactly what my future should be, but I think I'd rather face whatever repercussions come my way than continue to suffocate underneath somebody else's wishes for me.

"Vera," Paul, now nearing retirement, says as he stops by the entryway. He turns to look at me, wearing a smile on his face.

"Paul." I nod stiffly. Gone is the girl who dreams, who dares to question her life. In her place is what I need to be to see this dinner through and appease my father.

"Your father is in the dining room already." He holds his hand out and gestures for me to move ahead of him, so I do, leaving the doors wide open for him to close. My father has to pay him for something other than his hurtful jokes and opinions of his daughter, I suppose. Gloria was fired the minute I turned fourteen, and I've never heard from her since. Which says an awful lot of nothing good about how she felt about me.

My black knee-high boots click on the floor as I meander slowly down the hall. Taking a turn, I walk down another hall then after turning again, I finally reach the dining room. It's no different from the rest of the rooms. Aside from the gigantic oak table fit for a family of twenty instead of a family of two that sits in the center.

My father's head snaps up from the paper in his hand; he lowers it to the table and removes his glasses. His brown eyes rake over me from head to toe. If I didn't know better, I'd say he was wondering about my well-being. But no, probably just scrutinizing my fabulous taste in clothing. I opted for tight black jeans, a light blue vintage inspired blouse, and my black blazer, which instantly reminds me of the first time I laid eyes on Jared. I snuff out the memory and force my red lips into a smile. "You're home early."

He rises from the head of the table, and I take in his tall, large frame. Well over six feet tall and at almost fifty years old, Oliver Bramston's looks could rival those of men half his age. Too bad he's a raging asshole.

"Only a day." He brings his hand to my chin when I stop in front of him, tilting my face to the right and then to the left. My brows furrow while I try to work out what the hell he's doing.

"What are you doing?" I finally ask.

He stops, staring into my eyes for a heartbeat longer than I'd like. I try not to swallow, to cower at all, knowing he'll see it. "Just trying to figure out if you're actually my daughter or some other idiot woman who thinks it's funny to waste people's time."

I rear back, my eyes widening. "Excuse me?"

He takes a seat, gesturing for me to do the same in the one next to him. I do, wondering what Dexter has told him. Jesus, I should pay someone to key his precious fucking car for this. Because somehow, I don't think I'll be able to walk out of here with the same intentions I just walked in with.

"You know very well what I'm talking about." He folds his hands in front of him on the table, narrowing his eyes on mine. "You have everything a woman could want. *Everything*. But I'm not going to be around to take care of you forever, and Dexter? He's willing to do that."

I shake my head. "But I don't love him. It wouldn't last."

He slams his fist onto the wood table, and I cringe inwardly, trying desperately to maintain my outwardly calm composure.

"Love is for fools, Vera. And you're no fool. You're a smart woman; you'll figure out a damn way to make it last if you know what's good for you."

Good for me. Right. "He's not it," I whisper.

"What?" He raises his voice even more.

I clear my throat, averting my gaze to the table. "He's not good for me. You'd know that if you paid any attention at all." My lungs seize as I hold my breath in fear of what he'll say next. And though I feel his gaze burning holes into the side of my face, he doesn't respond. Dinner arrives a second later, thankfully giving me a few minutes of reprieve while my father eats. I move my steak and salad around my plate, my appetite long gone.

His cutlery drops to his plate a minute later, and I glance over at him. He wipes his mouth with a napkin. "Are you going to eat or just stare at it?"

Gritting my teeth, I cut into my steak and take a small bite. He nods. "Now." He drops the napkin beside his plate and picks up his glass of brandy. "You know what you need to do, don't you?"

I lift another piece of steak to my mouth, staring at him with clear disbelief that tears apart my indifferent mask. He takes my non-answer his own way, of course. "You'll make things right with Dexter immediately."

The food gets jammed in my throat. I thump my chest and reach for my water, guzzling it down and trying to breathe.

"Don't be dramatic." I swear he rolls his eyes, but I'm too busy trying not to die to see if I'm correct. Finally, it goes down, and I wipe underneath my watering eyes.

"Seriously?" I almost screech the word at him.

"Watch your tone. And you know how serious I am." He takes a sip from his glass.

He's insane. "I'm not doing it. You can't arrange things like that in this day and age."

I reach for my purse and am about to scoot my chair back to stand when he says, "I'm not arranging a damn thing. You two did that all on your own."

"You can't honestly think you can decide who I date."

"Oh, but I think I can." My blood turns cold with his dry laugh. "You like those designer clothes you're currently wear-ing? The access to large sums of my money any time you wish, hmmm?" He slams his now empty glass down on the table. "Of course, you do. Sit down and finish your dinner."

Don't. Just go. He wouldn't do it.

But that naïve voice in my head has a way of blinding me to things I don't want to see.

He would. He'd do it in a heartbeat. I should go anyway. I know I should. But that innate fear of the unknown, of what I'd do, has me sitting back down and picking at my food again.

Because I can't do it on my own. Not yet.

I need my grandmother's check.

Two months. Just two months and I'll walk away.

But what I'll do in the meantime, especially about Dexter, is anyone's guess.

CHAPTER NINE

"You look fabulous!" Isla sings when I open my front door for her.

Cleo agrees. "God, that dress. You look like every man's dark fantasy."

That makes me laugh while I close the door. I'm wearing a dark green skintight dress by Dolce & Gabbana that I picked up on sale last summer and haven't worn yet. It sits midthigh. I've paired it with my black boots and an extra-long, lacy black shawl that sits loosely over my arms and falls to the hemline of my dress. Isla's dress is midnight blue, long sleeved, and puffs out at the hips into a cute ruffle of gathered material.

"Cleo …" I start, but she waves a hand to stop me.

"Don't even. I love it, and that's all that matters." She grabs my clutch and phone from the entry table, tucking my phone into it as I continue to stare at her … overalls. Sometimes she gets a bit eccentric with her fashion choices. She's yet to learn that just because it looked good on a fashion runway or in a magazine doesn't mean it's going to look good once it's worn in real life.

"Whatever," I mutter, taking my clutch from her and fluffing my hair, which I've styled with loose curls at the ends. We make our way downstairs to climb into Cleo's Town Car and start the drive across the city.

"Here's to great sex and fan-fucking-tastic champagne!" Cleo hollers.

We lean forward in our seats and clink our glasses together before tipping the cool liquid into our mouths. Relaxing back into my seat, I heave out a sigh and try to relax. I need this—a night out. It's been too damn long since we just went out for the hell of it and had some fun.

The visit to my father's house the previous night is still much too fresh on my mind. What an asshole. Rage has me tensing all over, and I tip the rest of the champagne down my throat, moving for a refill to smother the feeling.

I haven't told the girls yet, knowing they'd be horrified. But that's not the only reason. Telling them will make it feel real. And I don't have a lot of freedom regarding the simple things like love, fun, and being myself. Breaking up with Dexter has given me a piece of myself back. I can't do it; I can't go back to him and beg forgiveness like some weak, pathetic girl who's solely reliant on men for everything she has in her life. Because although that is true, doing so would likely snuff out that tiny, flickering part of me that's telling me to hold on and stand my ground.

I highly doubt my father's going to allow me to wait two months. He did say immediately, after all. But a girl can dig her amazing heels into the ground and damn well try.

"Where are we going?" I ask, staring out the window at the bright lights that illuminate the dark.

"Cleo's got a thing for this guy who plays on open mic night at a bar near the slums," Isla informs me while she checks her lipstick using the front-facing camera on her phone.

That explains the weird choice of outfit then. "What about Cameron?"

Cleo shrugs, fidgeting with the stem of her champagne flute. "What about him?"

My brow rises. "Um, didn't you sleep with him last weekend?"

She lifts her eyes to me, narrowing them. "Yeah, so? You slept with that valet."

Isla snorts, and I do my best to ignore the feeling that the mere mention of him elicits. "Well, what's going on there?"

"Nothing." She averts her gaze out the window. "I just wanted to see if it'd be any better, then maybe I could erase the horrible memory of him taking my virginity." She returns her gaze to us, a mischievous smile pulling at her pink glossed lips. "You know, now that we're both not beginners fumbling around in the dark spare room at one of our family's dinner parties."

When she doesn't elaborate, I ask, "And? Was it better?"

She shrugs again. "Marginally. I did come, eventually."

We all laugh, and then I decide to dig further. I really don't want to go to a bar. "Who's this guy you want to see tonight?"

"Ugh. She's obsessed with him." Isla shakes her head.

"I am not. He just plays really awesome music," Cleo says.

Isla snorts. "Right. What instrument does he play then?"

Cleo's face screws up in confusion. "What's that got to do with it? He sings … He has a nice voice."

Isla laughs. "But he's gay; I swear I saw him kissing his boyfriend out front when we left last month."

"He's not." Cleo crosses her arms.

"His songs were about men!" Isla says in exasperation.

Oh, dear God. "Cleo, why don't we just go to that new club that's opened up down on Malone Ave?" I suggest as nicely as possible. I don't feel like getting felt up by some old shmuck or sitting on any sticky seats.

"Can't we just go for a little while? Please?" Cleo pouts, and gives us her puppy dog eyes.

"Oh, fine. But the second he's done, we're gone." I huff.

We get dropped off outside the Westbrook, which is crowded with people spilling out onto the street. There's tacky yellow and pink posters all over the windows and bricks, advertising cheap beer and open mic night. Shit. I'm trying to think of an escape plan when Cleo grabs both our hands and practically drags us through the doors. The smell of beer and pretzels and the sound of too many voices talking in one space smack me right in the face.

I'm going to need some alcohol asap.

We push through the crowds, finding a table that someone just stumbled away from, and take a seat on the stools. "Jesus, you can hardly breathe in here without drowning your lungs in someone's body odor or beer breath," I grumble.

"Relax. It'll be worth it once you see Nathan." Cleo fans herself theatrically with the drink menu.

"That's his name? I thought it was Nick." Isla's brow quirks.

Cleo waves her French manicured hand around. "Not important."

"Right." I smirk. "You want in his pants even though he probably bats for the other team, and his name isn't important."

She scowls at me. "Oh, hush. Let's get you sedated with some alcohol already."

I start laughing, but I'm in complete agreement with her suggestion and move to do just that when a drunken voice slurs, "Hey, pretty lay-dees. You're in my sheet."

Spinning around, I pin my gaze on a forty-something-year-old bald man with a beer gut that could balance a large bowl of Cheerios on it. "I'm sorry, was your name on it?"

He looks confused for a moment and scratches at his stained wifebeater. Christ, don't they turn people away who aren't properly clothed? I glance down, and sure enough, he's wearing flip-flops. It's not freezing, but it's still too cold to be getting around in his choice of clothing.

"Uh, why would my name be on the table?" he mumbles.

"Look, baldy. You snooze, or rather, drink too much booze, and you lose; now scram." I wave my hand in the general direction of anywhere away from us.

His bloodshot eyes widen, and a smile crawls across his probably once handsome face. "Hey, how'd you know my name? Maybe it is on the table after all."

"What?" My brows screw up in frustrated confusion.

"Baldwin. That's my name." He stabs a finger at his chest with a big grin, showcasing a missing eye tooth.

"That's nice, but you're missing two important facts here. Those would be; I don't care and get lost." I flick my hand again, and this time, he seems to get it. His face looks like it crumples when he turns to go, and something twinges in my chest as I watch him.

Jesus, I'm turning soft.

"Vera." Isla shakes her head, clicking her tongue at me.

"Well, he's not sitting with us, is he?" I say before climbing down to go grab us some drinks.

"Yeah, no thanks." Cleo's nose twitches with her distaste. "He smelled like moldy ground beef."

My feet pause, and I look over at her as does Isla.

"And you know this how?" Isla laughs.

Cleo shrugs. "What? It was an accident. I was sick in bed and forgot I'd gotten it out to make dinner with a few nights before. It was a long time ago, sheesh. But that smell …" She mock shivers. "It'll stay with me forever," she whispers, tapping her nose.

She's lucky I love her, I think to myself and shove my way through drunken groups of people clustered around the front of the bar. "Hey! No cutting line, lady!"

I throw whoever said that a glower and find a cute, clean-shaven face suddenly smiling at me. "Hey, no, you just, ah, you go right ahead. My treat?" He walks up to stand beside me, and I let him buy us some drinks before I ditch him and return to our table.

Forty-five minutes and three cheap glasses of wine later, there's still no sign of this mysterious probably gay and maybe Nathan or Nick guy. Though they've just started, and I must admit, the girl on the makeshift stage isn't half bad. She's beautiful, too, which is probably why she's got the full attention of most males here. Not a natural blonde, but beautiful curly hair regardless and big green eyes. She looks like a Barbie doll, only with extra ass and boobs. She's also got that whole country rock thing going for her, too. Boots, denim jeans, tacky belt, and low slung, hot pink tank top. But her voice … it's the kind you know you'll hear on radio stations in years to come.

"Thank you," she breathes into the microphone before handing her guitar off to someone while everyone claps. I sip the last drop from my third glass of wine, watching as she walks off stage and smiles hugely at someone. She then jumps off the last step, straight into a man's arms, and every inch of my body locks up as I take in that devious, crooked smile. That slicked back brown hair and those strong arms that held me all night just last weekend. It feels like yesterday for me, as thoughts of that night plague my mind like an addiction I've forced myself to walk away from.

But while it may feel like yesterday for me, it obviously feels like nothing to him.

I watch, my body still rigid, as he carries her over to the bar, and then they're engulfed by people trying to talk to country Barbie.

"So Dexter's finally leaving you alone?" Isla asks, staring down at her phone.

Blinking, I clear my throat. "Um, yeah."

"Oh, thank God. We were about to stage an intervention." Cleo smiles at Isla, who winks at me. I know they would, too, and that's one of the reasons my heart allows room for these two girls.

"Hey, is that …?" Cleo's brows furrow as she stares at someone to our right. I don't need to look to know who she's staring at, but I do anyway, just in time to see Miss Country Singer plant a kiss on Jared's lips when he lowers her to the floor—not even three tables away from us. "Yeah, it's him," I whisper, not being able to tear my eyes away. I don't know why I care so damn much. He's not what I should want, and he's definitely not something I'll ever be able to make my own. But it still stings. My hand lifts to my chest, as if to rub it, but I force it back down to my lap and endure it.

"Wow … he gets around pretty quick then." Isla scowls.

I try to shrug, but my shoulders are too stiff.

"But you two had such an amazing night, so why wouldn't he just come back to you?" Cleo asks.

"Strings, I guess. Nobody wants strings these days. Besides, we're from opposite ends of the city food chain," I mutter quietly.

As if finally feeling our eyes on him, Jared's gaze lands on us. The woman curls herself into his side then glances over to see what has his attention before trying to execute me on the spot with her eyes. I shoot him a wink, trying to act indifferent, and then turn back to the girls. "Act busy. Talk to me," I demand.

They jump right in. Cleo brags about the rare, limited edition Burberry bag she scored off eBay for twelve hundred dollars. Isla tells us about her latest bikini waxing nightmare. They keep talking, and I try to appear invested, but it's hard when I feel his searing gaze burning into my profile.

"Oh, shit. He's coming over," Isla hisses.

My heart thumps loudly in my ears when I lift my head to find him plucking the blonde's hands off him as he tries to walk over here. He finally manages, and she looks like she's about to stomp a cowgirl booted foot on the floor in a hissy fit.

"Frost." He stops right beside me. "Didn't peg you for a bar hopping kind of girl."

I'd roll my eyes, but they're busy drinking in his black Henley and his handsome face. "You should know better than to peg me as anything, Hero."

He grins, sliding those stupid teeth over his stupid bottom lip while he looks down at me. "Ladies." He turns to the girls.

Cleo waves, smiling brightly. "I'm Cleo."

Isla just glares at him, and he chuckles. "Okay, hi Cleo and …"

"Isla," I offer, smiling at her. She gets a little protective at times. It's cute.

"Don't you have company waiting for you?" I finger the stem of my wine glass while eyeing the woman who's looking angrier by the second as she watches us. He turns around, putting a finger up to gesture that he'll be a minute. She smiles at him then goes back to staring hate at us once he turns his back.

"That depends. May I have a word, beauty?"

Cleo audibly swoons. I raise a brow at him. "No, you may not." He laughs, the sound causing the wine to slosh around in my stomach. I need away from him. "Now move. I need to use the ladies' room." I adjust my dress as I stand.

He steps back, and I make my way over to the hallway behind the bar.

"Hey." He grabs my hand, and I spin around, venom filling my eyes. "Stop, just … give me a minute."

"Why? I have business to do …" I point at the door of the bathroom, trying to scare him off. "In there."

He crowds me until my back hits the wall then rests an arm over my head. I swallow over the knot forming in my throat at his heated gaze. "You don't wanna be doing any business in there." His other hand grabs my hip firmly. "Trust me."

I try to push at his hard chest. "Whatever. Back up."

"You don't really want me to do that." He frowns. "You weren't at the coffee shop this week." His head dips down to the side of my cheek, his lips skimming over it before I remember the blonde who just had her lips pressed to his. Fire fills my bones, and I manage to shove him back off me, probably only because he's caught off guard.

"You think I want your mouth anywhere near me when you were just sucking face with Dolly Parton's niece out there?" My annoyance helps me evade his comment about the coffee shop. There's no way I'd tell him that I didn't go because I was scared of seeing him. Worried that maybe he'd barely acknowledge me.

He chuckles. *Asshole.* Fuck him. I start marching back down the hallway until he grabs me again. "Stop doing that." I tug my hand from his and turn around to hiss in his face, not realizing how close he is.

"Don't tell me you're jealous, Frost?" He tucks some of my hair behind my ear while my eyes flit over his annoyingly smug features.

"I'm not. You wanted a one-night stand; you got it. Have a nice life and remember to wrap it before you tap it." I pat his chest and walk away before he can stop me again.

CHAPTER TEN

I don't talk to Jared again for the remainder of the night. But I do finally get to see Cleo's crush play on stage a half an hour later. She's right; he's totally gorgeous and has that whole Enrique Iglesias thing going for him. But if the man who's blowing him kisses by the side of the stage, the one he keeps smiling at while he's singing, is any indication, then yep, he's definitely gay.

"I can't believe I didn't see it," Cleo mumbles when we make our way out onto the street.

Isla pats her back, and feeling kind of bad for her, I blurt, "Hey, spank bank material, though, right?" I waggle my brows which makes her laugh.

"So right," Isla agrees. "Come on; let's all go stay at my place and watch *Mean Girls*."

I kind of just want to go home, but I'd never turn down open commentary while watching *Mean Girls*.

"Frost." My feet stop moving instantly. I could've sworn

I saw him leave with the blonde a while ago. A weird sense of relief fills my chest at the fact he's still here, which means he probably didn't.

"We'll catch you later." Cleo smirks. Isla looks hesitant to leave, but I give her a reassuring smile. "I think I want to go home anyway. I'll text you when I get there."

She nods but points two fingers at her eyes then at Jared, who just laughs, before she walks off with Cleo to hail a cab down the street.

"Already finished with your country star for the night?" My hands burrow into the pockets of my shawl. The air carries a bite to it that has me wishing I was at home in a hot bath with a book.

He straightens from the wall he was leaning against, eyes never leaving mine as he stubs out his cigarette and tosses the butt into the trash can next to him. "Stella? She's a friend." He swaggers over to where I'm standing underneath a street lamp with a poster for a missing cat taped to it. I tilt my head, looking up into his face as the light from the lamp extinguishes the shadows from his beautifully sculpted features. "With benefits?"

He doesn't hesitate to answer. "Yeah, sometimes."

White-hot jealousy ignites low in my stomach. That he would return to the same woman, give her something that he gave me … This is getting messy, and I know I should go. Yep, I should definitely move my stupid feet and go. But damn it all to hell, I can't. I want him, and I don't know why. Maybe it's because I've never done well with the whole sharing thing, being a spoiled, only child. Or maybe it's because I know I can't really have him, which only makes me want him more. I don't know, but whatever it is, when he wraps an arm around my waist and pulls me into his warm chest, the only thing I do know is that I don't think I can ignore it.

"Come home with me?" His voice is soft, like butter, wrapping around my self-control and completely smothering it. His eyes plead while his breath comes in short bursts that heat my lips when he lowers his head.

"Why didn't you leave with her?"

His dark brows lower. "I thought that would be obvious, seeing as I'm standing here with you."

Oh. Well, when he says it like that. "But I saw you leave with—"

"Frost." He cuts in. "I walked her out and waited here for you. She's pissed, but she'll get over it."

When I just stare at him, he lowers his lips to rest them over mine, whispering, "Say you're mine for tonight because I don't think I'm ready for our fun to be over yet."

My eyes flutter closed, and I nod. The movement causes our lips to brush together and bends me further to his will. I pull away. "Fine. But you're washing your mouth out ten times before I allow it anywhere near me."

He chuckles, grabbing my hand and walking with me down the street to a huge, old white truck.

"You can even watch me do it," he offers, opening the passenger door for me. I climb in and put my seat belt on before quickly firing off a text to Isla about my plans for the night, telling her I'll call her tomorrow sometime.

"Where do you work?" My eyes drop to the set of coveralls on the seat beside me. He watches the road, flicking the turn signal on and turning down a dark street.

"Surface Rust," he says. "We do anything from mechanical repairs to body work on both Harleys and older model cars."

"Interesting choice of name."

A tiny smile curls his mouth to one side. "So I've been told."

"So you're a mechanic?" That explains the dirty clothes he was wearing at the coffee shop. I turn in my seat to look at him better. "What's with the valet job, then?"

He shrugs, turning down another street. "I am that, as well as many other things, I guess. And the Hedgington calls when they need staff for events; the cash is too good to turn down." He seems to be thinking about something before he continues, "It was my foster father's business, Surface Rust. He taught my brother and me everything we know. He left it to us. We changed the name and a whole lot of other shit, too."

Don't ask any more ... "Your brother works with you, then?"

It appears my self-control is nonexistent when I'm in the presence of this man.

"He did. Does, I mean." He changes the subject. "What about you? Do you spend your days as a lady of leisure?" he asks with another curl to his lip.

"I don't, not exactly." I don't know why I tell him what I'm about to say next. Why I care what he thinks or knows about me. It just comes out. "I work part time for my father. But I think he still sees me as a spoiled child who doesn't know how to do anything."

He frowns. "What do you do for him?"

"I work in the accounting department at Bramston Inc."

He coughs out a laugh. "Sorry, what?"

It'd sting if his response wasn't expected. "You heard me."

He chuckles, glancing over at me briefly then turns into the driveway of a small, run-down yellow house. The paint on the wood exterior is peeling in places, and the landscaping is virtually nonexistent. But despite looking like it's in need of an extreme makeover, the lawn is mowed, no junk is lying around, and it all looks … tidy—quaint even.

"Home sweet home." Jared turns off the truck. "I know it's not anything like you're used to, but—"

I take off my seat belt and open the door. "I don't care."

After slamming it closed, I make my way to the porch and walk up the wooden steps to his front door. He unlocks it and swings it open for me to walk in ahead of him.

I scream when something touches my leg. Jared laughs, leaning down to pick up a fluffy ginger cat. "Toulouse, meet Vera; Vera, meet Toulouse." He holds it in the air in front of my face. "Shit, you're not allergic, are you?" He goes to pull him away, but I reach forward and surprise myself by hesitantly laying my hand on his soft head, patting him gently.

"Toulouse," I mutter quietly. "Like the *Aristocats*?"

He nods. "Yeah, ah, long story." He lowers him to the worn floorboards, and Toulouse looks disgruntled. He lifts his head to look at me, purring and trotting over to weave between my legs. It makes me laugh, and I can't help myself; I lean down to pat him again.

"He's very friendly," I blurt out.

I look up when Jared remains quiet. His eyes are on me, and he's frowning for some reason.

"What?"

He's quick to reply. "Nothing. You ever had a pet?"

I shake my head. "My father wouldn't allow it. He said they were a waste of time and money."

He lets out another disbelieving laugh. "That's a bit harsh."

My shoulders lift into a shrug. I stand and walk down the hall until I find his kitchen where I wash my hands while Jared mumbles something about going to wash his mouth out. I bite my lip, grinning, and walk back down the hall. I find his living room, which houses a few old recliners and a couch that looks as old as I am.

There's a giant flat screen sitting on an old coffee table. And where a coffee table should sit are three car tires stacked into a mini tower with what looks to be a wooden plank sitting on top. I feel him stop behind me, his hands land on my hips, and I stiffen. Warm, minty breath washes over my ear when he whispers, "Miss me?"

Goose bumps rise, blazing a trail over my neck and shoulders. "You'd like for me to say yes, wouldn't you?" My voice is quiet but challenging.

He nudges his nose into my neck, smoothing his hands over my stomach. "Fuck yes, I would."

Humming, I respond with a breathy whisper, "But then I'd have to ask if you missed me, and that's making things a bit too complicated, don't you think?"

Soft lips graze over my skin. "I suppose you're right."

He spins me around, barely giving me a second to look at him before his mouth is touching mine. With my stomach tumbling over itself, I wrap my arms around his neck and tilt my head, my tongue sneaking out to skim over his top lip. That's all it takes. Like an elastic band drawn too tight, he snaps, and the aftermath is devastatingly perfect.

My eyes close as soon as his mouth presses into mine with a force that has me moaning. His hand tangles in my hair, threading through the long strands roughly while his tongue dances with mine. Teeth nip my bottom lip, dragging over it before he pulls back, breathing heavy. I open my eyes to find his hooded ones on me.

Then he's pulling my shawl off and my dress up and over my head before throwing them to the floor behind me. I'm so turned on, so lost in this desperation gnawing at my insides, that I don't even care he might've damaged a five-hundred-dollar dress. Trying to unclasp my bra, I'm distracted as I watch him take off his belt. I grab his jeans, unzipping his fly, and then shove them down his muscular thighs to the floor, biting my lip as he steps out of them. He rips his shirt over his head then his arms are scooping me up and wrapping my legs around his waist.

His mouth comes back to mine while he walks down the hallway into a dark room. I don't take in anything about it; I've got other things to do like trying to suck his tongue into my mouth and sinking my fingers into his thick hair. He drops me to his bed, the black and gray sheets unmade beneath my bare legs.

"Pussy and tits out, now," he demands roughly. The usual playfulness in his features is now gone, replaced by a wicked kind of longing that makes his green orbs almost glow in the dark room as he watches me. He tugs his blue boxer briefs down, and my eyes zero in on his impressive length. It twitches and bobs against his lower stomach when he reaches into a drawer in an old wooden night table.

Condom, right. I snap out of it and kick my boots off then tug the straps of my bra down my arms, tossing it to the end of the bed before pulling my matching panties down my legs. He climbs onto the bed, sheathing himself, and then spreads my thighs wide open.

"Still bare." His eyes dart from my pussy to my face, wearing a pleased smile.

It makes me squirm, that and knowing he can probably see how turned on I am. "Touch me, already."

He tsks. "Frost, the second you walked in my front door, you handed over any power you thought you had. The only thing I want to hear from those sexy as fuck lips of yours are yes, please, more, harder, Jared, Jared your cock is amazing, and don't stop, I'm coming."

My eyes narrow, and I growl even as my stomach somersaults.

He chuckles, his eyes still fixated between my legs. "I'm not opposed to cursing either, especially from that mouth of yours. And don't try to argue." He releases my leg, running the rough pad of his finger over my slit with such gentleness that it's barely a touch at all. "This doesn't lie."

"Jared …" I don't even know what I was going to say because the look in his eyes when they meet mine halts all train of thought. His features grow taut with obvious restraint when his eyes roam over my body. "Holy fucking Christ, you really are too beautiful …"

I frown at his muttered words, not knowing whether to take them as a compliment, especially with the hard look that accompanied their journey past his lips.

He moves forward, sitting on his knees and raising my ass to rest on his thighs. I've never been in this position, so openly laid out, my legs spread wide, my ankles hovering in the air by his sides. My sex is mere inches from his defined abs. His finger, which is still trailing idle strokes over my mound, suddenly parts it, and his green eyes watch his every move with rapt attention.

I revel in the way his chest, coated in a tiny sprinkling of hair, rises then falls harshly while he plays with me gently. When he teases my entrance, I suck in a sharp breath.

"You know …" he says, eyes still pinned to his own ministrations while he trails wetness up to my clit and circles it. "I had planned to fuck you. Thought I would just bend you over and be done with it. That that'd be all I'd need to get you out of my system."

"Oh?" I ask, though it's more of a croaky rasp as he continues to tease my swollen clit and entrance repeatedly.

He nods. "Yeah. Just one more quick fuck. But you see, I failed to see the error in my brilliant idea. Because you're the type of girl who needs to be played with first." He huffs out a breath. "Shit, your body practically demands it." He thrusts his finger inside, and my eyes squeeze closed. "And I don't think I've ever enjoyed playing with my food this much before eating my fill."

My lungs constrict as all the air empties from them; his one thumb is now rubbing my clit while he thrusts the other slowly in and out of me. "When you're done with discussing food… maybe you'd like to make me …" I break off into a long moan, panting when he presses down firmly on my clit. Heat like molten lava spreads through every vein, every artery, as my body races toward climax. "Please make me come," I manage to finish with.

He removes his hands, and I whimper, my eyes flashing open to glare icy daggers at him.

"What did I say, Frost?"

Him and that stupid nickname. I could scream right now.

"Yeah, yeah, you said not to talk. But if you don't make me come right now, I'm going to scream," I warn him through clenched teeth.

He throws his head back with a loud laugh, and my frustration ebbs and disappears at the deep, hypnotizing sound of it.

This man. Where did he come from? I'm starting to feel a little scared but not for my safety. My heart pounds furiously while I stare up at his smiling face. I worry that that smile and the sound of his laughter might just stay imprinted in my memory long after this night is over. I knew this was a bad idea, yet I was unable to say no—not to him and not to my own selfish wants.

"Such a greedy, demanding princess, aren't you? And be my guest. I'd love to hear you scream; just make sure it's my name." He ducks his head and lifts my hips, bringing me to his mouth. My head thrashes around in the tangled sheets when his tongue opens me and swipes over my entrance before roughly flicking my clit. One, two, three times … and on the fifth swipe, I'm breaking apart, trembling and whimpering as pure bliss embraces every cell in my body. His tongue gently strokes, drawing out my orgasm and then his lips are kissing my mound.

Breathing heavily, I open my eyes when he lowers my hips to the bed and then kisses a path up my stomach to my breasts. "You're a sight to behold when you come … I think I'm going to keep you overnight," he says gruffly, taking a nipple into his mouth while squeezing my other breast. His hips lower, and his hard length rubs over the wetness between my legs. He moves over to the other nipple, giving it the same attention until his teeth scrape over the hardened peak and I start to squirm again.

I grab his head, needing his lips on mine more than I need to take my next breath. He doesn't put up much of a fight; no, he just smirks before nipping my chin and giving me what I want. I get feverish from the velvety feel of his tongue stroking mine and his coarse stubble grazing my skin. My legs wind around his defined hips. Locking my ankles together at his back, I then use my feet to push down on his smooth ass. He groans into my mouth when I rock and grind against him.

"Fuck …" He tears his lips away and one of his arms disappear from beside my head to move between us and align him. Then he's pushing forward, slowly working himself inside and bringing his arm back to hold himself above me.

He stares, watching me while I adjust to his size. I do the same, my eyes widening at the delicious feel of him filling me to the hilt and searing me in the best kind of way. His eyes are glazed over with barely contained control, his nostrils flaring as he blows a gust of breath out of them.

"You feel like fucking perfection," he blurts before frowning and then lowering his mouth to rest over mine. His hips rotate, stretching and getting me used to him before he starts to lose control. "Gonna fuck you now, beauty."

I nod, at a loss for words. This feels so good. *Too* good. And I'm not sure the words he requested I say would even come out of my mouth.

He rises on his forearm, grabbing one of my legs and hooking it over his shoulder. Then he's thrusting harder, deeper, faster. My brain turns to sludge as sensation overload takes me as its willing prisoner.

"Fuck, yeah," he rasps, eyes locked on my breasts, watching them bounce with the joining of our heated bodies. He lifts his hand to roughly palm one. My eyes shut, and I surrender to the overwhelming feelings, touches, sounds, and his scent, which is filling this entire room. I've always liked sex, what I've had of it anyway, but shit, I never knew I could love it or become mindless from it. I never knew it could be like this. Earth shattering in its intensity, magical with its ability to stop time, and heart seizing in the unexpected feelings it can awaken.

"Open your eyes."

They open to see him turn his head to kiss the inside of my knee hooked over his shoulder, his thrusts still deep yet slowing down. "You okay?" His brows pull tight as he clearly tries to keep himself under control while he waits for my answer.

"Yes, harder, please." The words leave my mouth in a barely

audible whisper, which only makes him frown further. I swivel my hips, trying to encourage him to keep going.

He stares for another heartbeat then slowly picks up speed again until he's fucking me with deep, fast, and measured strokes that have me burning from the inside out every time he hits that spot inside me.

He moves my legs around his waist and lowers himself back down, ducking his face into my neck and sucking. The sound of his grunts and groans as I start to clench tightly around him takes me right to the edge. His hand moves behind my head, tangling into my hair when he says in a hoarse voice, "Do it. I wanna feel you come all over my cock, beauty."

Then I'm free-falling into a fog of pleasure-shrouded ecstasy all over again.

His thrusts speed up then stop abruptly. I barely hear him over the sound of my moaning as he groans, "Shiiiit." His big body shudders over mine.

I wrap my arms around him after he collapses on top of me, running my nails up and down his back while we both try to catch our breath. After a few minutes, he says, "Yeah, I hope you like my cock as much as I think you do 'cause you're not going home tonight."

I laugh, and the sound feels too loud in the quiet room. He chuckles, kissing my neck before rolling over and bringing me with him to lay across his chest.

CHAPTER ELEVEN

Jared hands me a grilled cheese and takes a seat next to me on his bed. I switched on the small TV that sits on his dresser when he left to go make us some food.

He grabs the remote, and I grab his hand. "I don't think so."

He blinks, and I stare at his tired eyes. "What?" he asks.

I remove the remote from his hand and place it on the nightstand beside me. "Jason Statham is on. That means you keep your paws off the remote." I take a bite from my grilled cheese.

He guffaws then looks at me. "Wait, you're serious?"

I swallow, giving him a glare. "Deadly."

He tries to stop the laughter. His lips press together, his chest heaves, and then it finally escapes. "Shit, I'm sorry. But that's just—"

"Just what?" I snap.

"Never mind. If you like older men, that's your problem, Frost."

I drop my sandwich to my plate. "Problem? I see no problem with crushing on an attractive man with a fucking great accent." Picking my sandwich back up, I take a huge bite and stick my nose in the air while I chew.

"You like British accents, do you, love?" Jared asks in what has to be the worst attempt at one I've ever heard.

I cough and swallow just in time to avoid choking, dropping my sandwich and plate when I fall backward onto the bed and laugh louder than I think I've ever laughed before.

"Oh, my God ..." I swipe under my eyes, checking my fingers for mascara.

Jared drops down beside me on an arm, leaning over me with a soft smile on his face. "That's a damn powerful laugh you got there, Frost."

The smile wilts off my face. "What do you mean?"

He rubs his thumb underneath my eye, gathering the leftover wetness and sucking it from his thumb. "I mean ..." He lowers even more until we're almost nose to nose. "It always sounds dragged out from somewhere deep inside. Long forgotten, a little broken, but a whole lot beautiful."

I suck in a harsh breath; my eyes stuck on his. "You can be very sweet sometimes."

He frowns. "I can?"

With my lips curling, I nod. "You can. Surely, you know that."

He seems to think about it for a second. "Nah, I think you just have this uncanny way of making me spill my thoughts."

"Really?" My voice turns into a whisper.

"Really."

My stomach feels like it's vibrating. I push some more. "What are you thinking now?"

He grins, bopping me on the tip of my nose with his finger.

"Nice try, beauty."

I lift my own to trace the tiny scar under his bottom lip. "Where'd you get this scar?"

His gaze shutters momentarily. "Fight."

His reluctance to tell me more has my hand moving to the back of his head to bring his lips to mine. He tastes like cheese, but I guess I do too. I don't even care because underneath it is the taste of him. And I'm becoming so addicted to it that when he parts my lips to slip his tongue inside, my chest fills with the kind of soul-deep satisfaction I never expected to find from a man. Let alone a kiss.

When our breathing gets heavy, and our hands start to roam, he pulls back. "Eat." He pecks my lips and sits up. "You'll need your strength." He winks and returns to his food. We eat in silence, and he takes our plates out when we're done.

Eyeing his bare chest and arms when he walks back in, I ask, "What made you decide to get the tattoos?"

I lie down on my back, staring at him as he crawls across the bed to lie next to me. Bending his elbow, he rests his head on his hand. "I probably should've told you this before now …" He sighs, and I hold my breath in anticipation of what he's going to say. "But I have this weird obsession with the dead. What do they call it again?" He shrugs. "I dunno. But my dream job has always been to work in a morgue; maybe one day create some zombies …" I slap his chest, and he laughs, catching my hand and tugging me to him.

"You should've seen the way your eyes bugged out." He pokes my ribs, and I groan.

"Shut up. Some people do, you know? Have a fascination with the dead."

"Oh, I know. I really don't, though." He pauses. "You find that out in one of those books of yours?"

I tilt my head back to glare at him.

"Well?" he asks.

"Fine. Yes, I did. But still, you didn't answer my question."

His arm wraps around me when I roll over to face the TV, his finger drawing circles on the bare skin of my stomach. "A friend of mine was doing his apprenticeship years ago and needed a practice dummy." He snickers. "Lucky for me, he was actually really good. One of the best in the state now."

A tired laugh flutters out of me. "You're crazy. They're permanent."

"I know. But what's life without a little risk?"

He doesn't know, and how could he? How much those casually spoken words hit me right in the gut. Taking a deep breath, I relax back into him to finish watching the movie, which Jared begrudgingly admits isn't that bad, before I fall asleep.

Bright morning light filters in around the gaps of the sheet hanging over Jared's bedroom window. I lie here, tired but too awake to fall back asleep. I think that has something to do with the strong arm wrapped around my waist and the warm puffs of breath blowing over my shoulder blade and arm. His face feels like it's squished into the side of my back. Warmth saturates my chest. It's kind of cute, but I'd find it cuter if I didn't need to pee so damn bad.

I must've passed out during the movie because Jared woke me up with his head between my legs at some point in the very early hours of the morning. He then climbed on top of me, filling me and fucking me slowly, licking and sucking my neck the whole time. He must've been tired, but I'm beginning to think he likes slow and lazy as much as he likes hard and fast. My legs squeeze together at the memory. And as if he can sense what I'm thinking about, he shifts, groaning throatily and grinding his morning wood into my ass.

"Morning, Frost." His hand moves up to my breast to hold it firmly in his hand.

"Morning."

He squeezes it then rolls to his back, stretching his arms over his head. Not wanting to waste the opportunity, I get up, running out of the room in search of the bathroom.

His laughter follows me. "Where's the fire?"

I don't bother dignifying that with a response. Instead, I open and close doors and find two more bedrooms. One of them is filled with boxes and an old bed. I hesitate when I open the door to the third. The bed is made, and there are bike magazines and a romance novel featuring a man with a bare chest on the nightstand.

Letting my eyes roam for a second longer than what I'm guessing I should, I notice a framed picture on the dresser of a young couple as well as some coins and what looks like a set of keys.

My brows furrow, but my urge to pee is stronger than my curiosity, so I close the door quietly and keep moving until I find the bathroom a bit farther down the hall. After relieving myself and washing my mouth out with some off brand mouthwash, I wash my face and try to fix my sex hair the best I can. I grumble quietly, not having much luck, but it'll have to do.

I get dressed, walking out of the bedroom to the smell of coffee and following it to the kitchen, where I find Jared leaning against the counter and drinking some.

"You okay?" he asks.

My head bobs up and down, my gaze moving to the scuffed wooden floor.

Chin up, Vera. No one makes you feel uncomfortable.

I lift my eyes, though it's hard because he makes me feel a lot of strange things. Uncomfortable only being one of them.

Looking around the kitchen, I take in the old wooden cabinets and tiled countertops in the daylight. It's really kind of cute in a cottage kind of way. His appliances don't look too outdated except for the oven and stovetop.

He gestures to the other mug sitting on the counter. "I'd assume black if I hadn't already seen for myself that you add milk." He lowers his mug. "Sugar's over there if you want some."

I ignore the barb and take a seat on a stool. It creaks as I do but seems sturdy enough. Dragging my mug over to me, I try not to cringe. I don't know if I've ever had instant coffee. Feeling rotten over that tiny, insignificant fact, I bring the mug to my lips and try not to show my distaste for it.

Jared breathes out a short laugh. "You can hate it. Don't bother pretending on my account." He tips his mug back, draining the contents before turning to rinse it out and place it in the sink.

"Any caffeine will do," I mutter and drink at least half of it before taking it over to the sink to rinse it out and place it next to his.

He clears his throat, and I turn around to find him standing in the entryway. "I actually have to work today." He scratches his head. "I know it's a dick move on my part, but it's true, and I'm already a few hours late."

My eyes narrow. "But it's the weekend."

He shrugs, turning and walking away. "Yeah, but it's my business, and I can't afford to close shop on a Saturday. I'll meet you in the truck."

Oh. Heat crawls across the back of my neck. Biting the inside of my cheek, I try to snap out of it. It's not like I was expecting anything. Okay, I guess part of me was hoping he'd ask for more time. Or to see me again before he walked out of my life … *again.*

I make my way back to his room when I hear his loud truck start outside. Bending down, I pick up my purse from where it fell from his nightstand to the floor and is half hidden underneath his bed. My eyes snag on something pink. I reach over a bit farther and pluck out a pair of pink lace panties. Cringing, I toss them to the floor and move to the bathroom to wash my hands quickly.

Pink lace is not my thing, so I know instantly they're not mine. I try to ignore the jealousy scorching my insides and making my heart twist. Who knows when they could've ended up there, really. But just knowing he's been with someone else in his bed … I shake my head. Shit, what is happening? I'm starting to sound a little crazy.

I head outside and climb into his truck, doing up my seat belt while Jared backs out of his driveway. He hits the brakes when some guy comes running out from the shack of a house next door to his. He stops by Jared's window, asking for a cigarette and maybe a few dollars. Jared winces and tries to introduce us. I ignore him, though, looking out the window while Jared deals with him.

This really is a charming neighborhood.

The drive back to my apartment is quiet. Gone is the sexually charged energy that I've come to recognize when we're together. In its place is a cold, awkward kind of silence that has my ears ringing.

When he pulls up outside my apartment complex, it's almost eleven in the morning, and my stomach grumbles loudly.

He puts his truck in park and curses. "Shit. I'm sorry, I didn't even offer you breakfast."

I shrug, grabbing my purse and opening the door. "Don't worry about it; I'm not much of a breakfast eater anyway." God knows why I'm trying to make him feel better with that lie.

He seems to see through it, though, staring at me while I stand beside the open door. But he doesn't say anything. Not about that or anything else.

My thoughts scream at him. *Ask to see me again. Tell me you'll call me. Demand a kiss goodbye.* Anything other than just staring at me as if he can't decide whether I'm worth the trouble.

I step back onto the sidewalk. "Okay, well thanks." Slamming the door closed, I turn away and walk up to the gate, trying to ignore the crushing disappointment weighing down every step I take away from him.

CHAPTER TWELVE

After staring at the blank computer screen for who knows how long, I switch it off and grab my purse.

I don't care if it's half an hour too soon; Sally can kiss my ass because I'm out of here. Standing, I right my black, slim line pencil skirt then make my way down the row of cubicles.

"Vera!" Sally's screech follows me. But I don't stop until I reach the elevator and press the button. Her heels clipping on the tiles indicate she's gaining ground. I should be worried, but I'm more amused than anything. The doors open and I step inside, pressing the button for the ground floor.

"Vera." She stops the doors from closing with her hand.

"Sal." I stand stoic, my usual mask of boredom plastered on my face.

She frowns, her lips pursing. "That's not my name, and where do you think you're going? Those statements were due on my desk twenty minutes ago."

I press the button again, and the doors attempt to close.

She steps back with a huff as I inform her, "They're done and on my desk. Get them yourself."

Her wide eyes disappear behind the metal doors. When the doors open, I step out and make my way out to the street where I left my car this morning. Climbing inside, I dump my purse on the passenger seat and drop my head to the steering wheel.

It's only Monday, barely two days since Jared left me in a pile of confusion and disappointment. I'm not this person. Sure, I'm never rainbows and sunshine, but I'm starting to find it hard to recognize the face of the woman who stares back at me in the mirror each morning.

I have his number, so of course, I could just call him. But that's not me either. Chasing someone isn't typically my style. I don't chase anyone unless they're holding a mint condition vintage Chanel bag. And even then, I'll only speed walk. Unless there's a matching coat to go with it. Then I'll sprint faster than a runner trying out for the Olympics for the very last time.

Blowing out a breath, I turn on the car and make my way across the city.

After parking, I jump down from my Porsche Cayenne and try not to smile at the familiar sight of the bookstore. Always Booked needs a huge makeover. But then again, it's kind of perfect the way it is. Its old, shabby charm has a way of making you feel like you're always welcome. No matter who you are. I learned to appreciate that years ago.

"Badger?" I close the door behind me, the bell tinkling over my head.

"Vera?" His voice sounds from the back room. I walk toward it when he emerges with a sheet of paper and pen in his hand, his wire rimmed glasses falling askew. He lifts them to his head. His hair might be completely gray now, but he's still got a lot of it, and the glasses stand no chance as they sink right in.

He smiles, and I surprise myself by giving him a small one back. No matter how unsettled I'm feeling, Badger has a way of pulling smiles from me when I least expect it.

He puts the paper down and walks over to me, patting my shoulder and saying, "I've got a donation box that just came in. Ripe for the picking. I think I saw some Jane Austen in there." He nods toward the chairs up the back. "Sit down and I'll bring it over." He turns back to the storeroom.

"Stop. You sit down, and I'll grab it."

He sighs but doesn't argue with my firm tone.

I grab the box, eyeing the mess of the storeroom and thinking it might be time to actually help him sort this out, especially if he has no plans to retire soon. Stubborn old man.

Placing it on the floor between the armchairs, I take a seat and start rummaging through it, sorting out the sellable from the junk as I go and placing them in two different piles.

He laughs lightly, picking up an old copy of *The Baby-Sitters Club* and inspecting it. "It seems I've taught you more than I realized over the years."

"A bit of knowledge and a lot of common sense go a long way," I grumble.

"Oh, dear." He puts the book down, the old chair groaning when he reclines and folds his hands over his stomach. "What's got you in a mood today?"

I twist my lips, settling back in the chair and running my hands over a hardback copy of *Persuasion*. I already have this edition, but I hold it anyway. "Aren't I always in a mood?"

He tsks. "Don't be so hard on yourself all the time. What is it?"

I don't know what to tell him. But then again, I've always

been able to talk to Badger without judgment, so maybe this time will be the same. My shoulders droop with my sigh. "I kind of met someone."

A smile tilts his lips. "Kind of?"

"Yes. Kind of."

"So no more Dexter, then?"

"No more. For now."

His bushy gray brows furrow. "What do you mean?"

I stare off toward the front of the store at the old clock ticking away on the wall near the counter. "My father isn't happy about it. He's making ultimatums."

Badger's quiet for a minute. I glance back over at him, finding him staring down at the piles of books on the coffee table.

"I see," he finally murmurs. "But you've met someone else anyway?"

Sniffing, I fidget with the book in my lap. "Yeah, I have."

"Well," he says. "Come on, tell me about it."

A laugh escapes me. "Why?"

He rolls his eyes, and I laugh some more. He's an odd one, old Badger. "Why?" He huffs. "Because my life is these four walls and the pages of a good book. You're living. I want to know about it."

That last part makes me pause. "I'm living?"

He nods. "Yes. And it's about damn time. Only taken you what? Twenty-four years?"

Shaking my head, I lean forward to put the book down on the table. How ridiculous. "I've lived."

He hums. "Yes? So you know what it is to laugh so much you think you might pass out?" My thoughts flick back to Jared and the weekend. "Do you know what it is to see the sun rise and fall, and not only admire it but also appreciate it?"

I blink slowly, and again, he continues. "And most

importantly, do you know what it is to fall in love?"

He knows I don't. The frozen expression on my face says it all even if he didn't already know. "So tell me, my dear Vera. I want to hear about this man of yours or woman …"

A snort escapes at that. "It's a man."

He shrugs. "Never know. Whatever makes you happy, I say. Anyway, hit me with it."

He starts twiddling his thumbs, so I take a deep breath and begin with, "I met him on the side of the highway after Dexter took me to see that house a few weeks ago."

His brows rise and so do the corners of his lips. He nods for me to continue.

I stare down at my skirt, picking an imaginary piece of lint from it. "I freaked out. I can't even explain it." My head shakes. "I told Dexter to pull over; I don't know why. I just couldn't breathe all of a sudden and needed to get out. But when he finally did, I didn't expect him to take off and leave me there. I don't know what I expected. It was a dumb thing to do. But it seemed vital I do it, which I know doesn't make sense."

I pause, and Badger interjects quietly, "Sometimes the things that make no sense can lead us to our greatest discoveries."

Discovery. Is that what Jared is? Maybe. "Well, that's kind of what happened. He pulled over. This big guy in a leather jacket, sunglasses, boots, and all. He ordered me on the back of his bike. I didn't have many other options because my phone had no reception. So when I thought that leaving with him might give me a better chance of getting home and living to see another day, I got on and he took me home."

I look back over at Badger, who has a big grin on his face that tells me he wants to say something but is holding himself back until he hears the rest.

Smiling, I continue, "I kept bumping into him. First, at that damn coffee shop you love so much."

That breaks his silence. "You finally went, eh? Wasn't I right?" I nod, and he waves his hand. "Sorry, sorry. Keep going."

"Then again at the Halloween ball. That's where things kind of, well … took a turn."

He holds up a hand. "No need to explain that."

I grin. "I didn't think I'd see him again, not unless I went to that coffee shop, which I was too scared to do …"

"You? scared?"

"Terrified," I admit with a whisper.

He clucks his tongue, reaching over to pat my hand. His skin is soft and warm; I squeeze his hand gently. "My, my, I never thought I'd see the day. But you did? See him again, I mean."

Nodding, I tell him, "Yeah, the girls dragged me to the Westbrook last weekend. He was there, and we, ah, hung out again."

He's quiet for another moment.

"What?" I ask.

He shakes his head. "And you enjoy spending time with this man? He seems different from what you're used to."

Enjoy is one way to put it. I bite my lip to stifle my laughter. "I do. And he is. Very different. But he's … well, from the start, he's admitted he's not interested in anything serious."

He releases my hand to rub his over his jaw, sitting back in his chair again. "Ah, a man with commitment issues." He holds up a knobby finger. "Yet he keeps coming back."

"I don't think it's on purpose. It just kind of happens." I tilt my shoulder.

He laughs. "My dear, no, no. Despite what you may think you know, a man doesn't tell you that and keep coming back just because it's convenient." My eyes widen a fraction. "Vera, you're a beautiful woman, there's no doubt about it. But you really do need to give yourself more credit."

"What do you mean by that?"

"What's in there"—he points at my chest—"only amplifies what people see out here." He waves his finger up and down my body. "You just don't allow many people to see it. But even if you try to hide it with your indifference and sharp tongue, a good man will always find it. And if he's smart, he'll cherish the full package for the gift it is."

My heart warms so much; I'm afraid I'll start crying. Damn it, I never cry. I roll my lips between my teeth and look at the ground. "How can you tell?" I clear my throat. "What if you're wrong?"

He sighs. "Mirabelle and I …" Mirabelle was his wife, who passed away before I met Badger. "Let's just say we met when we were both very young. I did a lot of things I wasn't proud of. But she was a strong woman, and she refused to take my shit." I look at him then, having never heard him curse before. "Oh, don't look so surprised. I wasn't always old and wrinkly, you know." He winks. "Anyway, I shaped up, refusing to ship out. She gave me hell for a long while, but eventually, she came around. We never looked back." He smiles sadly. "And I'd give anything to see her again. Even for just five minutes. So you'll know because the right man will not let go."

Tears sting my eyes. He rarely talks about her, and I now think I know why.

Love has always fascinated me. All my life I've spent hours obsessing over it through the pages of books. The adventure, the magic, the risk, the beauty of it, never daring to hope that it might one day be something I could have myself. True, real love.

But looking at Badger while he tries to keep his composure, I suddenly wonder if it's worth it. Maybe I'm right to stick to my what-ifs and just carry on the same way I always have.

On my own.

I grab his hand, gently squeezing it again. He sniffs and gives me a watery smile.

And I can't help it; I need to know. "Would you do it all over again? Even knowing that you'd one day have to say goodbye and have your heart broken?"

He doesn't hesitate. "In a heartbeat. As many times as God would let me. Always."

He sees my struggle to understand and pats my hand. "One day, you'll see. It's not something that can be explained or read about in books. It needs to be experienced. Does it hurt? Absolutely and some days you think it might just kill you. But the joy far outweighs the suffering, that I promise you."

I'm lost in my thoughts as we finish sorting the books in silence. Lost in the possibilities and dead ends that bleed from them.

"Well, I'm going to close up." He rises slowly, using the arm of the chair to help him up. I stand too, gathering the books and carrying them down to the front counter for him then returning to grab the box to put in the storeroom. "Thank you, dear. Now, you must be tired after a long day at work. Maybe you should grab a coffee?"

I laugh. "Subtlety isn't your strong suit, Badger."

He shrugs. "Doesn't hurt to try things on every once in a while."

I smile and grab my purse, walking outside to an early evening sky of orange and pink. Pausing near my car, my heart jolts when I decide to hell with it and follow Badger's advice again.

I walk in and order a coffee from a waitress who wears a big smile and a name badge that reads Jenna. But two coffees later, and after reading five chapters of my book with my heart galloping wildly in my chest, he never even stops by. Of course, he wouldn't. It's dinnertime, for Christ's sake.

Giving up, I pack up and leave the little shop, buzzed on too much caffeine and feeling pretty damn stupid.

CHAPTER THIRTEEN

"Remind me why we're here again." I lift my champagne to my mouth, sipping and watching the other guests flock around Cleo's parents' large living room.

Cleo sighs. "Because it's practically mandatory."

"Yeah, but the caviar is good." Isla licks her fingers.

It's Cleo's parents' twenty-seventh wedding anniversary. It took some years, but I finally figured out that her parents would probably throw a party just for buying a brand-new car, so naturally, a wedding anniversary is a huge ordeal.

"Oh, shit. Ethan!" Cleo hisses.

I lean back against the wall, watching over the rim of my glass as Cleo and Isla rush over to stop Cleo's sixteen-year-old brother from trying to steal some alcohol near the buffet. I'm so bored I feel as though I might fall asleep standing up.

"Vera."

Nope, wide awake now. I turn my head to find Dexter, who runs a hand through his wavy brown hair as he approaches me.

"Dexter." I nod. "How's Lisa treating you?"

He stops next to me, huffing out a laugh. "Wouldn't you like to know."

"Not really, just trying to make a point."

"Point made." He adjusts his cufflinks for a second. "Where've you been? You know I wanted to talk with you. Is it really so hard to answer your damn phone?"

"It depends on who's calling, really."

"You and your smart mouth."

I shrug, downing the rest of my champagne.

"Look, I know I've made some pretty dumb decisions, Lisa being one of them." He stops fidgeting, giving me the full effect of his brown-eyed stare. Which still does nothing for me. "But I'm willing to own up to them, you know, to make it right."

"Mmmhmm." I tilt my glass toward him. "What a compelling speech. Excuse me while I swoon."

Irritation flickers in his eyes. Good, I wish he'd go be irritated someplace else.

"What do I need to do? Tell me, and I'll do it. Please."

The effort it took for him to say those words must have been extreme. His jaw relaxes as if finally saying them has freed him of some burden.

"You just need to leave me alone. There, easy." I shrug again and move away, walking over to join the girls when my phone buzzes in my purse. I place my glass down on a nearby table and open my clutch, digging it out.

Jared: Miss me yet?

My breath stalls. I'd wondered if he got my number that day at the coffee shop.

It's been a week since our last night together. I was

beginning to wrap my brain around the possibility that we were done. That he'd finally lost interest.

Glancing around the room briefly, I see Dexter's now talking to my father. That's not good. But at least he's leaving me alone. I move out of the room, walking to the kitchen before I reply.

Me: I was beginning to forget all about you, actually.

He replies instantly.

Jared: Then I'd better do something about that. What are you doing?

Me: Trying not to choke on all the egos filling one house. You?

Jared: I'm thinking I'm getting tired of trying to forget you and need to see you.

Elation fills my chest and has my lips curving into a small smile.

Me: You need to, do you?

Jared: It gets worse with every fucking minute.

Laughing, I type out my response before I can think better of it.

Me: Rescue me?

Jared: Tell me when and where.

I send him the address, and he says to give him ten. Tucking my phone away, I quickly find the girls and let them know I'm going.

"Oh, no fair. Take me with you," Cleo begs.

Isla glances over to where my father is now talking to hers. "Go now before he sees. I'll make something up if he asks."

"Like what?" I ask.

"I'll say that you went home, girl issues." She shrugs. "Works every time."

Cleo laughs. "So true."

I say goodbye, grab my coat, and make my way out the front quickly, worried my father will notice but too excited to care too much right now.

As I walk down the street, the noise of the party follows me like a looming shadow. But the sound of his bike rumbling in the near distance makes me glad I'm not waiting outside the house. At least down here, farther out of sight, there's less chance anyone will notice me disappearing on the back of a motorcycle.

A headlight flashes, coming over the small crest in the road, shining over me before the bike comes to a stop.

"Get on." He jerks his head behind him and holds out a helmet. I take it from him, fumbling with the straps for a second before finally securing it. He grabs my hand, and I soak in way more from the simple touch than I should as he helps me onto the back. My dark gray and black lace cocktail dress and black heels don't exactly make the best riding outfit, but oh well. It seems to be a recurring theme with me and this bike.

Once I have my hands wrapped around his waist, he tucks my clutch into his saddlebag then revs the bike. We drive past

Cleo's parents' huge home and continue down more residential streets until he pulls into a parking lot by the beach and turns the bike off. I climb off, passing him the helmet and almost squealing when he grabs my hand, yanking me over to sit on his lap.

"Hi." His cold nose brushes my cheek.

"Hi, Hero." I drop my head to his.

"What was I interrupting?" He runs his hands over my back.

"Anniversary party." I bite my lip. "I was bored out of my brain."

He hums. "Good thing I rescued you then."

We're quiet for a minute, and I wonder if we're just going to go ahead and get to the fun stuff or if we'll maybe discuss the way things ended last week.

"I'm sorry," he finally whispers, "for leaving like I did. Why didn't you call me? Hell, why did you let me drop you off like that and not spit any of your venom at me?" His voice is gruff and low; he seems almost angry.

My eyes lift to his, and I blink. "Um, well, you said you didn't want anything serious." I shrug. "So I tried not to get too serious."

He sucks his bottom lip into his mouth and stares. My hands lift to his shoulders, clenching as the urge to lean forward and suck that lip into my own mouth becomes all I can think about.

"And if I were to change my mind about that?" Vulnerability swims in those green orbs, and it leaves me a bit speechless. My stomach drops as what he's asking starts to sink in.

My father's warning blares through my head.

I can't. It wouldn't last.

But that's not what comes out of my mouth. Far from it.

"Are you asking for serious?"

His lips brush against mine, and I shiver. "To be honest, I have no fucking idea what I'm asking for. All I know is I can't get you to leave me alone." He laughs at my confused expression. "In my head. You're always there." He sighs. "Those fucking eyes." He moves his head back to look at me, brows furrowing. "Do you like haunting me, Frost?" he asks as though he's joking, but he seems genuinely frustrated by it. It makes me laugh, which wipes the seriousness off his face, and in its absence is his usual smile. But staring at his slightly crooked front tooth, the happiness rapidly filling my chest comes to a screeching halt when I remember the panties I found in his room.

"I'm sorry, but I don't think I can do the whole sharing thing, Hero."

The streetlight highlights the severe cut of his cheekbones when he scowls at me.

"What're you talking about?"

Smirking, I admit, "The panties in your room. I saw them when I was getting my purse from under your bed last weekend." I hold up my hand when he attempts to talk. "If I'm going to commit myself to something ..." *That could upend my whole life. Christ, what am I even doing?* "In any kind of way, I don't want to have to worry about other women."

He tilts back, scrubbing a hand over his face and glancing away briefly. I start to panic, thinking he's about to tell me something I don't want to hear. But what he says instead has me shocked and worried in a much different way than what I expected.

"Her name was Dahlia." He turns his gaze back to me, voice quiet but loud enough for me to hear over the sound of the waves crashing on the beach behind us. "They were her panties. She was married, and I know, that makes me an ass.

But I was going through a rough time and wanted a distraction. She was sweet and so damn sad. I thought it'd be fun to mess around with a hot married woman. I have no idea what made me keep the damn things. Other than the fact I started caring about her more than I thought I would, and I felt like being a dick." He chuckles quietly. "But fun has a way of going terribly wrong when you start to care about someone too much, and an angry husband is involved." He smiles, but it doesn't touch his eyes.

"Anyway. You've got nothing to worry about. It ended a while ago." He lifts a shoulder like he didn't just dump a whole lot of information on me that has my mouth hanging open. I close it, realizing that his comment about not wanting anything serious now makes some sense.

"Did you love her?" I don't know why I ask or where the question even comes from, but it's out. I try not to hold my breath, resisting the urge to close my eyes while I wait for his response.

"Did you love him?"

I heave out a heavy breath at his quick retort. "No."

He stares off at the empty parking lot, seemingly lost in thought for a few seconds. "I think maybe I could have. If circumstances were different, I guess." Scratching at his stubble, his eyes land back on me, a mischievous look filling them. "But it was very fucking obvious that it wasn't meant to be." He leans in to rest his nose against mine. "Which is something that's become even more clear these past few weeks."

I swallow hard, insanely and irrationally jealous of this Dahlia, yet thrilled he seems to think meeting me means more. God, he's got my emotions dipping up and down like a freaking roller coaster.

He grabs my chin, tilting my head and lowering his lips

to mine. I don't even care about our surroundings; I think it's clear he can make me forget a lot of things. His eyes stay open, his lips grazing over mine so lightly that my next breath gets trapped in my throat. "So damn soft," he murmurs against them.

Feeling brave, I lift my hand to the side of his face and rub my bottom lip between his. He groans quietly, blowing out a breath through his nose. To my horror, I giggle as the warmth tickles my upper lip. He takes advantage of it, eyes filled with mirth when he presses his mouth to mine firmly. His tongue sneaks out to skim over my lips, and I pull back, breathing heavy.

"I just needed a taste," he whispers.

Another laugh escapes me, and he grabs both sides of my head, tilting it and sinking his tongue into my mouth. I stop laughing, trying not to moan when he stops joking around and starts setting my body ablaze with his tongue rubbing against mine.

"Okay." I pull back again. "You've had your taste."

He glares, and I move to touch his face again, but my hand pauses midair before dropping back to my lap. He notices, grabs it, and lifts it to his mouth to kiss. Smiling, I place it against his cheek, rubbing my thumb over his stubble before moving it to his eye. "You have the most beautiful eyes I've ever seen," I blurt out on a whisper. My finger runs gently along his long lashes, and he scowls again, grabbing my hand and nipping my thumb. "Let's go with captivating. It sounds manlier."

Grinning, I tug my hand back and lean forward, pressing my lips to his again. It seems crazy to become addicted to the taste of a person. But when his teeth tug my bottom lip into his mouth for him to suck, I decide that everything about the time I've spent with this man is crazy. So I run my tongue over his top lip and sigh in contentment as my blood sparks, warming now that I'm finally getting my fix. His hands run down my jacket clad arms, not stopping until he reaches my thighs. Pushing my dress up more, he teases me by trailing the pads of his rough fingers over the sensitive skin on the inside of my thighs. He tears his lips away. "Fuck, we shouldn't do this here …"

"Touch me."

He doesn't need to be told twice. His lips come back to mine, his breath coming heavier in hot bursts that fill my mouth and cause my heart to beat faster. My panties are moved to the side, and I grin against his lips. "Want a new set to keep?"

His eyes open. "What?"

I climb off his lap and tug them down my legs before tucking them into the saddlebag of his bike. He pulls me to him again, helping me straddle him. "You're giving me your panties?"

He looks like I've just gifted him with a puppy. Laughing, I say, "Yes, I just did."

"God damn." His eyes then move down to my sex, just covered by the skirt of my scrunched-up dress. "Shit." He shoves the material up, his hands wrapping over the tops of my thighs, thumbs rubbing my mound gently. I grow even wetter from the soft touch. "Jared …"

"Hmm?" He lifts his gaze to mine.

I smile, but it's strained. "I need you."

He shakes his head, looking around the abandoned lot. "Here?"

I roll my lips between my teeth. "Well, yeah." I lean forward, licking then scraping my teeth over his shadowed jaw, and repeat the words he said to me last weekend. "What's life without a little risk?"

He moves me off him to unzip his fly and free himself. "You had me at Jared."

He grabs his wallet from the saddlebag, and I watch his cock jump as he rips a condom open and rolls it on. Shoving his wallet back into the bag, he then pulls me over his lap again.

He lifts me, and I give him a gentle squeeze, causing him to groan before I align him at my entrance and sink down. My legs rest over the tops of his thighs, winding together behind his back. He curses, hands reaching up to hold the sides of my face and weave into my hair. Once the burn subsides, I move, rolling my hips and running my nails over the back of his neck. His lips hover over mine, his eyes half closed. He exhales loudly when I lift as high as I can then drop back down. I keep going, moaning when a hand leaves my face to grab my hip tightly. He pulls me down and pushes up, grinding into me carefully in an effort to keep the bike steady.

"You're killing me, Frost," he rasps. "But I'm pretty sure dying shouldn't feel this damn good."

Whimpering into his mouth, all I can do is nod. My stomach tightens and my thighs start to shake when he holds me down on him, rocking and causing my head to spin. "You like me fucking you on my bike out here in the open?"

"Yes," I admit shakily.

He bites my lip, staring into my eyes. "You like getting a little dirty, don't you, princess?"

My hips jerk, and I swallow hard. "I do … but only with you."

He hums, the sound deep and throaty. "Good answer."

His hand leaves my face to grab my other hip, lifting me up and down. I start to moan loudly, my nails digging into the back of his neck. "That's it; tell anyone who can hear exactly what I do to you. Let them hear you come while you're stuffed full of my cock, beauty," he whispers across my lips.

"Fuck," I breathe, shattering and shaking while he rocks into me and slams my hips down on him at the same time. I become mindless, swamped in sensation and clinging to him desperately. He grabs the back of my head, forcing me to swallow his groan when he stills and comes. I run my fingers over his neck, and he shivers, groaning one more time and kissing me softly.

"I'm sorry." I pull back. "I think I left scratches."

His laugh is hoarse and wraps around my heart deliciously. "Scratch me all you want. In fact"—he presses his lips to mine, his thumb rubbing over my cheek—"I'll be mad if you don't."

We kiss lazily, and his softening cock jerks inside me. Pulling back, I give him a tiny smile before hopping off him with his hand helping to keep me steady. I right my dress while he kicks the stand down and tugs the condom off, tying it before tossing it in a nearby trash can. He zips up his jeans while he walks back over to me then fishes out his cigarettes from his jacket pocket. Lighting one, he puts the pack away and leans against the seat, pulling me between his legs. I watch in a trance as he inhales deeply.

"You're a fucking enigma, Frost."

It takes me a second to realize he said something to me. "Huh?"

He laughs and I grab the cigarette from his hand, taking a drag and sighing as the acrid taste of tobacco fills my mouth. Such a filthy habit. But I'm beginning to realize that I have a serious problem with bad habits. I pass it back to him. "You're nothing like you seem. Know that?"

Leaning against his thigh, I twist my lips. "Is anyone ever as they seem?"

He shrugs. "What you see is what you get with me."

That makes me laugh. "Sure, but I see more."

Smoke billows from his mouth when he replies, "Do you now?"

"Yep." I take the cigarette from him again, and he chuckles.

"Smoking's bad for you, beauty. Give that shit back."

"A lot of stuff is bad for me, yet I do it anyway." I take another drag and hand it back.

He squints at me, moving his arm around my waist to bring me closer. "And you do it so fucking well." He takes a deep pull, and I duck my head, grabbing his chin to tilt his mouth to mine. I inhale the smoke he sets free from his parted lips, and he groans, cursing quietly. He rubs his lips over mine before straightening.

"You and me, this week," he says. "I'm taking you out."

My eyebrows shoot up. "Taking me out where?"

He shrugs. "Haven't thought that far ahead yet, but it won't be anywhere fancy, so I hope you're okay with that."

I glower at him. "It doesn't have to be fancy."

He stares at me for a second, eyes narrowed slightly, and then nods. "Okay."

"When … and why?" I blurt.

Smiling at my embarrassing show of eagerness, he grabs my hand and kisses the top of it. "Wednesday. And because I've kind of made a mess of this already. Let me at least try to court you properly."

"Court me?" I grin widely at him.

He flicks some ash to the ground. "Yes, I'm going to court the fuck out of you."

"Right." I nod. "I don't care too much for courting, but I appreciate the gesture."

"You don't?" He frowns, grabbing the helmet from the handlebars and passing it to me. I step back, putting it on my head while admitting, "Not really. We could watch a movie instead? Or hey, maybe you could rub my back while I read a book. Now that"—I point a finger at him—"is my idea of courting."

He guffaws. "Shit, okay." He raises a thick brow. "Wait … you're not lying, are you?"

"I'm not much of a liar, no."

He hums deeply before stepping over to fasten the helmet for me. "I'm starting to see that. And many other mysterious things. Hey, maybe if you could just write all your preferences down, that'd—" My lips pressing firmly against his cuts him off. "Or you can do that," he murmurs. "In fact, feel free to do that anytime you want."

I laugh, and he chuckles, pecking me once, twice, three times on the lips before getting back on the bike. "But we're still going out Wednesday night. After that, all courting bets are off." He stabs his finger at me. "So be ready, Frost."

I bite my lip, trying in vain not to show everything I'm feeling on my face while he starts the bike. But when he throws me a wink and holds out his hand to help me on, I know I've failed.

CHAPTER FOURTEEN

L ooking in the mirror, I finish applying some red lipstick and stare at my reflection. My blue eyes are clear and bright, my pale cheeks rosy, and my lips, they tilt to the side as I think about the reason for these subtle changes.

After hearing nothing from him over the past three days, I sent him a text earlier asking if he still planned to see me tonight. I received a blunt response saying that it was nice of me to finally spare two minutes out of my busy schedule to text him and that I'm to meet him out front at seven and wear jeans because he's bringing his bike.

I laughed, not giving a shit if he was angry. He doesn't realize what a big deal this is for me, or what a colossal mess my life might become by taking this next step with a guy like him. I might not deserve this, and it might not work out, but I've always been greedy, so I'll take it all anyway. Every last drop.

At five minutes past seven, I decide I've let him wait

long enough and make my way down to the front gate of the complex.

I'm wearing my light denim skinny jeans, a long sleeve white peasant top, and an older pair of heeled brown boots. I've gotta say, it feels good not to have to stress over which dress or pair of heels to wear to whichever function or restaurant I'd usually go to on dates.

The sound of my heels clipping on the sidewalk echoes into the silent gardens. I close the gate behind me and pause to take in Jared, who's scowling at me. The scowl falls from his face when his eyes rake down my body.

He whistles. "Well, damn, Frost. I'm feeling a little underdressed now."

My brows scrunch as my eyes flit over his usual jeans and black motorcycle boots. He's wearing a dark red shirt under an old denim jacket. "I don't know if red is really your color. Clashes with those eyes of yours." I wink and finish walking over to him. He laughs, the sound rising above the noise of the traffic and causing a smile to settle on my face.

"Come here." He tugs my hand until I pull it away to rest on his hard chest. I place a finger on his lips when he moves to kiss me.

"If you're courting me, shouldn't you wait until the night is over?"

His eyes bulge, a crease forming between his lowered brows. "What? People actually do that shit?"

Still smiling, I inform him, "Yes, I'm pretty sure they do. You know, it's the gentlemanly thing to do."

He growls playfully and starts kissing my finger that's still on his lips, making me laugh. "Good thing I'm not a gentleman then." Grabbing the back of my head, he crushes his mouth to mine with a soft groan and my hand falls away. I weave them through his hair, rising onto my toes to deepen the kiss.

After a minute, he pulls away. "Still wanna watch a movie instead? 'Cause I've decided I'm totally down for that."

I place a kiss on his cheek, lowering his head so I can whisper in his ear. "Let's be real here; we probably wouldn't watch it anyway." I pat his chest and lean over his bike to grab one of the two helmets he's brought.

"Precisely why I think we should ditch this whole date thing." He moves my fingers aside to fasten the strap under my chin and pecks me on the lips before pulling his own helmet on.

"You got me a helmet?" I try not to sound like he's gifted me with a piece of jewelry instead of a plastic piece of head protection.

"I did," he says before climbing on the bike and spending several minutes trying to get it started. I bite my lip, trying not to make a comment about how long it takes. When its roar finally fills my ears, he revs it a few times and gestures for me to climb on behind him. I swing my leg over and wrap my arms around his waist. He squeezes my hands then turns the bike, looking over his shoulder for an opening in the traffic.

I never thought I'd admit this, not even to myself, but riding with him on this thing is becoming one of my favorite things to do. He turns, joining the flow of traffic, and I bask in the cold breeze that washes over my flushed cheeks.

The night is still young, the purple and pink hues of dusk fading into the darkness that will soon blanket the night sky. Looking ahead, I notice we're headed into the warehouse district. My stomach tightens, and I wonder when I was last here. I try to stay away from it, especially seeing as Isla's Mercedes had its tires stolen from near the docks years ago when she was picking up some empty boxes to help her move out of her parents' place.

The bike slows, and Jared turns, heading down a narrow street and around a bend. He then pulls into the parking lot of what looks to be a fast food place.

Huh. I never even knew this was here.

I must say the thought out loud because over the noise of the still rumbling bike, Jared says, "It's a hidden gem. Best burgers in the whole damn city."

He parks, and I instinctively let my legs drop when he turns the bike off. After releasing him and standing, I then take off the helmet, passing it to him when he climbs off the bike. I spin around, getting my first good look at the place.

The paint is coral in color, and there's a good chance it was once red or pink. A huge burger sits on the roof with the faded words, Shake N' Burger on it. Okay. I hope the food at least tastes better than the place looks. I knew we weren't going anywhere with candles and tablecloths, so I don't know why I'm surprised we ended up here. I just am. That might have something to do with not knowing this place even existed until three minutes ago. Maybe.

"Don't judge, Frost. You'll love it."

I throw him a glare when he reaches my side. "I'm not judging. I'm simply admiring the"—I wave my hand around—"chic look about it."

His chuckle is dry as he shakes his head and grabs my hand, tugging me across the parking lot and inside the restaurant. We're greeted by a bunch of turning heads and the smell of meat, onions, and fried food. And to my surprise, my stomach chooses then to growl. Loudly. Jared laughs again, and I glance away, a bit mortified. He brings my hand to his mouth and kisses the tips of my fingers. "Let's get you fed, beauty."

He releases my hand when we take a seat in an old vinyl

booth in the back. I can't help it; I cringe when I feel the sticky residue of something on it when I slide in on my hands. Jared notices, looking amused. "What?" I huff.

He picks up a menu and peruses it. "You. You act as if you've never eaten anywhere other than cafes and five-star restaurants. Shit, I'm surprised you even visit the coffee shop."

He's got me there. "A friend of mine has been telling me for years to get coffee there, and I finally did. But you're right; I haven't really eaten at many other places. Though I do visit McDonald's drive-through every now and then." Mainly once a month, when I find myself in desperate need of a Big Mac and chocolate sundae.

His eyes widen a fraction, and I stare at his dark lashes, resting just below his brows. "You're shitting me."

Smirking, I pick up a menu and decide to have a look my-self. "I'm not shitting you."

I look at the options, which aren't very creative. Just burg-ers, fries, onion rings, wedges, shakes, and breakfast meals. Oh, and milkshakes too, of course. Well, too much variety can make things difficult for some, I suppose.

Feeling Jared's eyes still on me, I glance up. "What?"

His head shakes. "Nothing." He waves down a middle-aged waitress, who beams at him and puts a finger in the air to indi-cate she'll be over in a moment.

I can't let it go, though. "No, tell me." I swallow thickly. "Please."

His lips pull into a small smile. "It's just …" He scrubs a hand over his cheek. "Don't you ever wonder what else is out there? What else might make you happy if you step outside your tower of cash and skewed perception?"

He doesn't know how big a step I've already taken. It's more of a leap really. "Who says I'm not happy? Besides, everyone loves money."

He shrugs. "Sure, it's great to have. But it's not everything."

I know. My chest hurts with just how much I know. He reaches across the table to grab my hand. "Hey, I didn't mean to …"

I shake my head. "No, I'm fine."

He stares, looking like he doesn't believe me. We're thankfully interrupted by the waitress, and he lets go of my hand to lean back in his seat. "Well, if it isn't Jared Williams, my boy. How've you been?" She slaps his shoulder with her notepad.

He smiles up at her. "Fantastic." His eyes move over to me. "This is Vera; Vera, this is Nita, wife of the guy who makes the best burgers you'll ever have the pleasure of tasting."

I give her a small smile. "Nice to meet you, Nita. Tell me, do you have soap in the facilities here?"

She frowns over at Jared, who winks at her, and she then returns her brown eyes to me. "Uh, yes, we have soap in the bathrooms. And nice to meet you, too, Vera."

She eyes me up and down, looking a little confused after her quick assessment. I don't know what I said that makes her look that way, so I mentally shrug and ask if they have wine.

"Um." Her eyes dart to Jared again then back to me. "No, but we have beer?"

I wince. "Yeah, no thank you. Water will do. Bottled if you have it."

Jared orders two burgers and sends her on her way. I see her glance back at us a few times on her way to the kitchen.

"What's her deal?" I mutter.

He shakes his head with a laugh. "Really, Frost? You think a joint like this would have wine?"

I shrug. "How the hell was I supposed to know unless I asked?"

"Never mind, she'll get used to you. Or you'll get used to this place because, high maintenance or not, I guarantee you'll be back." He stretches his arms above his head, and my eyes involuntarily roam over his chest and stomach. My own stomach dips when I catch a glimpse of skin above the waistline of his jeans, and remember the smooth, warm feel of it against mine.

"Thanks for ordering for me, too, Hero." Though I know the options were limited anyway.

"Don't mention it." He plucks a toothpick from the holder on the table to put between his teeth. "Wait, you're not allergic to anything, are you?"

I watch the toothpick in rapt fascination as he talks. "What?" I blink, shaking my head a little.

He grins, repeating the question for me.

"No, I'm not. Unless you count cheap perfume."

He nods, looking serious as he says, "Noted. No cheap perfume. Stay away from half the women in here then, Frost."

I roll my eyes, and he chuckles.

"You need to stop calling me that," I say only half-heartedly because really, it's kind of grown on me. Or maybe it's the way he says it as more of a term of endearment than an insult.

"Not gonna happen." He thanks Nita when she places our food and drinks down a few minutes later.

He starts eating as soon as she leaves while I just sit here, staring down at the humungous burger in front of me. I glance over at the bathroom door, watching some guy exit while still tugging up his jeans. Cringing, I grab my purse and quickly swipe some hand sanitizer on my hands, all the while Jared smiles at me around a mouthful of food. I look around for a knife and fork. Okay, I know I'd look stupid, but this thing is huge. I've never seen a burger like this before in my life.

Fuck it. I grab it, cringing again as grease and sauce drip

down my hands, and take a bite. My taste buds explode, and I don't even look up or give two shits about what Jared is doing until I'm done. I eat the whole thing like I haven't eaten in months. Because he's so right, damn it. It's probably the best damn thing I've tasted in months.

"Fuck me, Frost. You've gotta take off your training wheels before you try to win a race."

I wipe my fingers and mouth with a napkin.

"Oh, har har," I say after swallowing. "I'll be fine."

"You're tiny, though, all willowy looking and shit. Well, except for those tits and that ass." He grins at that. "Where's it all going to go?" His eyes narrow. "Shit, you're not gonna barf, are you?"

I laugh. "No, at least I hope not. And despite what you may think, I happen to like my food very much thank you." I surprise myself by winking at him and admitting, "So does said ass and tits. And let's not forget my hips."

I take a sip of water, watching and almost coughing as his eyes seem to glaze over. "I'm familiar with them, though I think I'll need to spend a little more time getting to know them, you know, just to make sure they haven't forgotten about me," he says quietly.

I put the bottle down, feeling all fluttery and weird in my chest. How the hell does this man, who screams bad news and is the total opposite of everything I thought I'd want, affect me like this?

Clearing my throat, I glance out the window into the parking lot, watching a small group of people as they laugh at whatever they're talking about.

I know it's probably kind of sad that despite all the opulence in my life, this date is the best one I've ever had. Considering I'm sitting on a sticky seat, just ate half my weight in carbs, and I'm not sure if that's really barbecue sauce on the wall by the window. Yet I can't bring myself to feel any sort of sadness over it. Only apprehension that our time together might come to a crashing end. But I can't deny myself of this. I'm sick of denying myself the things that really matter and could make me truly happy.

His warm hand lands on mine, causing me to startle and bring my gaze back to his. He tugs the napkin out of my fist, bringing it to the corner of my mouth while he says, "Ready for dessert?" He wipes my mouth, and I let him, too caught up in watching his lips as he talks. He lets the napkin fall, gently taking hold of my chin and dragging his calloused thumb over my bottom lip.

"Ready when you are," I whisper.

To my surprise and dismay, he actually orders dessert. Two banana splits. I can hardly manage to get through half of mine because it's huge as well. He has no trouble, though, barely muttering two words to me as he scarfs it down. When he starts eyeing mine, I nudge it over to him, watching in amused fascination as he demolishes that, too. "Aren't you a little old to be enjoying ice cream like a big kid who's just been handed a treat?" I ask. Yeah, I'm digging for his age. Sue me.

He shovels more into his mouth, mumbling to his bowl. "If twenty-six is too old for ice cream, then I'm done with this whole growing up thing."

We both laugh, and I rest my head on my hand, wondering if he's going to lick the bowl when he's done. He doesn't.

"When's your birthday?" I wonder out loud.

He wipes his mouth with the back of his hand. "Few weeks."

He throws some cash onto the table and grabs my hand,

helping me up and waving to Nita as we walk outside. The cold makes me wish I'd brought a coat, but he quickly fixes that when we get to his bike by pulling his jacket off and passing it to me.

"Thank you," I mumble, pushing my arms into the sleeves. He just smiles and puts the helmet on my head. I tug it on and pull the straps together, but then he gently swipes my hands away and does it himself again. I close my eyes until he's done, scared I'll attack him and make an idiot of myself right here in the parking lot with these feelings he's made rage to life inside me. He lets me know he's done by kissing me on the nose before he climbs on the bike. I wait while he kick starts it for a few minutes and then finally gets it running.

"Why don't you buy a new one?" My gaze skims over the rather old Harley-Davidson. "One that doesn't take forever and a day to start." I grin when his handsome features morph into an outraged scowl.

"Don't let her hear you say that again; she may be old, but she's sensitive," he says with so much seriousness that I burst out laughing, bending over to hold my full stomach.

"She's?" I gasp and straighten up, wiping underneath my eyes. "She's sensitive all right. How's that normally work for your street cred? Making women wait ten minutes each time you need to start her up?"

He grins, grabbing my arm and tugging me over to his side. The heat of his thigh seeps through his jeans and my own as my leg rests against his. He looks up at me, licking his bottom lip. "I wouldn't know or probably give a shit because you're actually the only one I've let on the back of this bike."

The smile drops off my face. My lungs deflate as air rushes up my throat and out my mouth in a huge exhale. He brings my hand to his mouth again, gently resting his lips on top of it. "You're beautiful even when you throw your venom and rich girl questions at people. But when you look at me like that … you're fucking breathtaking."

And it's official. This man is more than just bad news.

He's the very definition of the word.

CHAPTER FIFTEEN

Cleo fingers the sheer blue material of the dress on the rack, pursing her lips as she looks at it. "Cleo, stop trying with the blue. It's a hideous design anyway."

She turns her head, eyes falling on me and narrowing to thin slits. "But why? I want it. And your version of hideous and mine are completely different."

"Oh, so Jared isn't a walking, talking, tall, dark, and delicious drink of bad? Like you were just saying to me the other day?" Isla folds her arms over her chest.

Cleo shrugs. "No, we can agree on men, but clothes?" She holds up a finger. "Not so much."

She turns back to the rack of clothes, sighing and picking out a red faux leather dress to hold in the air instead.

"You said that?" I ask.

Isla snorts. "You're surprised?"

"Not really, no." Cleo's always had a way with words.

"I can hear you, you know." Cleo sends us a glare before

stalking off toward the other end of the store. I lean against the wall, trying not to laugh as Cleo holds her nose in the air the whole way to the dressing room.

"So … how'd your date go?" Isla waggles her perfectly styled brows.

I stare at the ground, trying to hide my smile. It's only been two days, but I still think about it way too much. "It was fine." It was amazing. But he didn't come in when he dropped me off, which shocked the crap out of me. He walked me to the doors of my building and kissed me sweetly then left.

"Sure." Isla jabs her elbow into my boob. "Now tell me how it really was."

"Ouch, bitch." I try to discreetly rub the side of my poor boob. She rolls her eyes, and I give in. "It was perfectly imperfect."

She scrunches her nose. "I'm sorry, what?"

"Yo! Hoe bags. Where are you?" Cleo hollers from the dressing room. We both wince as the other customers look toward the rooms and then us, disapproval stamped all over their pinched faces.

We join Cleo and tell her the dress is awful. But as usual, she doesn't care. I don't know why she even bothers to ask for our opinions anymore when she wears what she wants anyway.

"You'll look like Lady Gaga's long-lost soul sister," I tell Cleo on the way out. "All for the neat price of eight hundred dollars."

Isla laughs.

"Now, now, bitches. Let's not forget that Christmas is fast approaching. You'll both be receiving nothing if you keep it up."

I suck my lips between my teeth, trying to stave off the temptation to admit that her present from last Christmas is probably being used by someone who got it from Good Will to put out as a candy bowl on Halloween. Or as an ashtray. She has terrible taste all round. Even in kitchenware. But even my honesty should stop somewhere. And I know she's almost had enough of our teasing for one day.

"Whatever." Isla inspects her phone quickly. "Let's get some coffee. I'm exhausted, and Vera still needs to tell us about her date."

Cleo scoffs. "We've only been here an hour."

"Exactly. And I've found nothing I want." Isla sighs.

We grab a coffee and take a seat inside. It's getting way too cold to sit outside now.

"So perfectly imperfect?" Isla stirs some sugar into her mug. "Care to elaborate?"

"Not really, but I will." I take a sip of my coffee and wrap my hands around the mug. "He took me to some hole-in-the-wall diner in the warehouse district." I laugh at their gasps and wide-eyed expressions. "It's okay, wasn't so bad. In fact, the food was amazing. Best thing I've eaten in ages."

Cleo waves her hand around. "Yeah, yeah. Food is great. Back to the main feature please."

Smirking, I continue, "Well, we just talked a bit, ate, whatever."

"Whatever? No hanky-panky? Wait, did he bring his bike?" Cleo asks.

Isla gasps. "Which, by the way, everyone totally heard leaving the other night. God, have you had sex on his bike yet? Please tell me you have."

Panic sets my fingers clutching the mug tighter. "Maybe. But what do you mean everyone?"

Isla winces. "Yeah, that thing is loud. But don't worry, I doubt anyone would ever connect it with you leaving." That makes me pause. "So no hanky-panky?" Isla continues a little too loudly. "Christ, did I really just say that out loud?"

"You did," I inform her.

"Shit." She throws a glower at Cleo. "You and your weird-ness are finally starting to rub off on me after all these years."

Cleo guffaws. "Shut it, huss-burger."

"See, right there. You've gotta stop trying to make up new words."

"Why?" Cleo's voice rises. "I'm not going to apologize for having a unique personality."

I snort with laughter, trying to hide it behind my hand. Leaning back in my seat, I continue drinking my coffee while they argue about where Cleo's parents went wrong with her up-bringing and why they're even still friends. My phone buzzes in my purse. I fish it out and find a text from Jared.

Jared: Hi, beauty.

A huge smile takes over my face, I duck my head and re-spond while the girls keep arguing.

Me: Hi.

Jared: Miss me?

Me: Not really.

Jared: Liar. Where are you?

Me: Shopping with the girls.

Jared: Buy any more panties to give me?

I bite my lip to hold in my laugh.

Me: No. Your courting efforts have left me a little … frustrated.

Jared: I was trying on the gentlemanly thing for size. Turns out it doesn't fit. My junk hates me.

I cough as a laugh escapes.

Me: Kudos for trying.

Jared: Right? I deserve some kind of reward for that, don't you think? You don't have to work today?

Me: Only work Monday to Wednesday. Are you working?

Jared: At the garage. You didn't answer my question about the reward.

When the girls go quiet, I put my phone away and finish my coffee. "Drink up; I wanna go home and reorganize my bookshelves."

"Uh-oh." Isla raises her brows. "What has you anxious? Shouldn't you be happy?"

I spin my now empty mug around the table. "I am." And I think that's the problem. I feel like I'm blowing up an extra-large balloon, hoping like hell someone doesn't pop it.

The missed call from Dexter on my phone when I woke up this morning is a scathing reminder that I can only dodge real life for so long and that my time might be up before I'm ready. But I have no idea what to do.

Cleo snorts. "And you two call me weird."

They finish their coffee, and we wander back through the mall. It's busy for a Friday, but not so busy that I don't notice the big-breasted blond bombshell walking straight toward us.

Stella. Jared's karaoke night fuck buddy. Well, before me anyway.

Her eyes seem to glow when they finally fall on me, thinning ever so slightly before she smiles, her wide mouth showcasing almost all her white teeth.

"Well, hey, y'all," she drawls, and my ears protest at the high-pitched whine of her voice.

"Can we help you, sweetheart?" Isla's sugary voice drips with sarcasm.

Stella laughs, loud and obnoxious. "Why no, I just thought I'd say hello to Jared's new friend." Her eyes skate over me from head to toe.

I don't flinch or fidget. Let her look all she wants.

"Right. And you are?" I ask with a bland tone. I know exactly who she is. Cleo snickers next to me, nudging me not so subtly with her elbow.

Stella's eyes burn with barely concealed hatred, but she keeps the smile painted across her face as she answers. "I guess you could say I'm the one he always comes back to." She winks. "And don't you go forgetting it, honey. A man like him doesn't need to be rolling around in the hay with a snobby socialite like yourself." When all I do is raise a brow in response, she takes it upon herself to continue. "Come on now; you're from completely different worlds." She tsks. "That man will only tear your spoiled heart to shreds then run back to me before the pieces have even hit the ground. I've seen it happen more than you'd probably like to know." She shifts, planting a hand on one of her curvy hips. "I'm just trying to help you out here. Woman to woman. Better to be mindful of all this before things go too far, wouldn't you agree?"

The thought of Jared being anywhere near this cowgirl wannabe has the blood freezing in my veins until ice-cold rage settles throughout every stiff limb of my body.

But my indifferent, carefully crafted mask doesn't slip. "Are you done boring me with your annoying voice and your existence in general? Because I've got things to do, *honey.*" I throw the word back at her with brute force, a tiny smile tugging at my mouth. "Very hard, tattooed, green-eyed, and dark brown haired … *things.*"

Watching her face contort with anger gives me a sick sense of satisfaction even as I try in vain to stop her words from rattling around in my skull. Isla hooks her arm through mine, and I keep my head held high until we skirt around her. Her cheap perfume makes me want to sneeze and will probably take three showers to clear from my memory, but her words … I shake my head. Since when have I ever caved to people like her? Never. And I'm not about to start now. So as we walk through the automatic doors to the parking lot, I shove her annoying voice to the back of my mind. I'll erase that shit later.

CHAPTER SIXTEEN

J ealousy is an insidious thing. It can sneak up on you at anytime, anywhere. And many times, you thought you were just fine. Unaffected and unaware of it creeping, slithering, and festering somewhere inside you until your actions speak louder than your own knowledge of yourself.

I remember in fifth grade; little Jane Trundle came waltzing into class with a fabulous beret on her less than cute head. Pure annoyance had my eyes narrowing and my brows lowering as I tracked her every move across the room to put her ugly backpack away. And when she sat down next to her friends Hannah and Claire, they reached up to touch the maroon beret on her head with hushed whispers and smiles. By that point, the jealousy had already started to brew as ugly thoughts turned over in my head. *I'm prettier, my hair is longer, more luscious, and the maroon would look so much better with my black hair. She's not as popular, not as important as me. She shouldn't be on the receiving end of all this attention for a stupid hat that doesn't even look very good on her.*

At recess, I did something that taught me a thing or two about jealousy that would follow me for years to come. I walked past her and pushed her into the mud. Yes, I pushed a girl into the mud because of a beret. But at that stage, it wasn't about the beret. And while everybody else gasped, giggled, or asked if she was okay, I just stood there, arms crossed over my chest and triumph rolling off me in waves.

Until she started to cry.

It all changed when she started to cry. Something in my chest cracked open even as I tore my eyes from her sprawled-out, mud-covered form and walked away.

I didn't get in trouble. My father's influence reached far and wide even back then. But I didn't need punishment. My teacher took one look at me as I swallowed and walked off, and she knew. She knew that just because a heart may appear to be made from stone doesn't mean it can't break.

Jealousy comes in many different varieties. Different shapes and sizes. It rarely ever looks the same. But the effect it can have on a person, if they let it, will always be the same. Jealousy no longer strikes me with the materialistic. I quickly learned to squash that kind of jealousy by simply buying the same thing for myself. This feels different.

Even with Dexter fooling around behind my back, I've never felt jealousy of this magnitude. Only anger and embarrassment at his blatant disrespect for me. It feels malevolent, fierce, and entirely unwelcome. It's a fucked-up mixture of anxiety, longing, hurt, and possessiveness. All for a man who was never supposed to affect me this much, let alone have me feeling like I'm spiraling down into a dark pit of unknown danger.

Sighing, I close my book and put it away. I can't concentrate when my thoughts and feelings keep colliding. Stella's pathetic attempt at ownership of a man who isn't hers shouldn't still bother me, but this feels too out of control to try to tame on my own.

I lean forward to finally answer my phone when it rings again and am surprised to find that my mother has given up and it's someone else entirely.

"Hi."

"Frost, damn. Don't make a man beg for it. I'd almost think you didn't want to speak to me if I didn't know any better, of course."

And just like that, the sound of his deep voice stifles my worries. "I thought you were someone else. Sorry." I get up, switching off the lights on the way to my bedroom.

He goes quiet, and I hear him drop something that clangs in the background. "Oh? Was I interrupting something?"

I huff out a breath. "Hardly." I hop on the bed and lean back against my headboard. "It was my mom, if you must know." Something bangs again. "What are you doing?"

He curses. "Sorry, I'm still at work. Got a bike that needs to be finished by Monday at noon, and one of the parts came in two days late."

I pull the phone away from my ear to glance at the time. "But it's almost ten o'clock."

He grumbles, "I know. But talking to you makes that fact a little less painful." That makes me smile. "So tell me about this mom of yours. I've never heard you say anything about her. Was beginning to think you were imagined into existence by my own brain."

"You haven't spoken about your parents either," I remind him.

He scoffs. "Yeah, because there's no point. Back to you."

My brows furrow. "Well, there's not a lot of point for me

either. She left me for the Caribbean and her flavor of the month when I was a toddler. She calls me every now and then asking for money. Not much else to it."

His end of the line goes quiet. Not a sound in the background. Then he curses again, softer than last time. "Shit. I'm sorry I asked, Frost." He clears his throat. "I really wasn't expecting that."

Tilting my lips to the side, I ask snidely, "You pictured me having the pageant mom? The charity-attending, Botox-infused, meddler of a mom?"

"Well, yeah. Not gonna lie." He laughs, but it's short and gruff. "That's exactly what I pictured."

Figures. A part of me sings with satisfaction because I've proven him wrong about me yet again. "Enough about her. Why is there no point in talking about your parents?" I lie down and stare at the ceiling.

He sounds like he's resumed working, grunting in my ear as he hits something a few times. "They weren't around much growing up. Always off getting high somewhere. We didn't own a house and barely had clothes on our backs. They relied on their junkie friends to put a roof over our heads most of the time. When they'd move on to a new place, sometimes we'd have to spend days trying to find them. They'd forget about us."

My heart clenches. "Seriously?"

"Seriously. But it's okay. Felix and I, we eventually gave up trying to find them and just did our own thing for a while."

"Your own thing? Where did you live?"

"On the streets. Not for long, though. CPS got a hold of us pretty quickly."

I yawn and try to smother it with my hand. "And do you know what happened to your parents?"

"Nah, they're probably dead or in jail." His voice is

detached, but it doesn't do a good enough job of hiding the hint of anger I hear lurking beneath it.

"So that's how you ended up with your foster dad?" I ask what I already know.

"Yep. Darren was a good man, but it took two bad homes until we finally got placed with him when I was fourteen."

"Your brother too?"

"Yeah."

"Is he older or younger than you are?" I can't help my curiosity. The need to know everything about him tramples all over my fear of being shut down.

"Older, a little over a year."

"So what happened to Darren?" I've wondered but never had the nerve to ask.

Silence fills the line for a moment before he says quietly, "He drank too many beers at his friend's house one Friday night, as he usually did. He drove home half drunk and probably half asleep. His truck wrapped around a power pole."

I wince and my hand clenches, as though it wants to reach through the phone to touch him. To comfort him somehow. "God, I'm sorry."

"Don't be. It was some years ago now. They said he died on impact, so that's something at least." He changes the subject. "Anyway, you'd better get to sleep. I'm going to try to wrap this shit up for the night so I can get an early start on it."

Trailing my finger over the soft cotton of my duvet, I wonder when I'm going to see him again, or if I can dredge up the courage to even ask.

As if he knows what I was thinking, he says. "Tomorrow, I'll pick you up after I get done with work. Sound good?"

I nod then stop when I realize he can't see me. "I guess it does."

He breathes out a husky laugh. "You guess, huh? Have you been thinking about what my reward is going to be? You question dodging extraordinaire."

A quiet laugh leaves my mouth. "Maybe. But it was your idea, so maybe I'm the one who should be getting a reward. You know, for putting up with your hard to get bullshit."

He laughs loudly, and my stomach tumbles. "Hard to get? I told you—"

"Yeah, yeah. The gentlemanly thing to do. You and I both know it doesn't work too well for you."

He groans. "You're so right."

"Bye, Hero," My voice is quiet but laced with humor.

"Good night, beauty."

Jared sent me a text earlier, saying to pack a bag and be ready by four. It's already after three, so I finish dusting my bookshelves, pack an overnight bag, and then take a shower. I shave everywhere and wash my hair, moisturize, put on some light makeup, and dry my hair.

The buzzer blares, and I walk over to the door to press the button for the intercom. "Yes?" I ask.

"Let me in, or I'll huff and I'll—"

I snort and remove my finger, effectively cutting Jared off. After hitting the button for the downstairs doors, I quickly rush to put some nude gloss on my lips. I try to play it cool and smooth a finger over my brows, but when a knock sounds on my apartment door, I haul ass down the hallway and swing it open. Jared leans against the doorframe with one arm raised above his head. His lips twitch, pulling into a smile when he tilts his head, his green eyes dancing as they move over my face.

"Close the door," he suddenly says.

"What? Why?"

"Because sometimes when these eyes of mine land upon you, they have trouble believing what they're seeing."

"Oh." My voice is all stunned breath as it wheezes out of my lungs.

His hand drops from the top of the doorframe, and he takes a step forward, hooking an arm around my waist and crushing my chest to his. "Surely, you're aware that your beauty transcends all reason." My eyes close as his nose brushes against mine while he moves us forward and the door closes behind him. "Frost?"

"Mmm?" My eyelids flutter open as I try to surface from the dual effects of his compliment and his scent.

He chuckles. "And you said you didn't want to be courted." He lowers his voice to a whisper. "*Liar.*"

I slap his chest, stepping back. "Don't go and ruin it, asshole."

He catches my hand, pulling me back to him and brushing some hair behind my ear. The scowl on my face disappears. "Are you wet? I bet you're wet …" His hand drops to tug up my dress, and the scowl returns.

"Dick." I move away to get my bag from my room.

"I could say so many things to that, but I'm looking forward to sinking said dick inside you too much to risk it," he calls out.

I laugh quietly, grabbing my phone and bag before moving back down the hallway.

Dropping my bag by the door, I then try to find where he disappeared to. He's in my library, trailing a finger over one of my bookshelves. Standing in the entryway, I try not to twitch as I watch him. Those books are my Achilles' heel, so to speak. One of the only weaknesses I have.

"Quite the collection you have here," he murmurs, now running his finger over the spines of some of my old classics. It takes everything in me to stay still, to stay exactly where I am and not run over there to smack his hand away.

I know. I have issues when it comes to my freaking books.

But hey, if they're my only obsession, then so be it.

One must always be passionate about something. He turns, surveying the expensive armchair in the corner and the rest of my vast collection. And as my own eyes follow his every move, I can't help but wonder if my newest obsession will be more detrimental to my health than a library full of books.

"You clearly have enough money. Why don't you quit your job and open your own bookstore or something?"

"I don't know." I frown down at the beige rug while his words ricochet around in my brain.

I'm used to getting what I want. But having my own bookstore is just one of many things that I don't think I'll be able to get. I'm already in way over my head with him. It's ironic really. With him, I don't want to demand, kick and scream, or trample over someone to get what I want. I want him to want me back. Enough to accept me for who I am. Frosty layers and all.

"While I bet you make a hot as fuck accountant, you'd be even hotter with that whole librarian look." He pauses for a beat. "Or are you worried about what others might think?" I look up to find his hands in his jean pockets. His white shirt sits tight across his broad chest, and a crease forms between his brows as he studies me.

"I guess." I shrug. That's true. I've always been terrified of what people might think of me. But that fear is fading rapidly with every day I spend with Jared.

Deciding to change the subject before he keeps digging, I ask, "Is there any chance you washed your hands before you touched my books?"

His deep chuckle fills the large room and wraps warmly around my heart. "You're a puzzle, Frost. And figuring you out is way more fun than I thought it would be."

My stomach flips, and I glance away, not wanting him to see how his statement affects me.

"So …" He laughs quietly, turning back to my shelves. "You've gotta tell me, what inspired a woman like yourself to love fairy tales so damn much?" He swirls his finger around the top shelf, the one filled with my vintage collection of fairy tales. Everything from Grimm's to Walt Disney.

I try not to cringe at the offensive words. His question and subsequent reaction should be expected really. "Never judge a book by its cover, Hero. You never quite know what lurks within."

"Until you open it up and learn things you never guessed you would," he says so quietly that I don't think he intends for me to hear him. But I do. I hear those words with an intensity so loud that they travel right to my chest, causing my heart to thump violently.

"Ready to go?" He walks over to me. I nod, and his hand cups the side of my face when he stops in front of me. I swallow and slowly lift my gaze to his. Breath whooshes out of my mouth and into his when he lowers his head to softly plant his lips on mine. Grazing, rubbing, and teasing until he presses them firmly together, unmoving and unyielding. It's brief—all of five seconds—but it's probably one of the best kisses I've ever been given.

Resting his forehead against mine, he exhales heavily

before taking a step back. "Let's go then, beauty."

He grabs my bag and waits for me to lock up, taking my hand in his and lifting it to his lips as we both stare at the closed doors of the elevator until they open on the ground floor. He's parked his truck on the street; I climb in, and Jared dumps my bag beside me on the seat.

"What rough looking place with sickeningly good food are you taking me to this time? Or are we going to your place?" That would explain the overnight bag. I put my seat belt on.

He turns the truck on, putting it in gear and checking his mirrors. "I've got different plans for you tonight." He pulls out onto the street.

"Oh, well spit them out already." I turn to face him. He plucks his cigarettes out, and I snatch them from his hand. Lighting one, I take a quick drag before passing it over to him.

He grins, watching the road ahead. "All in good time, Frost. All in good time."

CHAPTER SEVENTEEN

He has different plans for me all right, and they apparently don't involve his bed, I think sarcastically as I shift myself around in the passenger seat of his truck. I have no idea where we even are. One tree blurs into the next, only interrupted by the occasional road sign.

"How much longer? And why the hell can't you just tell me where we're going?"

"You'll see soon enough."

I growl, legitimately growl. "We've been in this car for ages, Jared. I need to use the facilities."

He just laughs.

"What's so damn funny about that?"

He flicks on the turn signal, and we pull off some old highway we've been on for half an hour to a dirt road.

"Well, good thing we're here so you can use the *facilities.*" He snickers quietly. "You and that word."

I cross my arms and glare out the window. *Where the*

heck are we?

"Um, what are you doing? I'm pretty sure there's no civilization down here."

I grab the oh-shit handle as his truck lurches and barrels over some bumps and huge dirt mounds on the neglected dirt road.

"Here we are." He pulls up in front of a small grassy field sitting at the base of a small cliff. I try to swallow the apprehension down, opening the door to catch a whiff of salt from the sea and hear the waves crashing down below the cliff.

Jared lifts a massive bag and some chairs from the bed of the truck and walks over to the grass. How did I miss all that?

I watch in horror when he starts setting up what looks to be a tent.

Oh, no.

Oh hell, no.

"All right, this is hilarious and all, but I really need to pee. So can we go now?"

His brows lower as he looks at me over his shoulder from where he's bent over the tent on the ground. My gut churns. I can't do this. I've never been camping in my entire life.

"Frost … there's a bathroom behind you in the trees over there." He points behind me and returns his attention to the tent.

Fuck. I run my hands through my hair. "How do I put this nicely? Oh, screw it. Look, I don't camp. Ever." I glare at his back. "I don't do the outdoors, like, ever." I glance over my shoulder at the small, run-down building. "And I most certainly don't use bathrooms that are likely never cleaned. Ever."

He drops the small hammer he was using to drive a stake into the ground, rises, and walks over to me. I hold my glare and my stance. He can't make me do this. This is the stuff nightmares are made of. Speaking of … "Have you not watched *Wolf Creek*? Or any other horror movies? I'm too damn young to die, Jared," I snap.

He reaches up to gently slide his hands under my chin and over my jaw. "Vera, you'll be fine. I won't let anything bad happen to you. You trust me, right?" His green eyes implore my blue ones when he tilts his head down to my eye level.

I take a deep breath and slowly let it out. "I could still get bitten by a spider and die. That kind of thing is way out of your control."

He chuckles. "You won't get bitten by a spider."

I glower at him. "Oh, really? And what are you? A fucking fortune-tell—"

He shuts me up with his lips, and I sink into the kiss. His warm mouth slowly glides over mine in a way that has shivers raking down my arms and my worries flying out to the sea behind us. Damn him. Damn him and his amazing mouth.

He pulls back, smirking at me. "Go use the *facilities*, Frost." He walks back over to the tent.

I blink a few times, trying to remember why I'm mad.

"You're not going to let that go, are you?" I grumble and practically stomp my way over to the disgusting looking shed that apparently houses a toilet.

"Not a chance in hell, beauty," he says quietly.

I still hear him, though, and promptly raise both my middle fingers in the air to flip him off. His laughter follows me as I kick the door open and peek hesitantly into the dingy room. I find a switch by the door. Hallelujah, there's electricity. I sniff. Okay, doesn't smell too bad, but it's definitely seen better days. The shower's pretty moldy. The toilet is missing some of the lid, and graffiti decorates almost every surface. But I'm about to burst, so it'll have to do. I do my business and walk back to the truck, quickly rubbing some sanitizer into my hands before noticing Jared almost has the tent all the way up now.

Wow. It's kind of big. But as I walk over to it, my eyes widen so much they feel as though they're going to pop out of my head. "Where the hell did you get this thing? You'd be better off slinging a tarp over some sticks; it's that old." My gaze runs over the worn-out material of the tent. There's a hole in one side, and yep, there's another in the roof.

Great. Awesome. Fantastic.

"It was my foster dad's. So yeah, it's pretty damn old. He said he'd had it for most of his life." He picks up the hammer and drives the last stake into the ground. My gut twists and I wish I could take my words back, scrunch them up in the palms of my hands, and then crush them under my ballet flats.

"Oh … um, sorry," I mutter over the slight clang of metal on metal. "But you do know a snake could slide in through that hole and kill us, right?"

He drops the hammer and falls on his ass, laughing quietly as he looks over at me. The way the last orange hues of the sun fall over his hair, the sculpted cut of his cheekbones, and his beautiful eyes captivates me.

"What?" I finally ask. "It could. I've watched Bear Grylls, thank you." I cross my arms over my chest, and his eyes lower to them, his teeth sinking into his bottom lip while he slowly rises from the ground.

"Beauty, the only snake that will be sliding into any hole tonight will be mine. Into that sweet, warm, tight hole between your legs. Now, be a good girl and grab the cooler from the truck, would you?" He winks and turns back around to pull out what I think is a blow-up mattress and plugs a pump into it, rolling it out as it inflates. At least that's not a hundred years old.

His words disarm me so much that I blindly walk back over to the truck and yank the cooler from the back. I almost drop the damn thing on my feet, cursing myself out for doing what he asked after he legitimately just called me a good girl.

He finishes setting things up and pulls out some chips, chicken salad sandwiches, and then two waters for us to have for dinner.

"Only the finest chicken for my Frost," he says, handing mine over.

"Thank you," I murmur before his words sink in. I try to ignore them because I'm not entirely sure if he meant them the way I think or hope he does or even what to do with them.

"Did you bring marshmallows?" I lean over to look in the cooler.

"In the truck. Didn't know if you'd be the marshmallow type."

He takes a huge bite of his sandwich, and my eyes get stuck on his corded throat as he swallows his food. I shake my head, unwrapping my own. "Duh. It's one of the things I've never done but wanted to. Not camp, just roast s'mores."

He winks. "Then I'll make you a fire, milady." He takes a sip of water, and I start demolishing my food. The man knows how to make a mean sandwich; it's really freaking good.

Not even fifteen minutes later, I've got the marshmallows and sticks, and he's started a fire. I feel a little silly over how giddy I get, but my excitement to finally do this squashes it. He shows me how to best position my marshmallow on the stick then sits behind me, wrapping himself around my body and grabbing my hands to show me where to hold it and when to turn it. They're really not that great, but I eat three anyway because it's kind of fun. I turn my head, lifting my hand over my shoulder to place half of one in his waiting mouth. He licks his lips after he swallows. I brush a leftover bread crumb from under his bottom lip before turning back around, feeling warm from more than just the fire when I feel him grow hard behind me.

"Let's go, wanna show you something," he says, hopping up and helping me to stand. I frown, wondering where he expects us to walk to now when it's pitch black. He bends down, picking up a flashlight by the tent and tugging on my hand until I'm at his side for him to hook an arm around my shoulders. We start the slow climb up the grassy little cliff.

After taking a seat at the top, he folds himself around me again, and we watch the waves crash into the sand and rocks below. It's so dark and kind of spooky, but I feel safer than I ever have with his big body wrapped around mine. His scratchy stubble tickles the side of my face when he places a kiss on my cheek.

"Thank you," he says.

"What for?" I ask above the noise of the wind and water.

"I knew this wasn't exactly your idea of a good time, and I knew you'd probably freak out. But still, thank you for giving it a chance."

I have a feeling he's talking about more than just camping, but I try not to let my heart jump too much. Linking my fingers through his, I sink back into his body.

"There's still time for me to die yet, Hero. Thank me in the morning—*if* I'm alive and well."

He burrows his cold nose into my neck and chuckles. It makes me smile until his hand is moving my hair aside and his mouth is softly kissing my neck. I shiver, arching back into him and tilting my head, allowing more access for him to drag his tongue up to my ear to whisper huskily, "I want you."

"I know." I smirk, feeling him hard at my lower back again.

"Do you now?"

I nod, tilting my head back and asking with my eyes for his lips to touch mine. He reads the message just fine, and his lips descend to suck on my bottom one. He parts them, and his tongue slowly searches out mine in a lazy rhythm that has my panties rapidly growing damp. I moan when his hand reaches up to squeeze my breast. The roughness of the act compared to the soft, tantalizing touch of our tongues has my breathing coming faster and heavier.

His lips pull away, a mere breath from mine. Our eyes open and stay stuck on each other while his hand slowly moves over my stomach, dragging my dress up over my thighs. My legs spread automatically for him. A gasp leaves my mouth when I watch his eyes hood even more, and the rough pads of his fingers drag up my inner thigh to where I need him most. He doesn't waste much time with teasing, and instead, he tucks his fingers under the side of my panties to dip shallowly into my entrance, feeling exactly how much I need him.

"So fucking wet." He removes his fingers, his eyes never leaving mine, and I watch with rapt attention as he brings them to his mouth and sucks.

"Shit." I whisper my thought out loud.

His chest rumbles against my back with his groan. "You always taste so fucking good."

I don't get a chance to respond because his hand has returned, pulling my panties roughly to the side so that he can drag his finger through my folds. My eyes close on a moan that sounds so loud in the silence of the night even with the waves crashing down below us.

"Eyes open," he demands.

I obey instantly, and his finger slowly works its way inside, his eyes watching mine as he tortures me in the most amazing way possible. I never would've guessed that foreplay could be this good before Jared. I start squirming, trying to fuck his finger, but then he stops.

"What …?" I pant. "Please."

He growls, kissing my lips roughly before grabbing the flashlight, standing, and scooping me up into his arms. We're down the hill and inside the tent not even a minute later.

"Off." He puts the flashlight down and jerks his head to my clothes after placing me in front of the mattress. He leaves the tent, and I hear the hiss of the fire being put out. Then he's back and kicking off his boots. I kick my own shoes off then remove my cardigan, my dress following a second later. I watch Jared as I unhook my bra, finding a blinding white grin on his face when he moves his hand away from his mouth. That smile. Even in the muted, murky light of the tent, it still manages to make my heart stutter.

He tugs off his jacket then his white shirt, and my lashes lower, my eyes absorbing the pure male perfection that stands before me. I don't think I'll ever tire of looking at him. Those defined hips. The abs that sit underneath a wide chest. That tiny sprinkle of chest hair that matches the tantalizing trail under his belly button, which disappears into his briefs. His thick, tattooed biceps that bunch when he unzips his fly, shoving his jeans and said briefs down his muscular thighs. My mouth dries as my body heats to dangerous levels.

"Come here," I say, tugging my bra straps down my arms and tossing it to the floor with the rest of my clothes.

His head cocks to the side, his mouth curving. "But this view is so damn good."

He wants to play? Fine. "But why look when you can touch?" I turn and bend, sliding my panties slowly over my ass and letting them drop to my feet. Straightening, I lift my hair off my neck and step out of them before walking over to the mattress.

A low growl rolls through the tent. "Fuck me."

Then he's on me. Arms wrap around me from behind, taking me down to the blow-up bed and making it bounce. Laughing, I stare up into his face and smooth a strand of hair back that's flopped onto his forehead. Oxygen becomes an unfamiliar thing as I watch his nostrils flare and his heated eyes flick back and forth between mine.

"You're so fucking exquisite," he murmurs, voice quiet and causing goose bumps to rise over every inch of my hot skin. "You're not too shabby yourself," I admit with a smile.

"Yeah?" He uses his arms to lower himself over me, caging me in as they rest beside my head.

"Yeah." Then I go and blurt, "Why did you bring me here when we could've just hung out at your place?"

He takes a deep breath, letting it out through his nose and averting his gaze for a moment. The sound of the beach fills the silence as I wait with bated breath. I'm starting to regret asking, but then he finally looks back at me and says, "I may not be able to afford fancy restaurants, five-star hotels, or a red-eye flight to somewhere exotic." My eyes narrow, but I let him continue. "But … I can give you this. A night underneath the stars in a shitty tent and cold sandwiches. I know it's not what you're used to, or what you might want but—"

"It's exactly what I want," I cut in. With my heart racing dangerously fast, I let my next admission slip before I can think better of it. "You're exactly what I want."

His lips part. "Really?" His warm breath is choppy, mingling with my own, and I swear he can probably feel the butterflies swarming and swooping in my stomach, which is flush against his skin.

I nod, struggling to find the words. Using my hand at the back of his head to lower it, I press my lips to his. "This right here." I kiss him gently. "I think it's priceless."

His hand slides into my hair at the same time his tongue dips into my mouth, ravishing, claiming, and groaning. He rolls, taking me with him as our lips stay fused. Scraping his teeth along my lip, he then releases it to say, "If you're really mine, then I want to take you bare, with nothing between us." He starts trailing kisses over my jaw and up to my ear, nipping the lobe.

"I've never done that before," I admit with a hitch in my voice when his hands squeeze my ass cheeks.

"Never?" he asks.

"Never. But I'm on birth control."

"Fuck, you don't know how happy that makes me. I'm clean. Now sit on my cock." He reaches between us, and I rise a bit, positioning myself and slowly sinking down. My eyes stay glued to his face, watching his jaw clench tightly and his eyes squeeze shut briefly before springing wide open again.

This. The way those eyes blaze and hood within a matter of seconds because of what I do to him … It's enough to make me feel as though I'm free-falling out of my own skin.

"I hope you know," he groans when I grind down on him. "You're stuck with me now, Frost."

My heart warms at his declaration. It might not be candles, jewelry, and flowers, but it's him. And he's all I want.

"Fine by me, Hero." I smirk, and he growls, hands grabbing my breasts before rising to lean back on his hands and taking a nipple into his mouth.

"Yes," I breathe, rocking into him as my head rolls back. He moves on to the other, kissing and sucking and even nipping the tender flesh. His teeth and lips drag up my throat until he reaches my mouth. The way his arms wind tightly around my back to hook over my shoulders and tangle in my hair has me dropping my head to touch his tongue with mine. He groans, low and deep. An arm falls to my hips, moving me over him and making me cry out as I feel myself start to unravel. The friction, the heat of his skin, his taste of mint and tobacco filling my taste buds, and his scent send me spiraling. "Jared …" The words are both a plea and a prayer.

"Go on, beauty," he whispers gruffly against my cheek, gently kissing and rocking his hips into me until he hits that spot again and sends me over the edge.

"Fuck," he rasps, flipping me to my back, hooking my leg over his arm, and pounding into me while I'm still coming apart. He stills, grinding his pelvis into my clit and emptying himself inside me. I push my fingers into his hair, shuddering one more time as the last of my orgasm fades away.

"Please don't ask me to wear a rubber after that," he says with his face in my neck.

I laugh, smoothing my hand over his hair and using my other arm to squeeze him to me. "I won't." He hums sleepily into my skin. His weight presses down heavily on my chest, yet I can't bring myself to feel anything other than this bone-deep contentment.

CHAPTER EIGHTEEN

I wake to the feeling of lips moving up and down my exposed back, so I pretend to be sleeping. It's quite a nice way to wake up. *Then he bites my ass.* Legitimately bites my fucking ass.

I roll over, scowling up at his amused, handsome face.

"Really?" I snarl.

"Sorry, Frost. We gotta hit the road soon." He stares at my naked breasts. "But maybe we have time for—"

"Out!" I snap. "And don't return unless you have coffee."

"Not much of a morning person, are you? Figures." He chuckles, the sound husky and making me second-guess my command for him to go. He's not deterred by my glare and leans down to kiss my forehead, winking at me before leaving the tent.

I stretch and get up, pulling out my makeup bag and a maxi dress from my overnight bag, which he thankfully brought in and placed along the side of the tent. After getting dressed and brushing my hair, I then use my compact mirror to wipe my mascara off from yesterday and apply a fresh coat plus a bit of powder. I slip my cardigan on, grab my toothbrush, and zip my bag shut, leaving the tent to find Jared emptying a pot of water over the fire pit and a hot mug of something on a nearby rock. I hope like hell it's coffee and march over to inspect it.

"Coffee. It's instant but still coffee," he informs me, taking a drag of his cigarette and moving away to put the pot and cooler back in the truck.

I sniff it, shrugging.

I take a seat on the chair he's left out, placing my toothbrush on my lap and watch him disappear into the tent to deflate the mattress.

I'd offer to help, but oh, who am I kidding. I'd just get in the way anyway. I take a sip of my coffee, making a mental note to get him to stop at the nearest shop or café on the way back.

I have no idea what time it was, but I remember the early dawn light creeping in through the hole of the tent when he woke me up with his fingers between my legs. He fucked me slowly from behind until we both came, and then we fell back asleep, still joined in every way.

Standing up, I drain the rest of my coffee, trying not to cringe at the taste, and walk over to the truck to place the cup in the cooler in the back. Digging through his zipped-up duffel, I find a string of condoms and keep searching until finally, I find a tube of toothpaste. I smile. Nice to know he came prepared, just in case.

After he's done and I've brushed my teeth and cleaned up as well as I can in the dingy bathroom, he takes my hand and leads me over to a walking trail at the base of the cliff. "Where does this lead?" I ask, ducking around a bunch of branches that he holds back for me.

"The beach." He stops when we reach a set of very steep

steps that indeed lead down to the choppy beach below. I take off my flats and hold his hand tightly as we walk down them. Squishing the sun-warmed, rough sand between my toes at the bottom, I can't help but smile.

"It's funny, you know, considering we live right near the beach, that I hardly ever visit it."

He pokes me in the cheek, grinning. "You can tell."

My top lip curls. "I take pride in taking care of my skin, and not getting a tan is a choice I'm perfectly fine with, thanks."

"I didn't say it was a bad thing, Frost. In fact, that"—he turns and looks down at me—"your black hair and those big blue eyes are what drew me to you in the first place."

Oh. Heat climbs up my neck at the compliment. He thankfully makes no comment on my burning cheeks and keeps us moving down to the water. I hesitantly dip my toes in, shrieking at the frigid temperature. His laugh sounds carefree, unrestrained. And I don't want to take that from him, but I want to know more. Everything.

"Tell me about Felix." That bedroom at his house is imprinted in my brain, the way it looks as though it's waiting for someone to return to it. "Where is he?"

Jared stops moving and wipes a hand down his face. "This might be a conversation better had sitting down. Or better yet, not at all."

My frown conveys everything I don't need to say. I don't care, and I want to know.

He sighs, leading me over to the dry sand and taking a seat. I sit beside him, and he keeps my hand in his, fiddling with my fingers as he talks. "That woman I told you about? Dahlia?" I nod, trying not to clench my teeth together. He notices anyway and smiles at me. "I met her at the women's shelter where I was doing community service. My brother got into some shit early this year, and I dragged myself into it with him." He shakes his head. "It was his second offense but my first. So he's in jail, and I'm out here, trying to keep everything afloat until he gets out."

"The same shelter adjacent to the coffee shop?"

He nods. Well, crap. "When does he get out? And when can you stop working at the shelter?" I ask that last question for my own selfish reasons. He knows that but doesn't seem to care, only squeezes my hand again. "He'll hopefully be out before this time next year. And I finished my last shift a couple of weeks ago. She's not volunteering there right now anyway. But Christ"—he runs his teeth over his bottom lip—"I love it when your eyes light on fire with jealousy."

I scowl at him even though his husky voice is heating my body quicker than the morning sun shining down on us. "Continue."

He laughs. "Okay. What happened … it's pretty stupid. Growing up the way we did? With that kind of life comes friends in dark places. Felix and I, well, you gotta do what you gotta do to survive. If that means hanging with the wrong people to keep food in your mouth or avoiding shit from the same people you're hanging out with, then that's what we had to do."

"What did you have to do?" My voice is soft in an effort to let him know I won't judge and that he can trust me.

He stares out at the water. "I won't go into too much detail. Never anything too bad. The worst of it happened because of this guy named Ryan. We'd been with our foster dad for a while at this stage, and Ryan needed Felix's help. Darren had us working at his shop a lot, to help out and to try to keep us out of trouble. But trouble can find you no matter how good a home you manage to end up in." He blows out a breath. "He had Felix show him how to hotwire cars and other bullshit needed to steal them. Felix and I were still young, late teens.

He thought he'd show him, grab some much-needed cash, and that would be that." Jared laughs, but there's no humor in it. "Not the case at all. Felix ended up being roped into stealing the fucking cars, too."

"Grand theft auto?" I ask. I thought this shit only happened in movies.

Jared nods. "Yeah, they got busted after a few times. The third time, they didn't even get two streets away before the police were all over them like a bad rash. Darren was furious, but he got Felix out of trouble, seeing as it was his first real offense."

"The other guy?"

"Juvie. He had no parents around either; no one to try to get him out of it."

"Where were you when all this happened? Did you know?" I shift in the sand to face him more.

"I didn't know. And after, I didn't talk to him for weeks; I was so damn pissed at him." He smiles sadly. "Then when Ryan got out of juvie six months later, he'd formed some sort of fucked-up crew. They kept at it, doing dumb shit as the years rolled on by. Managed to make quite a fair amount of money dealing drugs and started stealing expensive as fuck cars from all over the state. Then Maggie fell pregnant ..." His mouth quickly slams shut.

"Wait, what? Who's Maggie?" The plot thickens, and my curiosity has my eyes glued to his profile. He curses. "Fuck it. May as well tell you." He scrubs a hand over his face and turns to face me while I try not to fidget or yell at him to hurry up and spit it out. Finally, he says, "Maggie was, is—hell, I don't know anymore—Felix's girlfriend. They met when they were in their senior year of high school. Different schools, though, of course." He smirks, and I don't understand why until he keeps going. "She had this strict, middle-income family. But her and

Felix, they were in deep with each other almost as soon as they met. So when her family told her to choose …"

"She chose him," I whisper, suddenly feeling like I know how this girl might have felt. Our circumstances may be very different, but having to choose between what you want and what others want for you? I'm all too familiar with that.

Jared nods again, averting his gaze to our still joined hands. "She did. She gave up a scholarship to a great college to stay with Felix, opting for community college and working part time so they could save for their own place. Darren died before that happened, though. Money got tighter, trying to keep a roof over all our heads, the business afloat and pay off the remaining debts." He shakes his head with a silent laugh. "Shit, we had no idea how to run it, only how to work there. But we learned. It took a while, and we lost a fuck load of money and made a ton of mistakes, but we did it."

"Your house, it was Darren's?"

He nods then blows a breath out of his nose. "Then a few months before Felix and I got busted, and he went to jail, Maggie found out she was pregnant."

I keep my mouth closed, entranced and shocked by the words leaving his lips and entering my ears.

"He did it for her, you know?" He sighs. "She begged him not to. Said they'd make it work, that she knew he'd probably get caught again. They fought about it for days, and he wouldn't budge. Said the money could set them up for a while, that they needed it. She threatened him, told him she'd leave him if he did that to her and their baby—risked it all in such a stupid way. But Felix's stress and this overwhelming need to make things right, to take care of his family blinded him. He was sick and tired of watching Maggie work long hours, sick of working at the garage and the way we were losing money instead of making it after we'd worked so damn hard ourselves. So he went back to Ryan and asked to be hooked up with a good job. One time, he said. One time and enough money to clear a chunk of debt and hopefully make a better life for them."

Holy shit. "But it didn't work out that way," I whisper, my heart hurting for the man in front of me and his family.

He bites his lip. "No, I guess it didn't, but … he's my brother, and when he wouldn't listen to Maggie or me, I wasn't about to let him do it alone. Too many risks involved with Ryan's crew and their dodgy deals."

I link my fingers through his, squeezing them. "You're a good man, Hero."

His lashes lower as he stares down at the sand between his spread legs. "So I've been told. I don't feel like one, though; not when I can't even do the one thing my brother needs. The only thing he wants."

I think I know what or who he's referring to. "Where is she now?"

"I have no fucking idea." He sighs again. "She left him not long before it all happened. Her sister swears she doesn't know where they are, but that she knows they're okay."

"And Felix still went through with it after she left him?" I ask the question that doesn't need answering.

He does anyway. "Well, yeah. He said he'd make it right; that once he had the money, he'd fix everything with her and it'd be okay. Besides, it was too damn late to back out at that stage."

It's then I realize how lucky I've been. I may not have had a lot of love in my life, not the kind he seems to share with his brother, but I've never had to know what it is to look at a situation with such hopelessness that I lose sight of what's important and risk everything. But then again, I've never had that much to risk in the first place.

A wave of shame washes over me, so huge it threatens to drown me whole. "Hey," Jared says. "What's up? Where'd you go just now?"

Tears sting my eyes. I'd almost forgotten what it felt like to feel them looming. To cry.

I close my eyes, taking a deep breath and opening them only when I'm sure the threat is gone. "Nothing," I mumble. "I'm just … I never knew. I mean, I *knew*, but hearing this, it makes me realize how good I have it."

He gathers me into his lap, smoothing my hair back off my face. "You're not as mean as you seem, Vera Bramston."

I cling to his black shirt, fisting it in my hands. "I've done some pretty shitty things in my life, Hero. I know better than anyone that I can be a real bitch, and you can't …" My voice hitches. "You can't change me."

He tilts his head. "And why would I wanna do a damn thing like that?" His lips press to my nose, and I melt into him, the simple touch sending tingles up my spine. "No one's perfect, Frost. But you? You're perfect for me. Just the way you are."

I shove my face into his neck, inhaling his scent of clean linen, tobacco, and a hint of bonfire. "Thank you," I whisper. "For telling me about him, about what happened." Because I know it was a big deal for him to open up to me like that.

"It made sense to tell you, especially if I'm keeping you around."

I lift my head, and he laughs. "I'm joking." He leans in to peck my lips. "I wanted to tell you. I just needed to …"

"Trust me?" I offer.

His eyes narrow. "Yeah, look, I know you're from a different part of the food chain than I am, but don't go thinking this is some game to me. I'm kind of crazy about you, Frost." His eyes burn with a vulnerability that has my stomach quivering and my heart wanting to dive from my chest into his hands. I want so badly to tell him that I'd never leave him like other people have. That I understand and he can believe in me. In us. But I don't.

"I'm not playing, Jared Williams. I'm kind of crazy about you, too."

I also don't admit that I think I passed crazy long ago. Fear holds us both captive, only allowing us to hand out parts of ourselves. Piece by piece, one at a time. Testing the waters before we lose ourselves beneath the undertow. No one wants to drown; they want to make sure it's safe. But I think we've now revealed enough to take another step forward and take a chance.

He kisses me softly, smacking my ass when he helps me up from the sand. He takes off his boots and socks then he picks me up. I loop my arms and legs around him, clinging to him tightly when he starts making a run for the water. "If you ever want sex from me again, you'd better think wisely right now," I warn.

He laughs in my ear and twirls me around as he walks into the water, the bottom of his jeans getting wet. I close my eyes and hide my face in his neck.

"No, no, no, please no. It's too cold," I chant.

He thankfully doesn't throw me in and walks back to the sand.

"Thank you, you big idiot." I kiss his neck.

He pulls my head out from his neck and gives me that crooked smile. "Don't thank me yet." Not even a second later, we're down in the wet sand, and he's crushing his lips to mine. I smack his chest, biting his lips and laughing like I'm high. "Oh, my God. This dress is worth more than some people's cars. I'm going to kill you."

He laughs. "Bring it on, beauty."

I experience a weird sense of Deja vu as we drive down the old dusty highway that will take us back to the one that leads to Rayleigh. It's strange that a month ago this man was a complete stranger to me. Some random guy who I thought might kill me when he rolled over to the side of the highway to save my dumb ass. I smile out the window, my eyes barely registering the blue, cloudless sky.

"Just so you know," Jared exhales, filling the interior of his truck with the smell of tobacco. "This whole boyfriend thing? Well, I've never really had a serious relationship. So feel free to smack me upside the head if I do something dumb. I'm a quick learner." His nervous laugh makes me trip over my own thoughts. Who knew this enigmatic bad boy from the city slums had a bit of an insecure side?

I smirk, trying to mask this expanding feeling in my chest. "So you're saying we're serious?"

He nods, taking a drag from his cigarette and flicking ash out the window. "Well, I, for one, am pretty serious about you."

"Yeah?" I ask with a grin.

"Oh, yeah," he says with a huge grin in return. "That ass is nothing to joke about and that smile?" He forces his eyes to roll back, and I laugh, reaching out to whack his arm. "And here we go already. I'm messing up, aren't I?"

"You're not. I want you exactly the way you are."

"Yeah?" He glances over at me.

I mimic his earlier words. "Oh, yeah."

He hums, taking another drag from his cigarette. "You're not as demanding as I thought you'd be."

"Okay, now you're nearing messing it up territory."

He laughs. "Should I apologize or just kiss you stupid?"

Smiling, I shake my head, grabbing his hand after he stubs out his cigarette. We're quiet for a beat, and I stare back out the window, trying to make sense of how everything is changing.

"Hey." He interrupts my thoughts. "What's up?"

I hesitate then decide to just tell him. "I don't know; I guess I still can't really believe this."

"What do you mean?" He turns into an old gas station and parks the truck.

Tilting a shoulder, I admit quietly, "That we're doing this. That … that you're mine."

He turns the truck off, looking at me with soft eyes. "Jesus, Frost. I've been yours since I saw you strutting down that highway like it was a damn catwalk."

He tugs me over onto his lap, and I laugh. "Shut up."

He grins. "You looked fucking ridiculous teetering around in your fancy shoes."

"Ass," I grumble.

He moves his arms around me, bringing my face to his neck and grabbing my ass through my dress. "You've got a fucking great ass. One day soon, I'm gonna squeeze my cock into it."

I shiver but don't admit that I don't do anal. And with the size of him? Yeah, no thanks.

"We'll see." I kiss his neck and open his door, climbing off his lap and hopping down to the pavement. "Coming? I need a coffee, or at the very least, something with caffeine."

He grabs his wallet and shoves it into his jeans pocket as he gets out, closing the door and scowling at me. "What?" I ask.

"I think we're about to have our first real problem. A fight even."

Placing my hands on my hips, I lift a brow. "We are, are we?

And why is that?"

He scoffs then does a terrible job of mimicking me, "*We'll see.*" I try not to laugh at the outrage on his face. "What do you mean *we'll see*? You can't have an ass like that and not let me play with it."

"Oh, you can play with it." I step into his chest, grinning up at him. "I said we'd see about fucking it."

He groans. "Say that again."

So easily distracted. I laugh, grabbing his hand. "Come on; I'll whisper dirty words in your ear after I get some caffeine in me."

"I'll hold you to that."

We walk inside, an old doorbell alerting the cashier behind the counter, who looks up from her magazine and gives us a warm smile. I return it, finding it comes naturally instead of forced for once. Though I think that has something to do with the male who currently has his arms wrapped around me from behind and is kissing my neck as I peruse the bags of chips on display. The song crackling through the old speakers hanging from the ceiling comes to an end, and a new one begins. "Why is it that old gas stations always seem to play old music?"

Jared's head lifts. "You're not complaining, are you? The eighties was full of great music."

I tilt my head back to raise a brow at him then grab a bag of Cheetos from the shelf. They fall to the floor, though, when he suddenly grabs my hand and tugs me to his chest. He grins down at me, his eyes alight with mischief again. I'm lost in the sea of green but come back to reality when he places his other hand on my hip and starts swaying us side to side between the fridge filled with soda and the aisle of savory snacks.

"Jared," I hiss. "What are you doing?"

I glance around, finding an older woman smiling at us as

she walks through the door.

"Don't tell me no one has ever taken you dancing in a gas station before." He kisses my nose then shocks me by twirling me around. He pulls me back to his chest and kisses my head.

Laughing, I say, "No, I can't say that anyone has."

His eyes flare wide open, his expression morphing into feigned shock. "Well, I'm appalled. A lady such as yourself should be danced with at every opportunity."

He then waltzes us up and down the aisle as the song plays overhead; tears are leaking from my eyes from laughing so hard. It's only made worse when he softly sings the words from Taylor Dayne's "Tell It to My Heart" into my ear. Then I'm almost choking, rubbing my face into his chest and shushing him.

He spins me three more times before the song comes to an end. Reaching up, he wipes the wetness from underneath my eyes while I just stare at him, stupefied and trapped underneath the force of everything I'm feeling right now.

He gently kisses my lips and whispers, "When you laugh, I feel it here." He grabs my hand and lifts it to his chest. He smiles softly at what I'm sure is my dazed expression before releasing me to grab my chips and a diet Coke.

Realization dawns as irrefutable as the sun rising. My blood boils and hardens throughout my entire body, traveling from my heart and straight to my brain, cementing what I think I already knew had happened.

But of course, it's next to a bag of peanuts in the middle of a gas station, of all places, that I realize I've fallen in love.

CHAPTER NINETEEN

"Sorry but your card has been declined." The barista pushes her black framed glasses up her nose, looking a bit uncomfortable. I've got no idea why, since she's not the one with malfunctioning credit cards. "Try this one." I hand her the black Amex.

She clears her throat. "Er, we just did."

We've tried them all. Except for my debit card. I pluck it out and hand it over, my gut clenching so tight that I'm scared it'll tear in half while she swipes it. It works, but there's no relief. Because that's my own personal checking account. With maybe a year's worth of wages in it, if that. Fuck. I stare out the window at the busy street beyond in a shocked daze, trying to decide what to do next. But my brain is frozen, just like my stiff body when I grab my to-go cup and move rigidly out the door. I turn right to go to work but think better of it when I see the bank across the street.

"Here. Hope you like lattes." I shove the coffee into a

homeless man's chest, not seeing whether he grabbed it in time before marching across the street and entering the bank. I withdraw everything, a whopping twenty-five thousand dollars and eighty-five cents.

Shoving the envelope into the bottom of my handbag and holding onto it for dear life, I make my way back home to put it away. After locking it in the mini safe that Cleo got me five Christmases ago, I sit on the couch with my head in my hands and stare at my phone, wishing I could do something about this mess. But I know I can't. My father's threats are never idle; I should know that better than anyone. Figures that, after the best weekend of my life, reality needs to even the score.

Well, it's even. And though I'm scared out of my brain, I think I'll be okay. The lease on my apartment is paid up until the new year, I own my car, and I have enough money to feed myself and pay some bills for a while.

Inhaling the deepest breath I think I've ever taken, I stand and let it out then make my way to the door. He wants to cut me off? Okay. I'll help him make sure that cord is severed properly.

Driving back to work, I park, grab my small box, and make my way to the elevator in the lobby. The echo of my heels clipping across the marble foyer sets my nerves jumping. The elevator dings, and I step out into the accounting department for Bramston Inc.

It's time for Sally to watch my fabulous ass walk out these doors for the last time.

"Vera, where've you been? You were supposed to be—"

"Save it, Sal. Got shit to do." I walk over to my cubicle and plonk the box down on the desk. Getting to work right away, I put my small number of belongings inside it. Pens, paper clips, a few dollar bills, stapler, calculator, more pens. As I open the drawers, I hear Sally's Mary Jane heels clomping on the floor as she rushes over.

Another calculator, glue stick, gum, tissues. Okay, so I don't need any of this crap. I just wanted to do this in person. I'm a little vindictive like that.

"Uh, what are you doing?" she asks from behind me.

"What does it look like, Sal?"

"For the last time, my name's not … Wait, are you leaving?"

Ding, ding, ding. There it is.

I paint a huge smile on my face, not even faking it.

"Oh, you can be quite clever when you really work for it, can't you? And yes, as a matter of fact, I am."

Slamming the drawer closed with my ass, I take a quick look around. That'll do.

"Bye Sal, it's been fun," I lie.

I walk back down between the cubicles toward the elevator.

"Oh, Vera! Here, you forgot your mug!" Sally comes trotting toward me.

"Keep it. It's a vintage Royal Albert," I call back while I step inside and press the button. "Sell it on eBay and use the money to pay for some proper skin care." I point at my nose, eyeing the nasty zit sitting on the end of hers as the doors close and she growls.

As I walk out of the lobby and onto the street, a huge smile spreads over my face. I'd whistle with glee if it wouldn't make me look like a goober. I make a beeline for my Porsche when I see a trash can. Walking over to it to dump the box inside, I change my mind when out of the corner of my eye, I see the same homeless man from earlier sitting in an alcove. He looks curiously at me when I drop the box in front of him. "There's probably a few dollars in there," I inform him before I make my way back over to my car and climb inside.

My brows furrow as I stare at my steering wheel. Damn, I

think Jared's fucking the nastiness right out of me. I can't complain, though; I like it too much to do a stupid thing like that. I only got three hours sleep last night, thanks to staying on the phone with him for too long and our weekend replaying on a constant loop in my head.

Shit. No job and fuck all money. Some might say I'm an idiot for quitting my job after everything that's happened today, but staying there is just another way for him to control me. I'm done being controlled. A whole sea of unpredictability yawns before me. But funnily enough, it's not as scary as I thought it'd be.

I park in the tiny lot and glance around as I walk over to the rolled-up door of the garage. "So this is where you work?" I inspect the dust already coating the tops of my black pumps. Jared looks up from where he's hunched over a bike, a wrench in his hand and a smile tugging at his lips. "Nah, I just like hanging out here with this smelly bastard in my free time." He jerks his chin at a large man with a huge beard, who grunts, "Fuck off."

Dropping the wrench, Jared chuckles, rising and grabbing a rag from his back pocket to wipe his fingers with. "Butch, this is Vera. Vera, Butch, one of the guys who works here."

Butch's head snaps over to me then, and I move farther into the crowded, oil-smelling interior of Surface Rust. Fitting name. There's actual rust on a lot of the tin siding of the poorly structured building. But inside? It's organized chaos. No clear space available except for in the center of the garage. Everything seems to have a home—even the various Harleys and an old car, which appear to be in various states of reconstruction or disrepair.

Butch scratches at his beard, which is so long it sits on top of his meaty chest as his eyes rake up my jean-clad legs to my cream blouse-covered chest. When he finally reaches my eyes, I raise a single brow at him. Busted. He grins sheepishly and looks over at Jared whose arms are folded over his chest while he smirks at me.

Butch clears his throat. "Sorry, ah, nice to meet ya, Vera."

"Charmed," I reply and move over to Jared. He unfolds his arms to fold them around me instead but then pulls back. "Shit, I'll get you dirty, Frost."

I lean up to brush my lips over his cheek. "Oh, you will be." I look down at my blouse. "And don't worry. I've had this thing for months."

"I'll just, um, yeah, got shit to do out back." Butch nods at us and walks out a door at the back of the garage that creaks loudly before slamming it closed.

Jared tugs me back to his chest with a low groan, skimming his lips side to side over my forehead as he inhales deeply. "Christ, I've missed you. Shouldn't you be at work?"

"It's only been a day." I laugh, but I'm secretly thrilled he does. "And, um, yeah, not going in today." I have no idea why I can't tell him. Why something stops me. Fear that he might think it's all the result of me being with him? Because it is, but it also isn't. It's been a long time coming; he just helped it finally happen. Albeit, unknowingly. *Later*, I tell myself. I'll tell him later.

"Longest day of my life." He squeezes me.

I laugh again. "What are you building?" I pull away to look at the bike he was working on.

"Uh." He scrubs a hand behind his head, his shirt riding

up a little. My eyes are drawn to that sliver of skin as if I can feel the smoothness of it beneath my fingers just by looking hard enough. "Probably not something you're interested in …" Jared trails off. That has my eyes unsticking and darting to his face. He folds his arms across his work shirt again, shrugging. "Sorry, I'm not trying to be a dick. But look at you and look at me." He smiles, but it's not convincing. "You don't really look like you belong in a place like this, beauty."

His softly spoken words are like tiny needle pricks right to the heart. He's right, though. I don't. But if I don't belong here, and I don't belong in my high-rise condo or fancy-ass life anymore, then where do I belong? My teeth sink into my bottom lip as I look down at my shoes. My beautiful shoes covered in a fine layer of dust. Yet I'm not cringing; I'm not cursing him out for working somewhere full of grime, dirt, grease, and countless other things bound to ruin my clothing choices. Because it's my choice to buy them, to wear them, and as I lift my eyes to the bike in front of me, I realize it was my choice to come here, too. I wanted to see where he worked and what he did. I can't really get mad at him for assuming what anyone else would. But still, my hand lifts to my chest, gently rubbing while I clear my throat. "Well, I wouldn't have come here if I wasn't interested, so are you going to just stand there or are you going to show me?"

The sharp bite to my voice has his eyes narrowing on mine. "Sure."

He tells me about the bike he's building for a client and the parts he's waiting on. And yeah, it goes in one ear and out the other, but I'm still entranced by everything that comes out of his mouth. The way he points at where the engine will go and crouches with a light in his eyes as he explains how they've had to order a new frame. It's then I realize that although he might've fallen into this job, this business he struggles to keep alive—he loves it. I'm hit with a case of irrational jealousy over this fact. I want him to talk about me with that same sense of wonder, interest, and devotion. With that gleam in his eyes. I want it all. But I don't think he realizes that, and I can't tell him.

I'm in love. In love with a grease monkey who fucks like it's his last day on earth and works in an old, decrepit shed. I'd laugh at how ludicrous it all is. This crazy turn my life has taken. But then he smiles softly at me as if knowing I'm not taking in any information he's telling me but, rather, listening and absorbing everything about him instead.

"You're not listening to a word I'm saying, are you?" His brow quirks.

"Sure I am."

He cocks his head to the side, eyes glinting.

Damn it. "Okay, I'm not learning a damn thing about the bike, but you?" I bite my lip. "You're a lot more interesting."

He throws his head back with a loud laugh then walks over to me. Tucking some of my hair behind my ears, he says, "I happen to find you very interesting, too."

"Yeah?" My voice is breathy.

He nods. "Oh, yeah."

The sound of his gravelly voice has goose bumps appearing on my skin. My nipples harden behind the cups of my bra. I step into him and wrap my arms around his waist, dirty shirt be damned. Our lips meet in a kiss that's gentle yet violent in the way it sends my emotions and hormones twisting into a painful mixture of need.

He pulls away, and my eyes flutter open, blinking and readjusting to the absence of his presence when he walks over to the other side of the garage. He uses another rag to wipe the top of an old wooden stool then carries it over and sets it down by the bike. "I need to remove this fender and a few other things then maybe we can grab some lunch." He taps the stool then bends back down by the bike.

I take a seat. "Why do you guys pull them apart like this in the first place?"

He drops the wrench and walks over to a toolbox by the wall. "What, the bikes?"

"Well, yeah." I fidget with my hands in my lap while I watch him. "Aren't they old anyway?"

He turns around and walks back over with a little plastic kit or something in his hands, bending back down to the bike.

"We enjoy it. Darren used to mainly work with old cars— you know, service them and do the odd repair here and there, too. But he always loved Harleys and would work on his own here at the shop when he could. Some people took notice, or heard, and started bringing theirs to him, too."

"But you know the stupid saying ... if it ain't broke, why fix it?"

He stops what he's doing and grins over at me. There's that weird twinkle in his eye I've learned he gets when he finds me amusing. "What?" I huff.

"You're adorable when you're trying not to show you're interested in something, know that?"

"Well, I do now."

He chuckles, going back to his tinkering. I'm momentarily hypnotized by the flexing of his thick bicep bulging against the confines of his shirt sleeve as he unscrews a bolt and gets to work on the rest.

After he's pulled it off, he collects all the bolts and chucks them into a small tin then rises and walks back over to his toolbox to put everything away. "Darren once told us that when he was younger, rebuilding choppers was done as more of a means of transportation than a hobby. He'd pick up bikes from the war era for next to nothing, bring them home or bring them into work, and fix them in his spare time. Now it's a little more expensive and kind of a growing industry. But I guess I just like the idea of feeling something I made rumble beneath me when I ride." He shrugs.

"Why?" I ask.

He turns around, leaning back against the workbench. "Hard to explain, but there's a certain beauty in creating something. In looking at the finished product and knowing you made it what it is. In the way you can so easily fall in love with an idea. Whether it's still a little rough around the edges or not, you commit to it, put in the time, the effort and keep at it until you get it just right. Just right for you. Because it makes you happy to not only see that finished product but because you also enjoyed every second it took to get it there."

I feel the breath whoosh out of me and stare down at an oil smear on the concrete floor. My heart constricts as I realize he hasn't just penetrated these cold layers of my heart and made me fall for him. No, he's now sunk himself in so deep that I don't know how I'm going to eradicate him. How I'm going to untie myself from these constricting binds he keeps wrapping around me.

And what's even scarier is, I really don't even want to.

My phone rings, breaking the tense silence and causing my gaze to move to my purse, which is on the ground next to me. I bend down and get my phone out, scowling at the screen when I see Dexter's name on it. I should probably just change my number now.

The phone disappears from my hands. Jared glowers at it before glancing at me. I lift my shoulders. "Don't even ask. You know I'm well and truly done with him." I try for a sultry smile, but I can tell it fails because his narrowed eyes drop back to the screen when it stops ringing and then starts right back up again.

He answers it. *Shit.* Not good, not good.

"Can't you take a hint?" Jared's voice becomes something I hardly recognize. Cold and gruff. It probably shouldn't send tingles racing down my spine, but it definitely does.

"Really?" He smirks at me briefly, but it's not playful. It's the kind of smirk that says he's pissed off but trying to keep his cool.

"Uh-huh. Sure, I'll pass on the message. Right after I'm done sliding my cock inside her tight pussy while squeezing those creamy thighs hard enough she's left with bruises. Because you know, we men have our priorities."

Christ. My cheeks heat, and I feel my panties grow damp. This shouldn't be turning me on because he's blatantly disrespecting me. Not to mention, probably causing a shitload of trouble for me if Dexter goes running to Father dearest. Oh, well. The damage has already been done in that regard, so let him do what he wants.

Jared hums, and I take a seat on the stool again. "No. Now don't call my girl again or I'll show you what getting on the bad side of a piece of shit city scum like myself can do for you. Fuck off and have a shit day."

I shouldn't be so caught up in those two little words, not after everything he just said. *My girl.* But now my insides feel like mush. He hangs up and turns away from me, running a palm over his perfect hair and causing some strands to fall on his face when he turns back around.

He passes me my phone, not looking at me. "Here. Apparently, you need to call your dad."

He's called me twice, and to him, that may as well mean

he's tried fifty times. But there's nothing to say, and I'm not going to do what he wants, so I didn't see the point in returning his calls. I take my phone from him and hop up to put it back in my purse. When I turn around, he's staring at me. His jaw clenches, and his eyes look like they're trying to see through me. "What?" I ask, my voice tinged with nerves.

He shakes his head and turns back to the bike, but his rigid posture and the tension radiating from him won't let me leave it alone. Walking over to him, I grab his arm, turning him around to face me. "Talk to me."

He sucks his lips into his mouth, hesitating, then finally says, "You know, this isn't easy for me."

I raise a brow, giving him a shaky smile. "And what, you think it's easy for me?" He has no idea of all the ways it hasn't been easy for me. But I'm not about to dump that information on him now. "What are you trying to say, Jared?"

He stares at me for an excruciating few moments. "I'm trying to say you can't fuck me over, Vera, because I don't know if I'll be able to handle it. What you've seen is what you get with me, and when you realize it's not as fucking fun as you thought it'd be, when you get sick of roughing it …" He trails off and turns around, placing his hands on the bench and dropping his head down.

He thinks so little of me? I don't believe that, though. He may be a smartass, but he's also a smart man. If he truly did think that way about me, he'd have left me alone weeks ago. I step closer to him and hook my arms around his waist from behind. He stiffens then seems to relax. I scoot under his arms until he's caging me against the bench with them. Lifting my hands, I frame his face, watching the way his eyes slowly soften when I rub my thumbs over his cheeks. "You're the greatest adventure I've ever had." The admission pours from somewhere deep in my soul. "But when you look at me, I feel it everywhere … mainly here." I tap my chest then lean on my toes to bump my nose against his. "If you were a book, I'd read you, touch you, look at you every day and never get bored."

I watch those green orbs widen at the same time his hands grab my face then his lips crash into mine.

CHAPTER TWENTY

We end up grabbing lunch at the coffee shop, and Jared says he'll walk me down the street to Always Booked before he heads back to work for the afternoon. It's been a while since I saw Badger, and I kind of want to fill him in on what's happened. Maybe he'll help settle this splash of fear that's still bubbling in my gut.

Jared folds his hand around mine, and we make our way down the street. "What time are you finished tonight?" I ask.

He flips his sunglasses down, shrugging. "No idea. I'd say come over, but it might be late …"

I start to nod then my heel suddenly gets stuck in a crack in the concrete sidewalk. "Shit."

I lurch, my ankle twists, and I'm certain it's going to break when I hit the ground. Jared's hand grabs my bicep tightly and thankfully stops my embarrassing, and what was sure to be painful, tumble to the ground.

He rights me then bends down, moving his sunglasses to

the top of his head. "Hold my shoulders."

Confused, I do as he says, and he lifts my foot out of my black pump then yanks my shoe out of the sidewalk. He then maneuvers my foot back into the shoe with so much gentleness that my heart clenches, much more painfully than the twinge in my ankle. He stands, my hands fall from his shoulders, and I try to balance on one foot while his eyes dart all over my face. "You okay? Does it hurt?"

Hesitantly, I put some weight on it, but it doesn't feel too bad. "I'm okay." I tuck some hair behind my ear, feeling kind of embarrassed. I clear my throat. "Uh, thank you."

He grabs my face with both hands. "Are you lying?"

Laughing, I shake my head. "I'm really okay. It's a little sore, but it's not sprained."

He bends back down and softly runs his fingers over my ankle. "It doesn't look swollen. But still." He turns around and crouches. "Better climb on, just in case."

I look around at the people passing us on the street. "Jared, no. Everyone will stare at us. I'm okay. Let's just go."

He scowls at me over his shoulder. "I'm not moving, Vera. I'll just stay right here, looking like an idiot until you hop on."

"Oh, fine." I huff loudly and bend down to climb on his back. A loud laugh erupts from me when he rises. "Hold on tight." My arms hook around his shoulders, my legs squeezing his sides. He hoists me up higher on his back then continues to walk down the street.

An elderly couple smiles at us, and I bury my nose into Jared's neck to muffle my giggle when the man winks at Jared.

I'm still laughing when Jared pushes open the door to Always Booked. Badger is standing by a shelf in the front of the shop and spins around, eyes widening behind his glasses.

The smile that takes over his face warms my heart. But

still. "Okay, Hero. Put me down."

Jared ignores me, pinching my ass when I start to climb down. "Graham, long time, no see."

Graham? I look around but then realize he's talking to Badger.

"Jared Williams. It's been a few years. Where've you been?"

"Oh, you know, just been busy being a menace to society."

Badger grins, tucking a book on the shelf and walking over to us. "It's a tough job that one, very time consuming."

Jared sighs. "Right? But someone's gotta do it."

Badger wheezes out a laugh, patting Jared on the shoulder. I use Jared's distraction to my advantage and jump down, almost falling on my ass. He turns around, glaring at me.

I glare back, and he smiles.

"Care to tell me why you've walked in the door with Vera, here, on your back?"

Jared glances between us, eyes narrowing when he realizes we obviously know each other. "Oh, well, she wanted to be a monkey, and she's my woman, so I gotta keep her happy, you know?"

Badger laughs again, leaning against the counter. "I take it you two know each other then?" I ask dryly.

They both nod, but Badger answers. "Yes, I've known Jared and his brother since they were this tall." He lowers his hand to his waist. "Little delinquents used to try to steal books from here until Mirabelle made them work for them."

Jared laughs. "She was a ballbuster, that one." Badger scowls at him, and Jared rushes to say, "Nicest ballbuster I've ever met. She also let us borrow books and made the best ham sandwiches I've ever tasted," he says to me.

"I take it this is the gentleman who rescued you from the highway?" Badger asks me.

I nod, smiling up at Jared when he coughs. "You've been speaking about me behind my back?" He tsks then looks at Badger. "All good things, I hope?"

Badger chuckles, and I point at him. "Not a word."

He mimes zipping his lips, and the two of them catch up quickly, Badger asking about Felix and how the shop is doing before Jared says he needs to go. He gently tucks my hair behind my ears and grasps my cheeks in both hands. "I'll talk to you later." He kisses my forehead and walks away, leaving my eyes fluttering as I watch him disappear out the jingling door to the busy street outside.

"Jared Williams." Badger laughs. "Well, I never would've thought it'd be him, but I gotta say…" He runs his hand over his chin. "I'm not mad it is."

I give him a nervous smile. "He's a good guy."

Badger nods. "He is. A heart of gold."

"My dad cut me off," I blurt out.

Badger's brows shoot up. "I'll make us some tea." I nod and follow him to the back room. He turns around. "But Vera?"

"Yes, *Graham*?" I arch a brow at him.

He shrugs. "You never asked." Blue eyes roam over my face. "Happiness looks good on you."

I've just climbed out of the shower when I hear a knock on the door. Shoving my arms into my robe, I quickly wrap my wet hair in a towel and move down the hall to see who it is. Only a few people have clearance to get up to my apartment without checking in with me first. Looking through the peephole, a green eye stares back at me, making me glad that I've now added him to that small list.

Laughing quietly, I shake my head and open the door for Jared, who walks in with two pizza boxes in his hands. The door closes behind him as he places the pizza down on the entry table. He whistles, crowding me into the wall. "So it's your shampoo." He sniffs the top of my head. "I knew it must be something like that."

I grab his hand and the pizzas, tugging him into my living room. "I thought you were busy with work?" I take a seat on the couch, placing the boxes on the coffee table.

He takes a seat beside me. "I am. I should've stayed, but I wanted to see you more." He leans in to pepper loud kisses over my cheek, making me giggle. What is it with this man turning me into a giggling schoolgirl? It's embarrassing, but he doesn't seem to care. He opens the boxes, and I take in his jeans and long sleeve white t-shirt with some band logo on the front. He must've gone home to shower first. I get up, quickly grabbing some napkins and two bottles of water from the kitchen. Taking a seat beside him again, I watch him pick up the remote and settle back into the couch, flicking through Netflix movies while he eats.

"Your ankle okay?" He puts *Pulp Fiction* on then pats his lap.

"It's fine." I arch a brow at him, and he huffs, pointing at my bare legs. I lift them, and he places the pizza box on the arm of the couch, using one hand to rub my legs while he eats with the other.

"See," he mumbles and swallows. "You just need a book, and I'm boyfriend of the year."

I finish chewing and swallow before responding, "I'd never touch a book with greasy pizza fingers. Besides, I think I said rub my back, not legs."

His head rears back comically. I laugh, poking my toes into his thigh. "Joking." I glare at his now unmoving hand. "Don't you dare stop."

He shakes his head with a smile, and we eat in silence until only a few pieces of pizza are left. Which are in my box. I scoot them over to Jared, who grins and demolishes them.

"I can't believe you know Badger." I take a sip from my water.

He wipes his fingers on a napkin and steals my water bottle from me, draining most of it in two pulls. "Yep. Can't believe you know … wait, Badger? You are talking about Graham, aren't you?"

I stand and remove the towel from my head, running my fingers through the tangled ends of my hair. "Yeah, I call him Badger."

He watches my every move. "Why?"

I grab the boxes and take them to the trash in the kitchen. When I return, I tell him, "I met him when I was a kid. He had dark brown, almost black hair with two streaks of gray running through it on either side of his head."

Jared smacks his thigh. "I remember that." He laughs. "Crazy that I've never met you before now."

"Maybe that's for a reason." I shrug, plucking our water bottles and napkins off the coffee table and taking them to the trash too.

He's standing, stretching his arms over his head when I return. "I think you're right. If I had met you before now, I would've undoubtedly fucked it up somehow."

I walk over to him and wrap my arms around his waist. His arms fall back down to my back, rubbing over the satin fabric of my robe. Spotting some pizza sauce on the side of his lip, I lift to my toes and grab his head to lick it from his mouth.

"You're a dirty tease."

"You had a dirty lip. I was just cleaning it for you," I whisper.

His eyes heat, and my stomach clenches. He slides my robe off, and it falls to the floor, leaving me naked. "Sit on the table."

"What?"

He directs me to the end of the coffee table behind me. I take a seat, and he tilts my chin up to look at him. "Fucking beautiful. Open; I want those lips around my cock."

He releases my chin and unzips his jeans, nudging my legs open with one of his. Shoving his jeans and briefs down to his ankles, his hard cock springs free, bobbing near my face.

I lick my lips, eyeing the pre-cum resting at the tip before grabbing the base and dragging my tongue over his salty slit.

Jared groans, his head falling back. I take my time, working him with my hand and taking as much of him into my mouth as I can. His head rolls forward, eyes watching me when he starts to thrust in and out, making me gag.

He curses and steps back, his cock leaving my mouth with a wet pop. "Lie down."

I scoot the remotes to the floor and lie down. He leans over me, staring at me before his lips lower to mine, gently grazing then moving down my neck to my breasts. He squeezes, licks, and sucks at them, and my legs instinctively wind around his waist.

"Can I take that picture now?" He lifts his head, squeezing my breasts and rubbing his thumbs over the stiff peaks of my nipples while never taking his eyes from them.

"Not today, Hero."

He sighs. "But I can see them anytime I want, right?"

I let out a soft laugh. "You can see me anytime you want, yes."

He nods, seemingly appeased with that, and lowers his

head to trail kisses over my stomach. My fingers sink into his thick hair, messing it up as my eyes try to keep track of what he's doing. His rough hands unwrap my legs from his waist before he reaches my mound. He kisses it and then spreads my legs further, dipping low to swipe his tongue up and down my folds. My eyes give in and close. He lifts my legs over his shoulders and then he's parting me with his fingers, teasing my clit mercilessly with his tongue.

"Oh … fuck." My eyes shoot open when he thrusts his finger all the way in and hooks it.

He rubs the pad over that perfect spot and flicks his tongue over my clit continuously. It takes all of a minute and then I'm coming, squeezing his head between my thighs as they shake and a long, loud moan leaves my mouth.

He rests his chin on my mound and gives me a small, crooked smile. "I think we need regular sleepovers. We should take turns. You clearly need me, and it's only been a day, beauty."

I laugh, and he lifts his head, smiling down at me. "Laugh it up, princess, but you know I'm right." He moves my legs behind him and thrusts inside me, hissing when he buries himself to the hilt. "God, fuck yes. I'm moving in, or you're moving in with me."

"A little premature, don't you think?"

He swivels his hips, and I moan. "Nah, I don't think so. When you know, you know."

Breathing becomes hard to do, and not only because of his slow, deep thrusts, but because of those words. "You know, do you?" I breathe out.

His nostrils flare, he bends down to rest his forehead against mine. "Knew weeks ago. I need this." He kisses my nose. "You. Everyday. Always."

I grab his head and devour his mouth with mine. He

groans when I bite his lip, sucking it into my mouth. His thrusts start to quicken, and he tears his lips away to straighten and look down at where we're joined. Running his fingers from my breasts to my belly button to where we're connected, he curses huskily. "I've never seen anything look this damn perfect." He drags his cock slowly in and out, watching his actions with a groan, and I feel another orgasm start to build.

I whimper, and his eyes flick up to mine. "You like that? My bare cock rubbing against every warm, tight inch of this pussy?"

Shit. "Yes."

His smirk is dirty and wicked. He thrusts harder, and my hands reach out to grab the sides of the table. "You're going to come again, aren't you, Frost?"

When I don't answer him, he stops moving, and I whine pitifully. "Yes, I'm going to …"

My words break off into another moan when his thumb circles my swollen clit.

He speeds up his thrusts. "Shit, yeah."

I've never been more grateful for my expensive taste in furniture. He slams into me, hard and fast, rubbing my clit and making me almost scream while my second orgasm rolls through me. My toes clench, and my fingernails probably break from holding the coffee table so damn tight. He stills, planted deep and groans loudly as he empties himself inside me. His body drops over mine, and he rests his head on my chest. I run my fingers through his hair while we both slow our breathing.

"You see I'm right, now, don't you?" he asks.

"Right about what?"

"Well, besides everything, the fact you need me. Time to move in, Frost." He turns his head, planting a raspberry on the side of my breast and making me laugh.

He stands, lifting me with him. My legs stay around his waist as he walks us to my bedroom. Still buried inside me, he slowly lowers us to the bed before withdrawing. He looks down at me and grabs my hand, placing it against his chest. "Again."

I smile, laughing softly and feeling his heart thud beneath my palm, fast and strong. "Hmm, that makes me wonder, where else do you feel me?" I drag my fingers down his chest to trace the indents of his abs through his shirt.

He doesn't answer me which has me frowning until his features soften. He blows out a loud breath, grabbing my hand from his chest and kissing it.

"Everywhere, Vera."

My heart skips three beats then starts to pound harder than anything that would be considered healthy. So loud I don't hear him when he says, "Every part of me."

But my eyes read his lips before they lower to mine.

CHAPTER TWENTY-ONE

S oft kisses pepper my face sometime between the sun waking and lifting into the sky. I wake up later that morning to a text message.

Jared: Be at my place by six. I'll make sure I'm home.

P.S. You're cute when you say my name in your sleep. ;)

I scoff, chucking my phone back on the nightstand and getting up to take a shower. I spend the morning cleaning and looking for jobs on my phone. It feels weird to sever that last tie with my father. But in a good way. Like I can finally breathe a little easier now.

Loud banging sounds on my apartment door, startling me. I put down my coffee and phone then walk down the hall, swinging it open before I've even checked who it is.

Holy shit.

What the hell is he doing here? I don't think my father has ever visited my apartment in all the years I've lived here. He walks in, not invited and not uttering one word of greeting. No, he marches in, slams the door, and sets those hard eyes straight on me.

Well, fuck.

"I warned you, and you know that my patience only goes so far. You've had your fun. Time's up."

Fear tears through me. "Excuse me?"

"You've made your point. You don't need my money or any help from me, but do you really need to tie yourself to the trash of this city?"

No. I swallow hard.

He laughs. "I expected better of you. You should know by now that not much gets past me." The false mirth disappears from his hard features. "But you've taken this little tantrum of yours too far. You're embarrassing yourself, and you're embarrassing me. End it with him. You've made your god damned point."

"No." I take a deep breath. "You don't get to decide how I live my life. Now get the hell out of my apartment."

I move to open the door, but then he says in the coldest voice I've ever heard him use, "It'd be a shame to see that tiny business that your street urchin can barely keep above water suddenly … sink."

My mouth dries. Jared's words from the weekend about his brother and all the hardships they've been dealt filters through my brain. Watching him work there, how much he loves it.

He wouldn't. Again, with that naïve voice. He fucking would, and he'd make it look like an accident.

"You wouldn't dare." I turn around and try for some false bravado.

He shrugs, adjusting the cuffs on his dress shirt. "Maybe I would; maybe I wouldn't. But are you really willing to risk it?" His hands drop to his sides. "That is the question here. How much does this grease monkey mean to you? You've seen where lust took your mother. Don't think you won't end up down the same long road of struggle. A life spent doing what you want is great until you can't afford to even feed yourself anymore and have to resort to begging." He raises a dark brow. "Is that what you want, Vera?"

"I'm nothing like her," I seethe.

He hums, clasping his hands together. "You're right. You may look like her, so much so that I can barely stand to look at you sometimes." I try not to flinch. "But you're right. You're nothing like her." He tilts his head. "Want to know why that is?"

"You're going to tell me anyway."

He nods. "Watch your tone." He takes a step closer, and I force myself to stand still as his expensive cologne and over-powering presence threatens to smother me where I stand. "It's because I raised you better. Harder. You're exactly who I want you to be. Ruthless, cunning, and smart." He lowers his voice to a menacing growl. "So use that brain of yours and close those fucking legs to scum that doesn't even deserve to look at you, let alone touch you. Quit ruining yourself, or I'll ruin him. Understood?"

"Why are you doing this?" I whisper. "Do you really hate me that much?"

He steps forward again, but I don't cower. "Cut the whiny shit, Vera. Your attitude lately makes you appear very ungrateful."

"You expect me to be grateful?"

"I could destroy him, and you know it. I'm merely just try-ing to ensure you stay true to yourself and you're taken care of, as only a man such as Dexter and his caliber could care for you."

"With money?"

His jaw clenches. "With security. I'm trying to protect you from making decisions with that useless organ in your chest when you should be using the one in your head."

I step back, moving next to the door. "It's no wonder she ran off."

He flinches. And while no one else would've seen it, I do.

His top lip curls. "That's why your stupid mother used to call, you know? For money. Just think about that before you decide to risk your piece of fun's only bit of livelihood he has left."

I shake my head as the thundering of my heart roars in my ears. This can't be happening.

"Do you know that she calls me now?" I admit, desperation and disbelief strangling my voice. "I send her your money because, like an idiot, I felt bad every time I saw you crumble after dealing with her. So I did it. She's probably going to be pissed she needs to contact you again, but shit happens, doesn't it?"

He slaps me. It happens so fast that one second I'm staring at him, and the next I'm blinking at the ground. "You have no idea what you're talking about," he growls.

Taking a deep breath, I lift my head and fill my stare with as much hate as I can muster. "Get. Out."

His eyes lower to my cheek, which is stinging like a bitch. I watch his Adam's apple bob as he swallows. When he doesn't move, I scream the words at him. "I said get out!"

He finally lifts his eyes from me and moves to the door. "Quit testing me, Vera. You don't want to know what else might happen if you do." The door closes behind him, and I drop my head into my hands, wondering how the hell everything can turn so horribly wrong in the space of ten minutes.

Staring at the screen on my phone, I sniff and try to mentally prepare myself for what I need to do. I should've known it could come to this. I *did* know. I just had no idea it would blow up in my face quite so badly. It seems my greed really does know no bounds, and now, well, I just hope he doesn't suffer the way I'm already starting to. He never dropped that four-letter word. One month. That's all it's been. He should be fine.

But unlike him, that's all it took for me to lose one of the most important parts of myself that survived after all these years.

My heart.

I sit up, take a deep breath, and finally dial his number.

He answers after three rings. "Hey, where are you? Didn't you get my text?"

It's six thirty, and I hear water running on his end of the line. "Frost? I've just made some macaroni; I'll save some for you if you hurry up."

Jesus. I can't do this.

You have to. "I saw your message, but I won't be coming over tonight, Hero. Or any other night." I try to sweeten my voice. "It's been fun, but I can't see you anymore."

Something bangs in the background, and he curses. "Wait, wait, what the fuck are you … oh real fucking funny." He forces out a laugh. "Hurry up and get your sweet ass over here."

I steel my spine, infusing as much strength into it as possible.

Do it. Like a Band-Aid.

"I'm not joking, Jared. I hope you didn't get too attached; you did say that you didn't want anything serious."

He goes quiet, too quiet. "I'm coming over."

He hangs up, and the blood drains from my face.

Fuck. No, shit, no. I can't do this in person.

I get up and grab my keys and purse, but when I reach the door, I think better of it and put them down on the entry table. He'd only wait or come back if I wasn't here.

God, why does that make it so much worse?

That huge part of me, the selfish part, is singing with glee that he cares so much. But I can't acknowledge it. I can't do anything about it for fear of what would happen if I do.

I sit on the couch and wait, smoothing my hair back and standing when, not even fifteen minutes later, there's a knock on my door.

He knocks again just before I swing it open. His gaze lands on mine. Shock and hurt stare back at me through green eyes. But I can't falter. I won't.

"It's over, is it? Just like that?"

I nod. "Yeah, I mean, I'm sorry." I shrug. "I probably took it a bit too far ..."

"Too far?" He laughs without any trace of humor and comes straight for me, grabbing my hips and kicking the door closed. His eyes dart between mine. "Why don't I believe you?"

Mask. Keep the mask on. I give him a sultry smile. "Because we were pretty good together, right?"

His brows lower even more. "Good? Vera, what the fuck is this shit about?"

I shift, trying to remove his hold on me, but his hands tighten. "It's that fucking guy, isn't it?" When I don't respond, he shakes my hips, his voice rising. "Isn't it?!"

I shake my head. "No, it's just time to stop playing around now."

"Bullshit," he growls. "What's going on?"

The truth sits on the tip of my tongue, but I can't tell him. Time to take this up a notch. "Nothing." *Everything.* "You're a good fuck, Jared, but there's no way I can have a future with you." I force out a laugh even though it hurts. "You knew that, didn't you? Don't take it personally; it's just the way it is." And it's never felt truer, now that I've admitted it out loud. I was stupid to think any differently. To think I could have it all.

He looks like I've punched him in the gut, staggering back a step and giving me enough room to finally breathe properly. But I feel no relief. Just this heart twisting sense of regret that I've done this to us.

"Don't take it personally, huh?" He huffs out a loud breath, rubbing a hand down the side of his face.

"You really shouldn't." I try to soften the blows I keep throwing. "You're a good guy. We're just not right for each other."

"Fuck me, am I fucking sick of hearing that." My brows furrow, but he continues, "So that's it then?"

My shoulders lift, my heart splintering as I stare into his glazed eyes. "Well, yeah. I don't know what else you want me to say."

"Say you're lying. That you're joking. Say anything other than the shit coming out of your mouth."

"Why?" I snap as though he's annoying me. He needs to go. Now. "It doesn't change the truth, does it? You said yourself that I might get sick of roughing it, and I guess I have. I'm sorry."

"You're sorry?" he snarls. "But you said I was your … your …" His hands clench. "You know what? Fuck this." He turns for the door, pausing with his back to me. "I knew you were different, but I didn't think you were really such a cold-hearted bitch."

The door slams at the same time I collapse against the wall behind me, crumpling to the ground and letting the tears run free.

CHAPTER TWENTY-TWO

Three days. Three days and an ungodly amount of chocolate and horror books. As soon as I saw that stupid four-letter word on any page, I slammed the book closed, and grabbed a new one.

No one ever tells you about the little things that accompany heartbreak. Just the sound of a motorcycle sends my heart jolting. But I'd know the sound of Jared's bike anywhere, so I know it's never him. This kind of hurt has me looking at so many things differently. The color green, or the way I stare at the sugar jar on the counter, remembering his love for a hot cup of sugar with a hint of coffee. Shit, just making a freaking sandwich has me wanting to scream. I had no idea of the ways having your heart broken could affect your day-to-day life.

But I've come to find that once it starts to fester, that hurt can turn just as toxic as the love you so ignorantly fell into. Filling your veins with anguish and your heart with poison until you can barely remember what happiness once felt like. Or even if you were ever happy at all. For maybe it was all just a dream. An imagining of something that will always remain elusively out of reach.

Especially for a cold-hearted bitch.

I don't blame him for his cruelly spoken words. I really don't. No, I blame someone who's much harder to take my anger out on. Myself.

Out of all the harmful things I could have ever done to myself, falling in love has got to be the worst. But some lessons need to be learned the hard way. Experienced, as Badger would say.

So I stomp on that ever-present urge to find my cure and beg for forgiveness, and instead, I walk into my closet in search of a dress. It's time to distract the hurt and become the girl I need to be for the night.

Blurring city buildings and lights stream past the passenger window as I shift, adjusting the material of my long black gown over my legs. It's more casual than most items I'd wear to such events, but it's still going to look better than half the other dresses at tonight's Bramston Inc. annual Thanksgiving charity gala, so I can't bring myself to give a damn. The pleats of the skirt shimmer when the light catches them through the window of the car, the deep V-neck cut over my chest a bit revealing yet still classy. It's a shame it'll probably never get worn again after tonight. I'll only associate it with sour memories, and I don't need any more of those.

Dexter reaches over the console, grabbing my hand. I recoil, snatching it back, and he laughs darkly.

The only thing worse than attending this event with Dexter—especially after I thought these days were long over—is having him touch me.

"Play nice and stop thinking so highly of yourself, Vera."

My eye twitches at the mere sound of his voice. "What do you mean by that?"

He flicks the turn signal on, turning down a back street that leads to the Hedgington.

"Do you honestly think I want to wind up trapped with someone like you?" He glances at me briefly. "Some bitch who doesn't give a shit about anyone other than herself?" He lets out a stunned laugh. "And let's not forget how fast the rumor mill is running with talk of you flying around Rayleigh on the back of some scumbag's motorcycle." Shock, thick and slimy, oozes into my bloodstream. "Open your eyes, Vera. I don't want to fucking marry you. I don't want to buy a house for you. I don't particularly want anything to do with you unless it involves getting between those nice legs of yours." He scoffs. "But you're even selfish with that, aren't you? You gave it to me so rarely that it's not really any kind of bonus at all."

Anger ignites, causing my teeth to clench together. "Cut the crap, Dexter. Why the fuck are you doing this then?"

"Isn't it obvious? Christ." He runs a hand over his combed brown hair. "And to think that your father says you're smart." He turns into the Hedgington, joining the line for the valet. Bile rises up my throat at the thought of potentially seeing Jared. But when we pull up, he's nowhere to be seen, and relief washes over me like a tidal wave.

Dexter turns to me before opening the door. "I want Bramston Inc., and your father is willing to give it to me, but being a man of strict tradition, he wants to keep it in the family." He opens his jacket, plucking his phone from his pocket.

"So behave, or my finger might slip and dial someone you really don't want it to." He gets out, and I try to pick my jaw up off the floor of his car. Shit. I'm such a god damned idiot. Inhaling one deep breath after another, I try to calm myself down.

He opens my door, and I take his offered hand, wiping my features blank before stepping out of the car. Pride and self-loathing are bitter pills to swallow, but I'll force them down and try to keep my head held high while doing so.

Assholes. The two of them are such fucking evil assholes. Tears prick the backs of my eyes, but I fight the urge to free them with every sliver of strength I have left.

He links my arm through his, smiling at a passing couple and walking us through the lobby. We hand over our coats then head to the ballroom, where we make small talk with a few people before sitting down to wait for dinner and the silent auction to begin. I see Isla over by the far wall talking with her father's business associate. She waves, giving me a weak smile. Her and Cleo both know all of what's happened. They weren't surprised, and even went so far as to tell me not to risk it and to just leave the Jared thing alone for a while. *Thing*. As if he's a toy I can put on the shelf for a while and ignore.

"For God's sake, smile," Dexter hisses into my ear after the auction comes to an end. "You look like you've swallowed a sour grape."

I feel like I'm going to hurl all over his lap, but I keep quiet and stretch my lips into a small smile. "Better," he murmurs. "You really are much more beautiful when your mouth is shut."

My eyes spring wide at his audacity. If he thinks just because he's finally told me about his ulterior motives that he can speak to me like trash, he's got another thing coming. I slap his arm as though he said something inappropriate, and I slap it hard. Turning my head, my lips a centimeter from his, I whisper, "You should really shut yours before I tell you and my father to go to hell and walk out of here."

He grins, his hand lifting to my neck. He wraps it around the side, his thumb smoothing over my jaw. "You and I both know you're not going anywhere." He presses his lips to mine quickly then sits back in his chair.

The next hour drags; I stay with Dexter the whole time, and Isla tries to join me when she can. When it looks like everyone is finally feeling the effects of the open bar, I decide I've had enough and excuse myself from the conversation. Dexter follows, catching my arm. "Where do you think you're going? We've barely been here two hours."

I pull my arm free. "You wanted me here. I came. Now I'm going."

He tries to stop me by grabbing my arm again, but I move away. "Don't. Please, Dexter, just… I've had enough for one night."

He blinks, obviously not expecting my softer tone of voice. He nods. "Fine. I'll call you soon. Make sure you answer."

I turn for the entrance, getting my coat and shoving it on while I move outside. My arm is grabbed again when I do. I spin around, about to scream at Dexter, appearances be damned, only to find it's not him at all.

Jared tugs me away from the front entrance of the hotel and around the corner near the gardens. My heart's fury is almost palpable. *Why* is he here? Tonight, of all nights.

"Jared, let go." I twist my arm from his grip, but he just grabs my upper arms, walking me back into an alcove and cleaving me open with the anger emanating from him.

"Don't waste any time, do you?" he snarls.

I avert my gaze to his scuffed, black boots, unsure if I'll be able to look at him without him seeing everything in my eyes.

"Whatever," I say with as much aloofness as possible. "Can you move? I need to go."

He lets go, only to move his forearms to either side of my head, trapping me against the cold wall. "Why, Frost? Is he waiting for you? I thought you would've been able to spare a bit of time for little old me, you know, considering I'm such a good guy and all."

His cold voice assaults every vital part of me. I shove at his chest, immediately dropping my arms back to my sides when the temptation to wrap them around him becomes too strong.

"Yes, he's waiting," I finally lie. "So go away."

He tsks, his lips hovering over my cheek. "But does he touch you like I do? Does he know how to make your legs shake like I fucking do?" He shoves his knee between my legs, and I suppress a groan, fighting the impulse to rock against his thigh.

"Jared, this is ridiculous. Stop it."

"No," he growls. "Fucking answer me."

"Hey, Vera. The car is here." I hear Isla call out from somewhere near the front entrance of the hotel.

His voice drops to a scathing whisper, his lips brushing over my skin when he says, "Do you think of me when he fucks you like the spoiled bitch you are?"

Pulverized isn't a strong enough word to describe the beating my heart just took. The pain has me desperate to escape, and I shove him hard. "Get off."

He steps back, and I can't help myself as my eyes shoot to his face. His features are only more devastating with the torment contorting them. "You know what? I think that's exactly what I need." His top lip curls. "Enjoy your perfect life, Vera."

He turns and walks away, thankfully before he can see my face fall. I suck in breath after breath, trying to cool the burn invading my heart and throat.

"Vera?" Isla steps around the corner. "Shit." She moves over to me, wrapping her arm around my waist. "Breathe, just breathe. Look at me." I do, and she breathes slowly, encouraging me to do the same. I do, slowly getting my heart rate back under control.

"Fuck, it hurts." I swipe under my eyes, removing the wetness.

She wipes under them gently. "I can see that." She curses again. "I had no idea you were in so deep. Why don't you just tell him? You could explain everything. Warn him."

My head shakes, and her hands drop. "Because then he'd almost have to choose between me and his shop. It was his foster dad's, and it's not just his; it's his brother's, too. Plus, he has some employees … It's too complicated."

She rubs my arms soothingly. "But at least he'd know."

I sniff. "Is he gone?"

She nods. "Yeah, walked straight past me without even looking at me before I came over. I saw you leave and followed you then heard you arguing and didn't know if I should interrupt." She scoffs. "Until he started being a dick. Is he always like that?"

I straighten from the wall, and we walk back to wait for her car. "No, you really think I'd fall for a guy who treats me like that?" I sniff again, climbing inside the Town Car and putting my seat belt on. Isla does the same. "I hurt him. But to be honest, I didn't realize he cared so much."

Isla's quiet for the rest of the drive to my apartment. When we're almost there, she says, "I think you should tell him. I think that going through with what your father and Dexter want might ruin something really good for you."

I close my eyes; my head tilted back to the roof of the car. "It's already ruined."

She pats my hand, and I lift my head when the car stops. "Call me if you need me, but just think about it, okay?"

I give her a weak smile and shut the door. She doesn't realize that's all I seem to do.

Think about him.

"I've done what you told me to, but I'm drawing the line at Dexter, no matter what you say or do." I hit the prompts, getting notification of my father's voicemail receiving my message. He's got to know he can only push me so far; he's asking too much, and tonight has felt like one bad nightmare after another. I hope Dexter chokes on his failed plans. If he thinks my father gives a shit about him, he's dumber than I thought. And I know my father cares more about me embarrassing him than he does about me making it work with Dexter.

Sighing, I stare at the screen on my phone, watching as the minutes go by until it hits three o'clock in the morning.

Throwing the covers off, I sit up, not knowing what I'll even say but knowing I need to do something. I don't even change; I just throw my coat on over my winter pajamas, slip my feet into my Ugg boots, and grab my keys before taking the elevator down to the garage. I jump in my car, giving it a second to warm up before I back out and make the drive across the city. Excitement trumps that nagging pain the closer I get to his house. Isla's right; besides, it should be his decision, and if he decides I'm not worth it … well, it might destroy me even more, but at least he'll know. He'll know that I didn't want this, that I wanted him.

A few strange cars are parked in his driveway, so I park on

the street, getting out and wondering what's going on.

I reach the door and knock, spying Toulouse through the curtains in the living room when he nudges them aside with his head. When no one answers, I knock again. Right, he's probably asleep, being the early hours of the morning and all. I turn to go, feeling like an idiot, when the door finally opens. Turning back around, I find a brunette standing there, half-dressed and yawning. "Uh, hi. Who are you?" she mumbles.

I move without even thinking, sliding by her and marching down the hall. After almost tripping over some guy who's half asleep on the floor, I throw open the door to Jared's room. But he's not in there. Turning around, I walk back down the hall, about to ask the woman where he is, when my peripheral vision spies a pair of feet hanging over the armrest of his couch as I pass the living room. Backing up, I walk over to the couch, my heart plummeting into my stomach when I find Jared, arms behind his head and staring up at the ceiling. He's not alone, though. Stella is draped over his chest, sound asleep.

He looks over, frowning at me. I glance around the living room, finding beer bottles, weed, and shot glasses on his miserable excuse for a coffee table and on the floor. "The fuck are you doing here?" he asks, his voice low and croaky.

My gaze falls back on him and Stella. She stirs and he moves to shift her off him. "Your fly is still undone," I inform him coldly before turning around and making my way out the front door.

He follows, snatching my hand before I can open the door to my car. "What, you had a change of heart all of a sudden?"

I yank my hand out of his. "I came to tell you that I made a mistake, but now I don't think I did. So why don't you go back inside. I'm sure you're tired after finally getting off after so damn long."

He backs me into my car. "Oh, don't worry Frost, I didn't fuck her. Not yet. But she sucked my cock, and she sucked it real fucking good." The smell of beer leaves his mouth, filling my nose. "Wanna know what really got me off, though?" I shake my head, trying not to register anything he's saying. His bloodshot eyes narrow to slits. "You. I thought about how fucking awesome it would be to break your heart the same way you've broken mine. Because even though you try to hide it, we both know you've got one. And fuck, did it feel good." He groans. "The thought of destroying it gets me so hard that it actually eases some of this pain in my damn chest."

Tears gather in my eyes, but he keeps going, "How's it feel, Frost? To know that someone else touched something you thought belonged to you?"

"Why don't you tell me," I deadpan.

His broken laugh cuts me open, but he stops abruptly. "Fine, I'll humor you." His voice lowers to a menacing whisper, and I never knew such a sound could exist. That a whisper could penetrate your eardrums and tunnel straight to your heart like an electrical current trying to zap what little life remains from inside you. "It feels like someone's raking their filthy fucking nails over your heart before they squeeze it in a vise so tight that you can't breathe. You can't think. All you can do is feel, and it's excruciating. Every breath you dare to take is a reminder you're still alive, still breathing, but for how long?"

When I don't say anything, his voice rises, and I startle. "How long, Vera? It's been only days, and it just gets worse. So tell me, how fucking long is it supposed to feel like this?"

His breathing becomes labored. "Answer me, damn it!"

"I don't know, but I want it to stop!" I breathe in a harsh lungful of cold air.

He staggers back a step, the anger slowly slipping off his

face. Pointing a finger at me, he sneers, "You did this. Don't forget that. So take yourself and whatever bullshit you came here to say home." He turns and walks back to the house, leaving me here with my heart exposed, broken, and so worn out that I'm surprised it's still beating.

My shoulders heave, my breath coming in sharp, white plumes in front of my face. He slams his front door, and I climb back into my car, driving home and slamming the door closed on hope.

CHAPTER TWENTY-THREE

"I'll cut his dick off while he sleeps," Isla growls.

"Do you think the bitch is still there? I think we should have a little chat." Cleo cracks her knuckles.

"Let's go key the fuck out of their cars," Isla suggests with eager eyes.

"Oh, they've picked the wrong chick to mess with. Where's my Amex?" Cleo mutters then starts digging through her purse. "I'm making some calls ..."

I groan, scrubbing my hands down my face. "Girls, no. I love you both more than Mac's new shade of red, but it won't make any difference. He's ..." I try to swallow over the feeling of my heart climbing up my throat. "It's over," I finish quietly.

Jesus that stings. No, it doesn't just sting. It fucking paralyzes.

"Man, that red is to die for."

Isla nods. "Mmmhmm, you must love us a lot."

I throw myself back on the bed in exhaustion. It's bad

enough I feel like I want to rip my useless heart from my chest, but I can't handle trying to calm them down at the same time. I just want to be alone. Even if I am grateful they give a crap.

"Look at her …" Isla whispers.

"Can someone legit die from heartbreak? Oh, my God." Cleo gasps.

"We'll take shifts …"

"I'm fine!" I snap then wince. "Sorry. I just feel like being alone."

Cleo scoffs, walking over to my bed and taking a seat. "Always with the alone thing. Tough shit, you can pretend you're alone." She lies down next to me.

Isla sits down on my other side and lies down too.

I stare out the window in my bedroom at the blinding midday sun, but I can't bring myself to close the curtains. Some part of me worries that if I do, the darkness festering and choking me within will team up with the physical and finally pull me right under. The fear is irrational—I know that—yet it's taken hold and buried deep. So bad that I even slept with both lamps and the hallway light on when I got home from Jared's. Well, tried to sleep.

Cleo and Isla remain silent. Tears leak from my eyes, falling to the duvet below my cheek. But like the two women next to me, I don't make a sound.

Being alone is what I know; it's what I like. But the fact they know I need them right now and can see through my bullshit makes me realize that at least not all forms of love are toxic.

I've immersed myself in fictional tales of heartache and how true love can conquer anything. But I never knew what it was like, and I never thought I would. I'd accepted that and made some kind of reluctant peace with it. But then a pair of green eyes stepped into my world and forced me to experience it first-hand. If I were asked to describe it, I don't really know if I could do it justice. It's something I'm sure is different for everyone.

But to me, falling in love felt like getting drunk off the finest of wines the world had to offer. One sip, just one taste, and you're hooked.

And even though you know what could happen, and that there are probably risks, you keep drinking anyway. Lost in the bittersweet warmth that slowly, deliciously spreads through your veins like wildfire.

It's both euphoric and deadly. Because too much, and you're on your ass, broken and alone, wondering how you'll eradicate this poison from your soul and still get out alive.

And if you do, you're left with only the bitter taste of what-ifs to keep you warm at night.

I now know what it is to fall in love.

And love is a burden I don't want on my soul anymore.

After two days of feeling sorry for myself, I'm desperate to try to see out the other side of this now fogged over window that once seemed so clear.

My unbuttoned coat billows behind me as I stand on the street and stare down at the opposite end where the coffee shop is. I wonder if he's there. If he's even thought about me with anything other than hate and revenge on his mind.

But wondering only leads to disaster. Wondering is for fools who hand their hearts over without knowing all the risks involved. My curiosity and that deep-seated desire to discover what else might lurk outside my gilded cage has come with a steep price. More than I could've ever dreamed to afford. But if

I could, I'd find a way. I'd sell my soul—any part of what's left of me—to get rid of this sickening heaviness in my heart.

My gaze slowly moves back to the front of Always Booked. I don't think Badger can help this time, but I don't know what else to do. So dragging my weary feet to the door, I open it and step inside. The bell jingles and everything seems as it should, but there's no sign of Badger.

"Badger?" My voice is hoarse from crying and being un-used, I suppose. Clearing my throat, I try again when I get no answer. "Badger?" I walk past the rows of mismatched book-shelves, finding no sign of him or anyone. It isn't like him to close early or leave the store unattended. He locks up if he leaves; he always does. I head to the back room, and that's where I find him, sitting on the old stool he uses to reach the high shelves. He lifts his head from his chest then drops it again. "Vera …"

Panic, raw and ugly like I've never known, twists my stom-ach in half. I rush over to him, grabbing his face and lifting it. His eyes seem sunken, and his soft, aged skin holds a pale blueish tint. "What's wrong? Talk to me."

He tries to smile then he drops his head and taps his chest. "It hurts. I think …" That's all he manages to say before he col-lapses on me. I almost fall to the floor, trying to keep him up-right. Gritting my teeth in fear and horror, I manage to lower him to the dingy carpet. I pat his clammy cheeks then dig my phone out of my jacket pocket when he doesn't respond. His chest is rising, and I feel a pulse, but his eyes won't open. Then I remember him tapping his chest. Maybe he's had a heart at-tack. Shit.

I dial 911 and put my phone on speaker before doing my best to turn him on his side. The first-aid course Sally made everyone take every two years, the one I thought was stupid considering we were accountants, now has me wanting to kiss her ugly shoed feet. I adjust his head while telling the operator everything I can through trembling lips. He can't die; he can't. I know he's old, but I need him. He's the best person I've ever known. One of the only people I have left.

I don't allow myself a moment to falter, not until the ambulance arrives and loads him into the back. Finding his keys, I lock the store and get in my car. But my hand is shaking too much to get the key in the ignition.

"Shit." I drop my head to the wheel, but it falls too low because the horn blares, scaring the shit out of me and some poor guy on his bike, who almost falls off as he rides past my car. I wince but know it was the shock I needed and turn the car on to head to the hospital.

Waiting rooms are miserable places to be. I realize while sitting on the hard plastic seat with a baby screaming in my ear behind me that I've never had to sit in one before. I went to the hospital once when I broke my pinkie finger falling down the stairs at home. But my father demanded they rush me in right away. I remember it like it was yesterday because I was pissed off. I was twelve, and my first and only worry was that I couldn't hold my books open properly with my right hand until it healed.

The clock ticks above my head. My feet shift on the sticky floor. I glance down, inspecting my black velvet ballet pumps. Huh. I don't even remember putting them on.

The clock says it's only been an hour since I arrived, but it feels like I've been sitting here for a week. Rigid, tired, and cold to my very bones.

"Do you think I could move in here?"

Badger laughs, the sound is dry but full of rich joy. "Here? And where do you propose you'll sleep?"

I fiddle with my bottom lip, staring at my shoes. "Here will do. The chairs are old, but they smell okay. I'll just sleep on them."

I look over at Badger when he doesn't respond, finding his keen blue eyes studying me. "My dear, you're only twelve years old. You can't leave home yet."

Home. He says the word as if such a place really exists. And if it does, I wish I could find it. "It's not a home. It's a maze of ice hallways and two-faced hyenas."

His head rears back, eyes widening. "You have quite the imagination." He leans forward again. "But tell me, why do you think that?"

I lift my shoulders to my ears and take a deep breath. My lungs fill with the scent of old and used books. I let it out, feeling more relaxed, and look over at the window. Tiny specks of dust dance in the afternoon sun over the section of children's books. "It's just ... always cold." Staring at the scuffed Disney copy of Cinderella that's on display, I blurt, "Do you think I'm an ugly stepsister?"

Badger tilts his head then reaches out to bop me on the nose. He pulls his hand back. "You know better than anyone that you're far from ugly."

My nose scrunches, my voice lowering to a whisper. "No ... I-I mean inside."

He scowls; his thick black and gray brows look like hairy caterpillars. "Who on earth gave you that idea?"

I glance away, my cheeks reddening.

"Vera, look at me." It's not a request but a command.

Badger hardly ever talks to me in that tone. But my father does, and my head turns back of its own volition. "I know you're *probably too young to understand this. But whatever you do, wherever this life leads you, always remember that only one person has the power to define who you are and who'll you become, and that person is you."*

That was the only day in my life I'd walked away from Badger feeling worse than when I had arrived. Funny that out of all the profound things he's said to me over the years, the most important piece of advice he ever gave me frustrated me the most. It eluded me. It didn't make sense at the time. I felt powerless, trapped, but I was also too young to understand. And so I ignored his words, thinking them futile. They served no purpose in helping me escape my father's clutches at the time, so they were forgotten.

Until now.

"Vera Bramston?"

I lurch to my feet in an instant. "Yes? Is he okay? What's happening? I know I'm not immediate family, but I'm all he's got, so please." I swallow thickly. "You have to tell me."

The nurse frowns, picking up a sheet of paper on her chart and looking down at it. She returns her confused gaze to me. "But it says here that you're his next of kin."

I nod, that makes sense. "Okay …" I nod again. I think I've lost control of my own reflexes. "Good."

She purses her lips and looks back down at her paper. "Yes, Vera Bramston, granddaughter of Graham Rodgers."

Rodgers. My brain tries to connect with where I've heard that name. Granddaughter. Erica Rodgers. My mother.

Wait. *Badger is my mother's father?*

"He's stable." She continues as if she hasn't just shaken me to the core. "He's asleep and will need to stay in ICU until we can determine …" Her words trail off into the clustered waiting

226 | ELLA FIELDS

room around us. I hear them, but I don't. All I can hear is that one word on repeat.

Granddaughter.

As we walk to his room, the nurse rattles off a list of things to me that I still don't hear, but I nod my head again. We stop in the doorway to his room. Well, I do, but she walks in. When she notices I'm still at the door, she gives me a soft smile and comes over to pat my shoulder. "I felt the same way when my grandfather got sick. But yours is showing some very good signs, so I think he'll be okay."

I can't speak; I just stare at his sleeping form lying in the hospital bed hooked up to an alarming number of beeping monitors. "I'll give you a moment. Holler if you need anything."

My head moves up and down yet again. Her sneaker clad feet squeaking on the floor indicate she's walking away.

Despair creeps into the hollowed-out void in my chest, filling it as each excruciating second passes until I can't breathe and I can hardly see.

I march back down the hall with my hand over my mouth as though I can stop any more of this torture from finding its way inside me. I can't handle any more. I just can't do it.

I drive home with my lips between my teeth, breathing shallowly through my nose. Once back inside my apartment, I move to the only other place capable of providing comfort. Heavy, dark oak bookshelves, all of them larger than anything else in this apartment, line the walls, and I've arranged the books alphabetically, by author. It's all perfect. But now it feels all *wrong*.

Storming into the room, I make a beeline for the first books I can get my hands on. I don't even look at them. I just start tearing them from the shelves.

Ripping, shoving, and crying, I tear pages upon pages from

them so violently that my nails break. *Good*, I think amongst the chaos of my brain. I don't need pointless tales of something I can't have. I'm so sick of trying not to give in to the hopelessness that lives inside me that I try to forget with every page I read. It's never worked anyway. They've let me down, crushed me by warping that naïve part of me that still believed.

I can't believe. I've seen firsthand what believing will do. I've *felt* it. I'm still fucking feeling it. When you've had everything you've ever wanted, you're not allowed to have anything that truly matters.

So I won't.

They don't matter. None of these carefully crafted stories with their beautiful words matter. None of them.

Not anymore.

Paper flutters to the ground around me while my breaking heart rages and wars within. I want it out. I need it gone. My hands rip and shred. The sound of someone weeping fills my ears. Wetness cascades down my face and down my chin, falling to the pages on the floor below me. I move onto the next row and then the next. I keep going until my legs weaken, and my hands and fingers are stinging. My whole body starts to shake with the force of my anguish, and I give in, falling to the rug on the floor, surrounded by my heart's demise. The sole reason for everything that's happened to me lies in perfect ruins around me.

It feels like part of me just took its final breath.

I've never felt more alone.

CHAPTER TWENTY-FOUR

I wake up in a pile of debris. My heart sinks when I sit up and take stock of my surroundings. Remembering what led to this destruction has panic rising to the forefront of my mind. I stand on shaky, cramped legs. My neck is stiff, and as I move my hair back off my face, my finger lands on something sticky. I hope like hell it's not drool. But if it's not, then it's probably snot. Shuddering, I drop my hair and walk out of the room, closing the door behind me without a backward glance. After showering and grabbing a breakfast bar, I head back to the hospital.

Not even the fluorescent lights in the corridor can send the darkness that accompanies my every step scattering. The nurse at the front counter said he's still in ICU, a place I've never stepped foot into until yesterday. Not that I took much in. Even now, the beeping, the hushed murmurs, and the sorrow stifling the air doesn't touch me.

Pausing outside his room, I peek my head in, only to be

met with one of the best sights in the world. His smile.

"Vera ..." His voice is hoarse, but it's enough to have tears filling my eyes in a second. I walk right to him, trying to remind myself to be gentle and not to run. I dump my purse on the floor and drag the chair over to his bed. Grabbing his hand, I lift it to my cheek and close my eyes, absorbing the warmth from it. The reminder. *He's here.* He's okay.

He tsks. "Don't tell me those big fat tears are for me. Not from the girl who'd rather eat dirt than shed a tear in front of anyone."

I sputter out a wet laugh then drop my head to his bed and let the tears fall. He removes his hand from mine, using it to smooth my hair back from my face. "Shhhh, it's okay. The old ticker just needed a bit of a reboot is all. Nothing to worry about."

He continues to soothe me, and I feel like the biggest bitch in the world. I lift my head, swiping the tears from my cheeks. "I'm sorry. You're lying here, and I'm ..."

He lifts his hand, halting me. "Don't even finish that sentence."

My lips curve into a smile then I remember all that I discovered. "Why didn't you tell me?"

He frowns. "Well, I didn't know there was anything wrong myself—"

"No. Erica."

His eyes close as soon as her name leaves my lips. He reopens them and sighs. "I don't know. I always meant to eventually, but if I'm being honest, your father is what stopped me every time." He looks over at me; his blue eyes tired but full of affection. "And my own selfishness, of course."

"What's he got to do with it?"

"Everything." He stares at me. "I couldn't believe it, that

day you walked into my store." He shakes his head, smiling. "I knew about you, of course. It's just … we were warned, when we tried to see you after your mother left, not to try again."

"Why?" But I think I know why. They're a reminder of what my father lost. Just like I am.

"The day Erica brought your father home to meet us, I never expected it to last. But Mirabelle and I played nice and kept our mouths shut. And it soon became apparent that your father was quite attached to our Erica. A year after they met, they were married. Ten months later, you arrived."

I've never even seen wedding photos of my parents. The only picture I've seen of my mother is a crinkled copy of her in her early twenties that lives in my father's study, locked away in his drawer.

"You don't think she should've married him?"

"I can't really answer that. But I will say that Erica, since the time she learned how to walk, has always had an adventurous spirit." He smiles again as if remembering. "She'd never sit still for long. Used to drive your grandmother crazy. I used to think it was our fault, that maybe her quiet childhood and afternoons spent in the bookstore had her longing for something different."

He shifts, and I move to help him sit up, propping his pillow behind him. He thanks me and continues. "Anyway, she never contacted us after she left, besides the odd Christmas or birthday card. The last time I saw her was at Mirabelle's funeral. She left again right after with some new fellow on her arm."

"What did my father say when he told you to stay away?" I ask.

He looks like he doesn't want to answer, but he does anyway. "I'm not proud of it, but you've got to understand, that bookstore was Mirabelle's life. The only thing she ever wanted, and I couldn't afford to buy her a new one, but I saved. I worked hard and saved every penny I could to buy her that one."

My heart breaks further. But after everything that's happened, I'm not surprised. "He threatened to take it from you."

Badger nods, tears brimming his eyes. "I'm sorry. I tried to think of something else we could do, but we'd put everything we had into that store, and you've seen for yourself that it barely covers the basics. Mirabelle was furious with me because she wanted you. She was ready to set fire to the store just to spite your father." He laughs quietly. "But she knew—we both did—that we were powerless no matter what we did. The more we tried, the angrier he got."

"So you stopped." It hurts, but I understand. No one wins against my father.

"We did." He averts his gaze. "You look just like her, you know."

"I know."

His eyes meet mine again, and I don't know how I didn't see it. So many people have blue eyes, but something about looking into Badger's eyes has always felt different. Familiar. Now I know why. "I'm sorry … but you've got to know, that day you walked in? I'll never forget it. But if I had told you when you were young … And then when you grew up, I just never could bring myself to risk it."

"He can't control whether I see you or not anymore."

"No, but you can. I didn't know how you'd react, not after keeping it from you for so long."

Taking his hand in both of mine, I give it a gentle squeeze. "It's okay."

His shoulders seem to deflate as if me knowing this secret has freed him. I'm not mad; I'm disappointed I never knew, but it feels good to know I'm not as alone in this world as I thought.

I only wish he would've told me sooner, especially if it's caused him unnecessary stress.

He sucks in a sharp breath, and I straighten with worry that something's wrong. "What happened to your hands?"

Oh. I stare down at them for the first time since yesterday. They're covered in tiny paper cuts, and some of my nails are blunt while a few others remain long. "Nothing."

"Vera …"

"A story for another time." I throw one of his favorite sayings back at him with a tremulous smile.

He snorts, patting my hand. "Nice try. Is it Jared? Where is he?"

Pain radiates throughout every cell in my body at hearing his name. I mustn't do a very good job at hiding it because Badger hums in understanding. "Oh, my dear. Whatever's happened, I'm sure it'll work itself out."

Blinking away tears, I draw in a deep breath, terrified of the words that leave my mouth. "No, it's over. It was a mistake to begin with." I lift my shoulders, but the effort costs me strength I didn't know I had. "I'll be okay."

I don't know if I'm trying to reassure him or myself. I don't know much of anything anymore. Who I am, what to do, or when this hurt might let up.

The door opens and in walks the same nurse I met yesterday. "Good morning, good to see you're back. I'm Ashley, by the way." She smiles at me and moves over to Badger, checking machines and whipping a thermometer out of her pocket.

"What's going on? Do you have any idea what's caused this?" I sit back in my seat, making sure there's enough room for her to move around me.

"The doctors have already made their rounds this morning, and they suspect a heart attack. They want to run some tests later today, but for now, everything is looking okay."

"What other tests?" My tone turns harsher.

"Vera," Badger admonishes.

I shush him and turn back to the nurse who only smiles at me again. "They just need to check some things and make sure there isn't a blockage—"

"And if there is?" I cut her off, not caring if I sound rude.

"Surgery. But we won't know until we do further testing."

Seeing my face no doubt pale, she smiles down at Badger. "You've got a worrywart over here. Care to tell her you'll be just fine?"

Badger chuckles, and the sound has relief flooding into my bloodstream, warm and welcoming. *He's okay.* I just need to keep reminding myself of that. "Sorry," I mutter.

"No need to apologize." She checks something on his chart then gives us a wave. "I'll be back in a little while; hit the buzzer if you need anything."

I watch her go and then it hits me, like a sucker-punch right to the gut. These hospital bills. He can't afford them. And neither can I. Not anymore.

"Hey." Badger brings my attention back to him. "Would you mind reading to me?"

My stomach curdles because I don't know if I can. But looking at him, at his blinking eyelids that look like they might close any minute, I know I could never deny him. Even if it hurts. Because he's saved me in more ways than I could ever hope to measure or dare to even think about.

So I grab my phone and open my reading app.

CHAPTER TWENTY-FIVE

Three Weeks Later

"Vera, I'm fine. Go on, go home." Badger waves a hand at me. I stand by the door to his bedroom, watching him take a seat on his bed.

"Don't forget your—"

He shakes the pill bottle at me with a smile. "I won't; I'm not willing to face your wrath again." He winks. "Go; I'll be fine."

I hesitate, as I always do at the end of each day I'm here. He needed bypass surgery to clear a blocked artery and was in the hospital for over a week. I've since taken over the running of the store and discovered that he does indeed live upstairs. I'd always wondered but never had the courage to ask.

Walking into the room, I bend down and place a kiss on his forehead. He closes his eyes, a soft smile pulling at his lips. "I'll be in first thing in the morning; call me if you need me." I point at the cell phone I bought him on the nightstand.

He waves me off, and I head back down the rickety, winding metal staircase. My phone rings in my purse just as I'm reaching the front of the store. I grab my purse from behind the counter and dig it out, sighing when I see the number.

"Vera Bramston?"

"Yeah, yeah. It's me. I'll have the bill taken care of within the week. I just sold my car, and I'm waiting for the check to clear." I lock the door and grumble into the phone, "So back off, it's coming." I promptly hang up and dump my phone back into my purse.

Daylight is turning into night at rapid speed. The days since Badger's heart attack have passed quickly, but the nights, they're long, haunting in both time and the memories they bring with it. Being at the bookstore makes it easier to ignore the crushing pressure that still sits on my heart, squashing it and squeezing the life from it. But at night, nothing stops it from dragging me under all over again. I thought time would make it better, not worse. But I've learned the hard way that time can be your worst enemy. And I've played the willing victim by allowing it to take so much from me in this life of mine already.

Despite his threats, Dexter never did call. I can only hope, even if it's mixed with a bit of naïvety, that my father got my voicemail and took me seriously for once. Even though the silence from them makes me a little nervous, I'm not silly enough to go looking for answers I might not like.

Christmas lights flicker on in storefronts and restaurants along the street while I walk down the sidewalk to my car. I curse quietly, trying to locate my keys that've fallen somewhere to the bottom of my purse. Then I hear it ... the same voice that fills my dreams and nightmares every night without fail.

"Well, hey. What's up, Frost? Run out of hundred-dollar bills to wipe your ass with?"

Air. I'm outside, yet there's suddenly not enough air. I don't answer him. I'm frozen, keys in hand and simply just trying to breathe.

"What, too good to talk to me now? Or does your boyfriend forbid you to speak to anyone who can make you come multiple times in one night?"

My eyes squeeze closed. The temptation to turn around and look at him becomes too much. It becomes all I can think about. I can almost see that devious smile behind my closed eyelids.

Do it. Just look at him and be done with it.

I open them and spin around, wiping all expression from my face. He looks exactly the same. Same leather jacket, same amazing hair, and the very same green eyes that I'll probably see behind my closed lids for the rest of my life. How is that fair? That he should get to walk around as if nothing affects him. Like I didn't affect him the same way he's affected me. Crushed me. Ruined me. Poisoned me for life.

"Where is he anyway?" He feigns interest, glancing around. "Though I guess the douchebag did leave you behind on a busy highway. I'm guessing that sweet as pie personality of yours doesn't leave a lot of room for actually giving a shit about you." He snorts. "I should know."

My eyes sting with the threat of looming tears. "Are you done?"

He cocks his head to the side, hands buried in his jean pockets as he stares at me. He straightens from the wall he was leaning against, and his eyes seem to take on a foreign shade of green. It doesn't take long to realize why. They're full of hate.

"Yeah, I was done weeks ago. You know that." His clenched

jaw tightens.

Fuck this. I keep walking to my car—a five-year-old Volkswagen Golf—and open the door. I need away from him before I can allow myself to crumble. Every step hurts; every step that I feel him take behind me is another crack in my heart. I open the door and throw my purse in. "Aw, don't go yet; it's been …" He stops then asks from behind me, "Where's your car?"

I lean against the doorframe, heaving out a forced, disinterested sigh. "Sold it."

His beautiful face contorts with confusion. "Why?"

Laughing, I decide, fuck it, why the hell not? I've still got my pride, but being too proud is something I can't afford to be anymore. Literally. So I tell him. "I needed the money. Have a nice life, Jared." I fold myself into the seat and close the door.

I've just started the engine when the passenger door opens, and he climbs in.

"What the fuck are you doing?"

He looks straight at me. "Explain."

"Get out."

"Not until you explain."

"Get. Out. Now." The words are a growl. It's getting hard to even look at him without bile steadily crawling up the bottom of my throat.

"I'm not moving until you tell me."

Our eyes stay glued in silent battle, and of course, I lose. A given when it comes to Jared Williams. I'll always lose.

"My father." I turn away to look out the front windshield. "He threatened me and cut me off."

He scoffs. "And what, you being the good little girl you are, did exactly what he said?"

"When it concerns you, yes." I close my eyes as soon as the

words escape, not meaning for them to, not intending to tell him that much.

"Bullshit," he seethes.

I shrug. "Believe what you want, I don't particularly give a shit. Now get out." He doesn't move. "Jared, please …" My voice breaks. I glance over at him in time to see realization dawn on his face.

"No." He breathes the word out, more of a whisper to himself, a quiet last-ditch effort at denial than a response.

I answer anyway. "Yes."

"When?" His Adam's apple bobs as he swallows over the word.

"Does it matter?" Christ, nothing matters anymore. I've ignored my coffee shop cravings, bringing my machine in from home to make some at the store in hopes that I wouldn't have to subject myself to this. That I wouldn't have to see him again.

"It does. When?"

I put my hand on the stick shift. "You know when. After we returned from camping."

He curses, and I think he's about to punch my dashboard, but thankfully, he doesn't. He opens the door and gets out, walking up and down the side of my car with his hands in his hair.

I don't wait for him to get his shit together. Nope, I reach over to close the passenger door before stepping on the accelerator and getting the hell away from him.

CHAPTER TWENTY-SIX

Not even a hot shower can warm me after seeing Jared. But I remain standing under the hot spray until the water runs cold. I dry myself and dress in my winter pajamas, digging through the drawers in my walk-in closet in search of the huge, fluffy, hideous bathrobe Cleo bought me years ago for Christmas. It might be ugly and hot pink in color, but it's so damn soft and, dare I admit it, comfortable. Her presents have really started to become useful this past month.

After pouring myself a glass of wine, I take a sip and a seat on the couch, wincing at the cheap taste of it sliding over my tongue. My gaze falls on the boxes lining the walls of my living room. My lease is up next month, and even though my inheritance from my grandmother will arrive next month on my birthday, I've done the math. Numbers might be boring as hell, but my degree will come in handy in making sure I can survive and still live comfortably on my grandmother's money while working at the bookstore. So I've been apartment hunting.

Both Isla and Cleo have offered for me to move in with them if I run out of time.

Which I just might. Between running the store and running from myself, it's hard to focus on much else. I thought I knew exactly who I was and how much control I had over my own life. I was unforgiving with my harsh outlook on reality; my vision clouded with inexperience and judgment.

But the simple fact is—I had no idea.

Nobody has any idea of their true self until they hit that pivotal moment. Until they come across that tree in the middle of the road, blocking the way out.

It's like you're submerged under a vast, never-ending pool of water, constantly swimming and trying to surface before you run out of air.

Rock bottom.

I always thought only idiots who were just too damn lazy to sort their shit out and get on with life used that stupid saying. A few years ago, I almost gave some drunk who was crying into his beer at a club in the early hours of the morning two hundred dollars just to buy a pair and man up.

Boy, am I glad I didn't.

Because the true idiot here is me.

I may not be the nicest person in the world, and I can accept that. I can own up to my mistakes and take responsibility for them. But I've come to realize I'm not a bad person either.

Looking at it all, and I mean really sifting through those things better left alone, I've discovered I'm just like everybody else underneath the finery that covers me.

Unfailingly and bare nakedly human.

Part of me desperately wants to put an end to this madness.

You can't break that part so easily, the kind of girl I used to be.

But he broke who I was becoming.

And I don't know how to fix her.

Loud banging has me sitting straight up in bed. I'd be pissed, but it's not like I'm sleeping much these days anyway. I'm sick of the torture I experience every time I close my eyes. No thanks, I'll just try to stay awake. I'll pick the devil I know—reality— over the devil that toys and teases me with cruel words in my dreams.

Still wearing the huge, fluffy robe, I tuck my feet into my slippers and wander down the hall. Whoever it is knocks again, and a sinking sensation in the pit of my stomach has my feet pausing near the kitchen. I glance at the time on the microwave and see it's just after one in the morning. Shit. It's him. I know it is. Which is only reaffirmed when he hollers at me through the door. It's muffled, but I still hear it. "Vera, open up. Please."

My phone starts ringing from the bedroom. I glance back down the hall to where the sound is coming from then back at the door. He keeps banging, knowing I'm going to answer to stop him from waking up my neighbors. Damn it. If the couple across the hall weren't in their sixties, I wouldn't give a shit.

Keep telling yourself that.

I growl at my own thoughts and stomp down the hallway, pulling open the door and hissing at Jared, "What the hell do you think you're doing here?"

He stumbles back a step then rights himself and comes straight for me, bypassing me and walking into my apartment. "Hey! Get out."

He shakes his head and continues walking down the hall. I

let the door close and run after him, stopping him when he gets to my bedroom with a hand tugging at his jacket.

"Whoa, baby. You want me to take it off, all you gotta do is ask." He slurs a little and turns around. Bloodshot eyes stare down at me, and the acrid scent of tobacco mixed with whiskey drifts over me. "You're drunk."

He smirks, and I want to punch him. "Why, yes. Yes, I am." He pinches the air with his thumb and pointer finger. "Just a little."

"Jesus fucking Christ."

He chuckles. "Fuck, I love your filthy mouth." He steps closer, dropping his head to my shoulder. "Missed you."

My stupid heart rejoices, but I don't give it what it wants. I push him away. "Go home; you're wasted."

He stumbles again, and I quickly right him. Even if I feel like letting him fall to the floor, I don't feel like paying for the damage his big body might inflict on the wall behind him. "Why'd you lie to me?" His eyes narrow on mine when I take a step away from him.

"I came over to tell you …" I stop and cross my arms over my chest, sighing. "God, this is pointless. What's done is done; just forget it."

He laughs, but the sound is hoarse and a little broken. "Forget it? You fucking ripped my heart out and stomped on it with your expensive as fuck heels."

"I didn't know that would happen; I just did what I had to."

He nods. "Yeah, well, thanks a fucking lot."

I arch an incredulous brow at him, and he steps forward. I retreat until the backs of my legs hit my bed. "You should've just told me the truth."

"Please." I roll my eyes. "There was no point after what I walked in on." Fire fills my bones, and I relish in its burn, gritting my teeth.

He lurches forward, arms reaching for me, but thanks to his inebriated state, I dodge him. He falls face first into my bed with a groan. "Fuck …" He rolls to his back and stares at me. The look on his face is the very definition of defeat. Too bad I don't give a damn.

"Jared, get up and go home already."

He groans again, rolling to his side and blinking lazily at me. Great, he's going to pass out. "Can't," he mumbles. "Took a cab."

"So I'll call you another one. Up, now." I swing my hand around in the air and point at the door.

He chuckles. "Come here. Lie down with me."

Is he serious right now? Of course, he is. "No."

"Can you at least get me a glass of water then?" He licks his lips. "My mouth's too dry to kiss you the way it is now. Probably tastes like an ashtray, too. But don't worry, a bit of water should fix it."

"Water? You're seriously asking me for water?"

His eyes close, and he nods.

Oh, my God. I turn around, leaving the room and cursing him out the whole way to the kitchen, where I get his stupid glass of water. But when I return, he's out cold.

"Jared." I shake his shoulder. Nothing. Not even a flicker of his eyelids. Great. I fight the urge to tip the water over the asshole's head and place it down on the nightstand instead. Grabbing a blanket from one of the boxes in the living room, I lie down on the couch.

Where I proceed to stare at the ceiling until the sun rises.

At around seven in the morning, I hear the toilet flush in my en suite and sit up, running a hand through my hair and cringing at the ache in my tired muscles. Today should be fun.

But I'm used to it by now.

I fold the blanket and head to the kitchen to make some tea. Jared emerges five minutes later; his face rumpled from sleep and last night's binge drinking session. I don't say a word to him; I don't even know what I'd say. I sit down at the counter and sip my tea, scrolling through my phone and hoping he just leaves. "What happened to your library?" He leans a hip against the other side of the counter.

My lungs dry out. I still haven't stepped foot in there since I tore it apart.

He sighs. "What happened? Tell me the whole fucking truth, Vera."

"My library, my business."

"Not the library, your dad. What did he do?"

Scrunching my nose, I admit, "Well, nothing. I did what he asked me to and ended it. Your business is still standing, I assume?"

"He threatened you with my shop?" He groans. "Shit, Vera. Why the fuck didn't you just tell me? It would've been fine; we could've …"

I look at him then. "Do you know who he is?" Jared nods and tries to talk again, but I don't let him. "So you know it wasn't worth the risk. I'm not sorry I did it because I know him. And when I got too weak and tried to tell you anyway, you crushed me beyond repair." I turn my attention back to my phone. "So I guess we're even. Now get out."

"Vera, fuck, I'm sorry." The words are rough and edged with remorse. "Would you please look at me?"

"Why?" I pretend the picture of a donut and coffee that Cleo's posted on Instagram is way more interesting than the man standing across from me.

"Because I'm trying to tell you I'm sorry, and that I couldn't hate myself more right now."

I take a sip of my tea. "That's nice. I hate you, too. The door is that way." I lower my mug, gesturing toward the door with my head and still not looking at him.

His laugh is coated with sleep and nerves. "You can try to freeze me out all you like, Frost. I'll just keep trying to make you melt again, anyway."

"Stop." I lift my head, trying not to flinch from the full effect of having him stare at me like that. Like I'm his reason for existing and he's tired of trying to keep doing so without me. "You're not allowed to do this to me, not after everything that's happened. I have no idea why you're even here. You said it yourself, it was over weeks ago. Three weeks, if we're being technical."

"Because you fucked up and then I really fucked up. But I need you …"

"You don't need me. You've made that perfectly fucking clear," I lose my cool and hiss at him.

"I do," he almost growls.

"Why?" My breath hitches. "Son of a …" I shake my head. "Why can't you just go and leave me alone?"

"Because I fucking love you!" he roars.

My heart seizes in my chest, and my phone falls from my hand to the counter. "*What?*"

His chest heaves up and down. He runs a shaky hand through his hair, messing it up even worse than it was when he walked in here. "I'm in love with you, Vera Bramston."

Rage like I've never known fills my aching heart; its raw and all-consuming haze blurs my vision and floods my bloodstream. How dare he? How fucking dare he tell me he loves me now and like this? The bastard.

I'm so blinded by my fury that I don't even see him

rounding the counter. I only realize he's wrapped his arms around me because his scent invades and tries to override my anger.

"Get the hell off me." I try to break his hold, standing from the stool and trying to shove him away. When that doesn't work, I start slapping at his chest until I'm practically punching him. "Just go, asshole. And take your lies with you."

"Vera." His voice is firm, but I don't care. I shove away from him, finally. "I'm not lying. Look at me."

I stare at his scuffed boots instead. Wondering if he wore them all night, or when he fucked Stella. Because I know he probably did. It's been weeks since we were together.

That has my head snapping up. He opens his mouth to spout that four-letter word again, but I beat him, venom coating every word that leaves my mouth. "Did you tell Stella you loved her, too?"

He flinches as if I'm the one who destroyed him. And yeah, I might've done that, but I was never with anyone else.

"Frost, I'm sor—"

"Don't fucking call me that."

He blows out a breath, taking another step forward. I back up against the wall, warning him with every ounce of hatred I can infuse into my glare not to come any closer.

And still, he steps closer. I run for it, bolting down the hallway to lock myself in my room, but a stupid box in the doorway means that Jared's walking right in after me before I can spin around to close the door.

This is maddening. Why the hell won't he just leave? "Haven't you done enough to me, to my life? Why can't you see that?" The volume of my voice rises and so does my heart rate.

"I haven't done nearly enough. That's why I'm here. That's why I won't be going anywhere. You'll keep seeing me, hearing from me, and hell, hopefully think of me the way I constantly think about you until you fucking come back to me." He growls those last words, hurling them across the room until they hit me square in the chest.

"I don't think I can forgive you, so don't bother wasting your time. Go find your little Dixie chick, I'm sure she can fix your broken ego again."

"Stop, just fucking stop. If I can forgive you, you can forgive me, and I don't want Stella. I don't want anyone but you."

"Well, you'll have to excuse me if I don't quite believe you, on account of seeing differently with my own two eyes."

His head drops and he stares at the floor for a second before returning his eyes to mine. His voice is quiet when he says, "Jesus … I fucked up okay? I fucked up. I didn't know, Vera. You never told me …"

"You would've found out the truth if you'd have talked to me instead of running your mouth and fucking someone else."

"Stop!" he thunders. "I know what I did, but I never did that, I promise."

"Why should I stop? You think it's hard to hear, do you? Try hearing the person you love tell you all about how someone else got them off." I laugh manically and point a finger at him. "That's hard to hear. Now get the hell out of my apartment before I call the cops."

He visibly flinches. "You wouldn't," he says, vulnerability bleeding from his green eyes.

Fuck. His stupid probation. How the *hell* did I wind up falling for a guy on probation?

"You love me?" he asks quietly, walking across the room until he's standing in front of me.

"Did. Past tense. Now please, go."

"You're lying." His nostrils flare, his eyes flicking back and forth between mine. I swallow hard. He needs to leave before all my flimsily reconstructed walls crumble into dust.

"I'm not. We've both caused enough damage, Jared. Let it go."

I walk by him and down the hall, snatching my phone from the kitchen then opening the door. He follows, frustration pulling those beautiful features tight. Just when I think he's going to leave without any further assault on my heart, he whispers, "I'll see you soon, beauty."

My bottom lip trembles. I slam the door as soon as he's over the threshold and shut my eyes over the tears.

CHAPTER TWENTY-SEVEN

"Ugh, answer it already," Isla groans when my mother calls my phone for the third time tonight. I don't know why it's only now that I realize I don't have to put up with her crap anymore, but nevertheless, it forces a genuine smile from me. I reject the call and block her number then toss my phone back into my clutch.

Looking in the mirror, I tug my skintight black dress down over my thighs then make sure I've tucked the girls away properly. Grabbing my long, gray knit cardigan, I pull it on then adjust my pantyhose before slipping my feet into my boots and bending over to zip them up.

"You're going to freeze," Cleo says behind me, zipping up the fly on her checkered skinny leg pants.

"Better than looking like I'm wearing your grandma's handbag on my legs." Besides, a little cold has never hurt me before.

Cleo scowls, and Isla laughs from my bed, scrolling

through her phone.

"Bitch. I think I liked you better when the grease monkey was giving it to you on the regular." Cleo slaps a hand over her mouth as soon as the words escape her pink glossed lips.

"Cleo." Isla stands, chucking her phone into her purse. "We don't talk about he who shall not be named."

"I'm sorry. But hey, I didn't say his name." She raises a brow and points a finger at Isla.

Shaking my head, I give myself one last look in the mirror before deciding that I'm as ready as I'll ever be.

When the girls said they're sick of my moody, mopey ass and that they were taking me out, I didn't protest. I kind of agree with them. It's time to stop living in self-pity. That and I could do with the distraction after Jared's departure from my apartment yesterday morning. I haven't heard from him since, and the need to keep reminding myself that's a good thing is becoming tiresome. I miss him. I want him. I still love him. But I also hate him.

I'm not sure if I can move past what's happened, so I guess there's no point in obsessing over it. I need to keep waking up every morning and just keep going. Snuff out that part of me waiting on him to follow through with his promise to see me soon.

"Don't worry about it." I grab my clutch. "He actually saw me a few days ago when I left the store."

They both gasp. "What the hell? Details." Isla places her hands on her hips. She's wearing the cutest peach dress, and I think I might have to borrow that one. *Borrow*. I try not to panic. Because I'm currently a little broke.

"Yeah, like now," Cleo demands.

After rolling my eyes, I tell them what happened as we head downstairs to the street. Cleo hails a cab, wearing a huge grin on her face. "Wow, I just knew it wasn't over. This is so exciting."

Isla shoots daggers at her. "Whose side are you on?"

Cleo shrugs, dropping her arm when a cab spots us standing here and pulls over. "The side that wins, of course."

A snort escapes me as I open the door and hop in the back. "And just who do you think is going to win?"

Isla gives the driver the address to the new club that's opened downtown.

"Ja—oh, that was close." Cleo laughs at herself. "But for real, he's got your heart, Vera. You need to get that shit back or get him back." She tries to wink, and Isla reaches into the back to pinch her arm. "Hey, ow!"

"Shut it, traitor." Isla scowls before turning back around.

Cleo shrugs again. "Sorry not sorry. Just saying it how I see it."

"You mean you're telling it like it is?" I raise a brow.

She purses her lips, huffing. "Whatever."

We get out of the cab five minutes later and walk briskly up to the doors of the new club, Sensual, showing the bouncers our IDs before getting waved in the doors. Someone curses loudly in the long line wrapped around the side of the newly remodeled building. Money might not buy you happiness, but it certainly has its benefits. That and Cleo's father is part owner of half the buildings on Malone Avenue, including this one.

Sensual is one way to put it. The whole place is painted a sickly, vibrant red and black with lace trimmings for decoration and curtains. Framed semi-pornographic artwork decorates the walls.

I grab Cleo's arm as we near the stairs to walk up to the VIP section. "Is this some kind of kink club?" I whisper-hiss.

She throws her head back with a laugh. "No. Well, at least

not that I know of. Daddy told me the owner is almost sixty and a bit of a perv, though."

"Lovely," Isla mutters when we near the top and give the security guard our names. He directs us to a curtained-off corner where a large section of the floor is glass to view the dancers and some of the crowd below. "Oh, my God, is that woman in a cage?" I stare in fascination as we take our seat after giving our drink order.

"That's insane. Look at her go. Do you think her nipple tassels ever fall off?" Isla asks. "Hmmm, I doubt it. She's probably double side taped the shit out of them," Cleo surmises.

Once our champagne arrives, we sit and people watch through the glass floor while drinking.

"Wow, yum." I turn the bottle the waitress left in the ice bucket on the table. "This is so good." Then again, any expensive champagne would taste better than the cheap wine I've been drinking lately.

"Right?" Cleo lifts it out, topping off our glasses. "Let's get some more of this bubbly in our tummies."

"So have you found an apartment yet?" Isla asks.

After taking a huge swallow, I admit, "No, but I haven't had a lot of time to look. I really need to get my ass moving."

Isla nods, taking a sip of her champagne. "You know you've got us. Don't panic."

Cleo nods, too. Warmth fills my chest, part champagne but mostly affection for these two women who would do something so huge for me. Even if it'd drive me crazy to live with one of them. I know I'd probably drive them crazy, too.

We finish the second bottle the waitress brings over before making our way downstairs to the dance floor. It's been a long time since I felt like dancing. But tonight, I feel like I need it.

I tip my head back, downing the rest of my drink and passing the glass to a waiter who's walking by. We move through the swaying bodies, the bass from the remix track pounding into all my senses. It feels like it's waking me up. But it's also making me think I'll probably wake up with a splitting headache in the morning.

Cleo and Isla grab my hands and start swaying their hips to the Prince remix. A slow smile crawls across my face, and I start dancing too. We aren't left alone for very long, though. A group of clean-shaven guys who look like they've barely turned twenty-one sidles over and starts dancing behind us. I don't care, though. Not even when one of them grabs my hips and starts moving with me to the beat. Which is surprising. I'd usually have turned around and slapped him by now. But it feels good—that taste of vengeance on my tongue, slithering into my body and through my limbs, reigniting some of my soul. Until his hands move to my ass, making me cringe.

"You've got the best set of buns I've ever felt," random guy yells near my ear.

I spin around, about to tell him he's ruined the moment and to scamper off, but someone else does it for me. "And if you touch those buns again, I'll make sure you won't sit on yours for a month. Beat it, kid." Jared shoves the guy away, who raises his hands in surrender and retreats into the crowd.

"What the—" The fury emanating from him shuts me up. He grabs my hand and starts pulling me away from the girls.

"She'll see you ladies later," he yells out to them. I send them an apologetic look, but Cleo's all smiles and glee, clapping her hands and giving me a thumbs-up. Isla looks skeptical but doesn't come after me, so I guess she's not too worried.

He nods to a security guard, who steps aside for us to walk down a blocked off hallway. I hear a moan from behind one of the doors and again wonder what the hell kind of club this really is.

I yank my hand out of Jared's when he opens a door. "Stop. What are you doing here?"

He just gives me a hard look. "Get inside."

"No. Why?"

He runs a hand over his hair. "Christ, Vera. Because I'm not talking to you out here, and I fucking know you'll run the second I get you out of this club. Get in."

I cross my arms over my chest, raising a brow at him. He huffs out a disbelieving laugh. "Fine. Have it your way, beauty." Then he's picking me up and carrying me into a room that houses a few chairs and what looks like a bench seat. He kicks the door closed behind him, locking it while I do my best to kick him. "Put me down, now!"

He lowers me and pushes me against the wall, crushing his chest to mine. "Why were you letting that guy touch you? Do you really hate me that much?"

He's caged me in with his arms. My breasts push against his black shirt. I lift my hands to his shoulders, trying to shove him off me. "I can do what I want, just like you probably have. And yes, I do hate you that much."

He winces, his green eyes closing briefly then opening and imploring me, but I don't know what for. "I never slept with Stella. I couldn't. I haven't been able to sleep with anyone." He lowers his forehead to mine. "Not when every damn thought I have is of you."

Relief. Warm, sweet relief wraps around my heart, squeezing out some of the damage. But it's not enough. "I don't care." I try to push him off me again, giving up with a groan. "Answer the question, already. What are you doing here?"

He doesn't hesitate to admit, "I followed you."

"You *what?*"

That smile, and that stupid crooked tooth, everything about that mouth. My eyes soak all of it up without my permission. "I was coming to see you, saw you leave, and followed you." He shrugs, pushing his chest further into mine. My nipples tighten, and I almost groan again with frustration. This is torture. "I don't give a damn if that makes me sound crazy. I'll be anything I need to be to make sure you're always mine, Frost."

I don't respond. I can't. I close my eyes, needing to block him from one of my senses before this loose hold I have on my self-control snaps. "Please, just stop this."

The soft brush of his nose and the warmth of his breath ghosts over the skin of my neck, making me shiver. "You don't really want me to do that."

Stiffening, my eyes shoot open at those familiar words.

He laughs softly. "That's my girl. You remember, don't you?" He kisses the underside of my jaw, and my head tilts back to the wall, my resolve fraying. "We're pretty hard to forget. Wanna know why?"

He licks my fluttering pulse, and I moan out a garbled, "No."

He hums. "I'll tell you anyway … because like any story that involves two people who fall in love, you're my happy ending, and I'm yours."

Tears fill my eyes. He can't do this. He can't say all these perfect words and try to turn something that ended the way we did into anything other than what it was—ruination. I wrecked us, but he killed us. He almost killed me. I can't forget that. "Nice speech. Did you find it in the dollar store along with your country plaything?"

A broken laugh erupts from deep in his chest. He lifts his

head, staring down at me with narrowed, determined eyes. "You can try to hurt me as many times as you want, but I'm not going anywhere." His hands lower from the wall, drifting down to my hips. They squeeze them then move further down to tug my dress up and over my hips.

I remain frozen, full of disbelief. "You're the worst thing that ever happened to me."

His fingers trail over the clips of my thigh highs, moving up until he reaches my panties. "W-what are you doing?"

"I'm gonna fuck the hate right out of you." He rubs his finger over the damp material.

"No, you—" His mouth slams into mine, his teeth and tongue tugging my lips apart for him to gain entry. He licks my teeth, my tongue, the roof of my mouth, any inch of me he can get to. The thread snaps, and I melt into him, my hands moving up his shoulders to his neck and crawling into his hair. He groans, tilting his head and sucking my tongue into his mouth.

His hand fumbles between us, and I hear his fly unzip. He lifts my legs, hooking them around his waist. Then he's moving my panties to the side and inserting a finger inside me. "Shit …" I tear my mouth away from his, struggling for breath and rational thought. It seems both have abandoned me when I need them most.

His finger disappears, and he hoists me higher, his cock nudging at my entrance before he slowly sinks inside with a drawn-out groan. "You think you can do without this? Without me?" Teeth sink into my neck. "Answer me." His voice is a throaty growl.

"Y-yes," I whimper, squeezing my eyes shut.

His lips graze a trail to my ear, his hands squeezing my thighs in a bruising grip as he thrusts hard and grinds into me. "You said you weren't much of a liar." He grunts. "Yet you seem to be lying through your perfect teeth every chance you get."

A shaky breath leaves me at his whispered words. He's right. I've turned into a dirty fucking liar. But I'll lie forever if that's what it takes not to be broken again.

"Are you going to talk, or are you going to fuck me?"

He chuckles, his nose running along my jaw. I tilt my head back, keeping my eyes closed. "Oh, I'm gonna do both, my beautiful Frost."

Frustration and panic start to drown out my need to come. I'm such an idiot. Why the fuck am I even doing this?

Fingers tilt my chin down. "Open your eyes." Gone is the cocky smartass and in its place is the softly spoken man who thaws my heart within seconds.

"Vera." My eyes open. He blinks, and I melt even more. "I love you." Those eyes are capable of stripping me of all rationality. But his words … They have the ability to render me hollow.

He starts thrusting slowly, never taking his gaze from mine.

"Your smile." *Thrust.*

"Your laughter." *Thrust.*

"Your strength." *Thrust.*

"The way you glare at me first thing in the morning." *Thrust.*

"The way you care so much that you feel the need to act like you don't care at all." *Thrust.*

"The way you ruined us to try to protect something that you know means a lot to me." *Thrust.*

"The light in your eyes when you're happy—truly happy."

His breath washes over my lips, warm and drugging. "Wanna know what I love most of all?"

My head shakes, and a tear slides down my cheek. His thumb scoops it up and brings it to his mouth where he rubs the salty wetness over his bottom lip. The slow, deep thrusts keep coming. And I had no idea emotion overload could send you racing toward an orgasm like this. But it's the best kind of slow build I've ever experienced.

"Your darkness. Because it's not really dark at all. It's beautiful, it's honest, and it's your heart." He kisses my nose. "And your heart is mine."

I close the distance between our lips, my mouth attacking his like it's trying to absorb every bit of him inside me. He spreads my thighs open wider, and his thrusts fall in sync with the savage dance of our tongues and lips. It's rough, it's dirty, and it's destroying me in the most exquisite way.

What feels like seconds later, I'm falling into spine-tingling bliss. My hands twist into his hair as I try to stop myself from drowning in the overwhelming sensations wracking my entire being. He slams into me three more times then stays buried inside with his lips fused to mine, groaning my name down my throat and causing my legs to spasm violently.

"Fuck," he rasps, trailing his lips softly over mine before skating them over my cheeks. His hands let go of my thighs to hold the sides of my face. Dropping soft kisses over every inch of skin he can reach, he says, "I'm sorry."

Love. What a word. You can fixate on it, study it, try to capture it, but ultimately, that tiny, woefully inadequate four-letter word is not enough. It's merely a word, trying to capture something too powerful within a group of simply structured letters. It's wrong. Love isn't a word, and it's not anything you can describe. It's simply a trap. And once it's caught you, good luck ever trying to get out. I know I probably never will. Doesn't mean I'm going to give in, though. Its power has proven too much for me, and I've had enough of feeling powerless tonight.

Jared finally steps back, grabbing my arms and helping me

to stay upright. "Frost?"

I step away and look down at my dress, righting it and my cardigan. I can feel Jared's cum leaking out of me with every move I make, which is a bit gross but weirdly satisfying too.

He just stands there, staring at me while he zips up his jeans. The wary look on his face has my stomach clenching with guilt. Like he knows I'm about to walk out of here and leave him alone with his useless I love yous.

He'd be right. I smooth my hair back, take a shaky breath, and stalk to the door. "Bye, Hero."

He doesn't stop me, just whispers, "I'll see you soon, Frost."

But it lacks the conviction I've come to now expect from him. And that alone has my feet almost stumbling over themselves in the hall on the way out.

CHAPTER TWENTY-EIGHT

The weekend passes in a blur of reality television, some more packing, and a bit of apartment hunting online. I've lined up two places to look at this week, both cheap, and both combined probably wouldn't house all the stuff I have. I'm going to have to sell some of it anyway but doing so feels like I'm giving away another part of who I was before this whole mess began. Letting more of me go, in any shape or form, makes me wonder what will be left. Or if what remains is enough.

Head held high, I walk into the coffee shop Monday morning for the first time in almost a month, not caring if I see Jared. I've survived this much, so I'll survive whatever else he throws at me.

"Hello, woman who owns my heart."

Okay, maybe not that. Eyes widening, I spin around to see him leaning by the doorway. A few onlookers give us curious glances that quickly turn into smiles when he stalks over to where I'm standing in the line. "Would you mind not feeding me your cheesy verbal garbage in public places?"

That has scowls and looks of outrage thrown my way. "Oh, please," I mutter at them.

Jared just laughs as if it's perfectly okay to be shut down in front of seven, maybe eight people. Wrapping an arm around my shoulders, he winks at the few seated near and standing close to us. "She loves me; it's written all over her face." He points to my face, and I narrow my eyes at his finger, shoving his arm off my shoulders. "She's just a little bit grumpy until she gets her morning coffee." They all start laughing as if we're playing around.

Let them; I don't really care. "Hey, you're back. What was it now, hmm …" Jenna taps her chin, and Tori, the one who doesn't like me, sidles up next to her. "A latte. That's L-A-T-T—"

"Okay, you can spell. Congratulations. Now how about that latte?"

Jenna coughs to hide her laugh while Tori shoots her annoyance straight at me via narrowed eyes. I move aside and wait for it with my arms crossed over my chest. Jared orders his then stands right next to me. "So, have a good time Friday night?"

I twist my lips, humming. "I'll say. I met this guy who took me home and rode me hard all—"

He steps in front of me, placing the palm of his hand over my mouth. "Don't." His brow twitches, and I try not to smile at his show of irritation. "Not funny, and if that ever happens, it'll be me who's riding you hard, and you know it." He removes his hand, and I flip him off before grabbing my coffee and storming out of there as quickly as I can.

"Yes, I'm calling to let you know that the check I was waiting on has cleared. Do you accept credit card installments or do I need to write a check out to the hospital?"

"Oh, um, this is for Graham Rodgers, you said?" I hear papers shuffling on the receptionist's end of the line. "Because we've received payment already, I think. Hang on let me just … oh, yes. Here it is. Paid in full as of last week. It says here we tried to call you to let you know."

I stare down at the counter then start blinking like there's dust in my eyes. "I'm sorry, what?"

"It's been paid."

Pinching the bridge of my nose, I mutter, "That's impossible. By who?"

"Hmmm, I'm not really at liberty to discuss such details, but seeing as you seem to all be family, I think it's okay. It was paid by Oliver Bramston."

No. Fucking. Way. "*My father?*"

She clears her throat. "Ah, you'd be the better judge of that than I would. But that's what it says here."

"Okay." I nod my head to no one and take a deep breath, letting it out slowly. "Thanks, bye." I hang up, and before I can think better of it, I dial the demon himself. Something I thought I'd never do again. But I need to see what the hell he's playing at now.

It only rings four times before he answers. "Vera, I'll call you back. I'm in the middle—"

"No, you hang up now, and you won't hear from me again. You'll talk to me now or never."

I lean against the counter. My hip digs into the old wood, but I hardly feel it.

He says something to someone then the sound of a door closing reaches my ears. "Okay, you've got my attention, but there's no need to be so fucking dramatic. I raised you better than that."

God, same old same. "Yeah, there kind of is, considering you practically disowned me for not staying with my ex-boyfriend, threatened my new one, oh, and then you slapped me in the face."

He doesn't say anything for a while. I start to think he's hung up on me, but then he sighs heavily. "Sorry is a stupid word that doesn't make up for anything. But I am sorry. I never should've laid a hand on you. But that guy, you deserve better than a—"

Swallowing hard, I try to keep my wits about me, and stop him right there. "Why did you pay for Graham's hospital bills?"

"You found out about that, did you?" He continues when I don't answer the obvious question. "Because I know how much he means to you, and despite what you may think, I don't want to drive you away. I've only ever wanted the opposite. I just have a shit way of showing it."

Dumbfounded is one way to put how I'm feeling. *Unbelievable.* My brain trips over the first part of what he said more than anything else, though. "You knew about me seeing Graham?"

He laughs dryly. "Why do you think you've been allowed to see him for all these years?"

"Allowed?"

"Yes. I've known about it since you were in your early teens, but I couldn't bring myself to stop it."

Jesus. I swipe a hand down my face. "Why didn't you ever say anything about it?"

"Why didn't you?"

"Because I had no idea he was my grandfather," I retort heatedly.

He sucks in an audible breath. "You didn't … You mean, he didn't tell you?"

"No." I glance over my shoulder when I hear Badger making his way down the rickety staircase at the back of the store. "He was worried if I knew, I'd slip and say something, and then you'd never allow me to see him."

He ignores my snide tone. "How is he?"

"You really want to know? Or are you just dodging yet another thing you're at fault for?"

His voice drops an octave in warning. "Vera, I may have made some mistakes in my life, but I'm still your father. You will show me some respect."

"No, I think I won't. I'm going now. Oh, and Badger's fine, by the way. Thanks for paying the bill; I'll have the money wired to you when your mother's check clears next month."

I go to hang up when he practically yells, "Vera!" I put the phone back to my ear. "Please, just … Will you come for dinner one night soon? Dexter knows he's to leave you alone. I've also reinstated access to all your credit cards."

That explains Dexter's disappearing act. But … Money. It all comes back around to the same damn thing. I'd be lying if I said my shoulders didn't deflate with relief, though. "You don't get it, do you? Your money isn't important to me. Not anymore. The only reason it was in the first place is because it was all I knew. I know better now. I know more. I've experienced more." I smile at Badger when he arrives at the front counter. "So I don't want it, and I don't need it."

He scoffs loudly. "Surely you can't be surviving that well without a job and without money, Vera. Don't be stupid, just come to dinner. I don't want anything. I just want to see you."

But after everything that's happened, I don't know if I can believe him.

Chewing on my lip, I eye my purse sitting under the counter, where those well-used cards lie in wait. "I have a job. I have enough money to survive, and I'll let you know about dinner. Bye, *Dad*." I hang up before he can respond, dumping my phone on the counter and heaving out a huge gust of breath.

"Your father?" Badger asks with a note of shock in his voice.

"Uh-huh." Still staring at my purse, I grab it and get my wallet out. Plucking the cards out one by one, I stare at all three of them in my hands. I'm still staring at them when the bell over the door tinkles. Glancing at the wastebasket, I open the drawer in front of me and pull the scissors out. Then I proceed to hack into the hard plastic as best as I can, chopping them in half and then in more halves until my hands start to hurt. Chucking the scissors back in the drawer, I grab the wastebasket and tuck it under the edge of the counter before scooping the remains of my father's hold on me into the trash. I dump it back on the ground, dusting my hands and turning around to find two sets of eyes on me. One blue and one green.

They both start slow clapping, and I try not to growl. Blowing a piece of hair that's escaped my ponytail from my face, I huff, "What do you want now?"

Jared points at a tool bag on the counter. "Fixing some shit, need to make sure old Graham here takes it easy." Badger chuckles. "You okay?" Jared asks.

Shrugging, I move over to the pile of books by the register, pretending to sort through them. "Great, never been better."

Jared snorts. Right freaking behind me. Man, he's sneaky. "You're even more beautiful when you're mad. Like a fire trying to contain itself," he whispers into my ear. "In fact, it makes me wanna make you so mad just to see what happens when you explode." He nips my ear. "All. Over. Me."

Goose bumps scatter over the skin of my bare neck, racing down my back. I squeeze my thighs together. "Go do what you came here to do, or go away."

He quickly kisses my cheek, and I give him my best glare. He doesn't care, just smiles and walks off to the back of the store.

I turn my glare on Badger next, who's busy trying to look like he's minding his own business by fiddling with the little Christmas tree at the front window. "You." I narrow my eyes at him.

He looks around, playing dumb. "Me?"

"Yes, you." My hands fall to my hips. "Why is he here?"

He walks over to me slowly, almost cautiously. "I called him, wanted to see if he'd have a look at these stairs of ours. They're older than I am."

Betrayal blinds my vision. "Why would you do that to me?"

He shrugs and leans against the wall. "Because I love you, and he's good for you."

My tense shoulders drop, and I feel more layers of ice melt away from my heart.

"But he … he hurt me, Badger. Badly."

His blue eyes soften behind his glasses. "I know, dear. But he also made you happy. The happiest I've ever seen you."

I sniff. "I don't need him. I'm happy on my own."

Nodding, he says, "You will be. I know you'll be very happy on your own moving forward. I couldn't be more proud of your decision to leave your father's shadow behind. But … love brings a different kind of happiness. And I'd hate to see you live with regrets. Those pesky things can be a terrible burden on the soul."

Tell me about it. He doesn't understand, though, and I

don't know how to explain it to him.

"He did something that I don't know if I can forgive."

Badger hums, rubbing at his chin. "I'm not trying to make excuses for him. I don't know what he did. But … just know that we're all human. It's in our DNA to make mistakes." He looks over at the back of the store where the sound of drilling keeps stopping and starting. "We're always so quick to judge someone from the mistakes they've made. When really, we should be judging what they do after they make them instead." His gaze swings back to me with a pointed look. He straightens. "I'm going to grab a coffee before bingo, want one?"

I shake my head. Not even coffee can help calm the erratic dance of my nerves nor the turning in the pit of my stomach.

He leaves and I stare toward the sound of Jared banging on the stairs. I want to walk over there and have him make me forget all this has happened. I want to feel the touch of his lips on mine. I want to see the way his eyes change with every expression that moves across his face. But I don't do any of that. I stay right where I am for over an hour, serving the few customers in a distracted daze.

Jared walks back up to the front after lunch with his tool bag in hand. He drops it by the door. "Where's Graham?" He looks around. "I'm done, fixed some loose shelving, too."

I keep my bored mask in place, biting the side of my cheek to stop from spewing out how grateful I am. "He's gone to bingo."

He raises a brow. "Bingo?"

"Yup. He decided he needs to live a little more before his number is called."

He chuckles. "Wow. Well, bingo isn't for the faint of heart."

I don't respond. I'd almost forgotten how easy it was to be roped into his orbit, almost forgotten that I hated him for a second there.

A woman walks up to the counter with her daughter. "Hi." She smiles. "Do you have a new copy of this book?" She holds up a dog-eared edition of *Harry Potter and the Chamber of Secrets.*

"Can you not read? You're in a bookstore, after all. The sign outside says very clearly, new and used. So if there's no new copies on the shelf, you're fresh out of luck." My irritation doesn't bode well for business. Oh well. People will have to get used to me and my moods. Besides, the man beside me is mostly to blame anyway.

She just blinks at me.

Jared rushes in to say, "You'll have to excuse her. You see, I recently broke her heart and she's still a little bitter about it. Want me to see if we can order one in?" He then turns his panicked face to me. "Wait, you can do that, can't you?"

Scoffing, I relent, "Sorry, he's ruined my life. Leave your details on the pad there and I'll order one for you." I don't even look at her; I keep my gaze stuck on the nuisance next to me. "Why are you still here?"

"Because you are," he fires back.

"But I've made it clear I don't want you here."

He lifts his shoulders. "We both know you do."

I guffaw. "You're so full of shit."

"And you're too damn beautiful for your own good."

With my heart slamming against my ribcage, I feel myself slipping again. "This is crazy."

"I'll say." He grins.

"What's it going to take for you to realize I don't want this anymore?" As soon as the words slip past my lips, I regret them.

He frowns. "Sometimes, Frost, you don't get to pick the things you want in life. They have a way of picking you instead.

And for whatever reason, you picked me and I picked you. You can fight me the rest of your life as far as I'm concerned. I mean, I'd prefer it be while you're naked, but I'm not fussy." He shrugs. "You've invaded my heart, and there's no cutting you out. I've got no choice but to wait, so I will, for as long as it takes."

My pulse screams through every part of my body. My shocked, liquefying body.

Someone clears their throat, and I turn to see that the woman and her daughter are long gone and that Badger has returned.

Jared steps closer to me and places a soft kiss on my head. "I'll see you soon, beauty."

As soon as the door closes behind him, I walk to the back of the store and lock myself in the bathroom.

CHAPTER TWENTY-NINE

O n Wednesday night, I find myself standing in my living room, glancing around at all the boxes lining the walls. Everything I don't need daily is packed. Well, almost everything. I've put it off long enough, and so I grab some boxes and walk down the hall to my library. I close my eyes, take a deep lungful of air, and let it out at the same time I open the door and step inside. Bracing myself for the destruction I caused all those weeks ago, and what I know it's going to do to my already ravaged heart, I open my eyes to discover something very different instead.

The boxes slip out of my hand. All the mess has been cleaned and the books are back on the shelves. The broken, torn apart ones are arranged in piles on the rug. Piles that make up giant letters. Letters that spell *I love you*. He's even used the scrunched-up pages to make an exclamation mark after *you*.

It's hardly the grand gesture most girls would want after having their heart broken, but it's the grandest one anyone has ever made for me. I step closer, looking down at the books I've wrecked; the same ones he's painstakingly tried to piece back together enough to do this for me. Tears gather in my eyes, my nose stings, and my chest starts to rise and fall faster and faster. I drop to my knees, and for the second time, I fall apart in this room. But as the tears run down my face, splashing onto the taped-up cover of *Wuthering Heights*, I realize it doesn't feel like I'm falling apart. I feel like I'm finally letting go.

Not only of the hurt Jared and I both caused, but of the hurt I've lived with my whole life. The kind of hurt that embeds so deep inside, you don't even realize it's there. Not until someone comes along who not only sees it, but accepts it and has the patience to wait for you to acknowledge it, too. It's excruciating, letting a part of yourself go. No matter how much you need to or how awful that part may be. It's still a part of you that you've carried within yourself for far too long.

It kept me company, that hurt. It gave me what I needed to protect myself in any situation. But nothing can protect someone from falling in love. From living.

It's time for it to go. I run my hands over the books, the tape Jared used, the glue you can hardly even see, and the piles of pages that still have yet to find their way back home.

And I now understand why people say that goodbyes are always hard.

No Christmas lights decorate this part of town. It's almost pitch black. The kind of darkness that blocks out the stars and makes you feel like it's about to envelop you in its eerie embrace. I don't let that stop me, though, as I lock my car and walk briskly up the driveway to the steps of Jared's front porch.

Squaring my shoulders, I quickly swipe under my eyes, trying to stop the falling tears still somehow escaping. I cleaned my face before I left, but I guess they're not finished. It figures that after I spend most of my life not shedding a tear over anything, I'll spend days on end in tears in the space of a few months.

The door swings open before I can knock, and Toulouse meows, walking over Jared's slipper clad feet. Slippers. He's wearing grandpa slippers. He notices me staring at them and shrugs. "Don't judge. It's cold."

I sniff, trying not to laugh. He's giving me no shit about showing up here in the middle of the night with a tear-swollen face. That somehow makes me fall even more in love with him. He nudges Toulouse back with his foot; the cat gives him an annoyed look before turning his butt into the air and walking off into the house. "Come on, it's fucking freezing." He grabs my hand and pulls me inside. After locking the door, he turns around, still holding my hand.

I step closer to him. "Thank you."

Understanding dawns, his sleepy eyes opening wider. "You saw the books? I was going to lay down shirtless, you know, to give it everything I've got, but then I realized I had no idea when you might walk into that room again. I could've been in there for days, and I'd be no good to you if—"

I throw my arms around his neck and kiss him. I kiss him like it's the first and last kiss we'll ever share. Because he's given so many firsts to me, and it's painfully obvious he's going to have all my lasts.

My green-eyed hero.

My endless adventure.

My everything that matters.

He picks me up and carries me into his room. My lips break away from his to rain kisses all over his face. He chuckles, falling to the bed with me falling beside him. "You're cute when you're not angry with me anymore, know that?"

Grinning, I trail my finger down the center of his face, and he nips it when it reaches his mouth. "I want you to get rid of that couch."

He nods. "It'll be gone come morning."

"Where's your phone?"

"Nightstand, I think." He pauses. "Why?"

I don't answer him and, instead, roll over to grab it. Once I've found Stella's number, I follow the steps to block it, hit delete, and toss his phone down on the nightstand.

Jared chuckles quietly. Rolling on top of me, he undoes the buttons on my coat, tugging my arms through when he's done. I slip my hands under his black t-shirt, rejoicing at being able to touch his warm, smooth skin again. "I'm sorry," I whisper. "I know I should've told you from the start, but I was so scared he'd—"

He shakes his head, pressing his lips to mine. "Shhh, I get it. I wish you had told me, but I get why you didn't, and honestly?" He lowers his voice to a whisper. "It's the cruelest, but most selfless act anyone has ever shown me."

Tears clog my throat, but I manage to get out, "I think he'll leave us alone now, but I understand if you don't want to risk it. I never wanted to make you choose."

He rests his forehead against mine. "He can lay the world to ruin for all I care. I've got insurance."

A laugh erupts from me. "Yeah, but it's not enough. Your brother, the bikes, your employees…"

"Hey, stop." I blink. "It'll be okay."

I nod, letting out a huge breath. "Okay."

I start tugging at his shirt, and he sits up, tearing it over his head, and then lowers himself back over me, kissing my chin then pecking my lips.

"I'm sorry. Whatever you do to me, whatever happens, I'll never let myself do something like that again. But I swear I didn't …"

"Shhhh." I give him a pained smile. "I believe you."

He lifts his head, wincing and cursing softly. "It's just … I've been let down quite a few times in my life, and it's almost ingrained in me to think the worst of those I care about the most." He blows out a breath. "Almost like I'm sometimes just waiting for them to prove me right." He rolls his lips between his teeth for a second. "I shouldn't have done that with you. I should've pushed past the impulse to believe the worst, but it became all I could see. Then it became the worst thing I've ever done."

More tears. He kisses the wetness from my cheeks. "I'm so fucking sorry."

I sniff. "Okay."

"Okay." He nods, a smile trying to pull at his mouth.

I laugh, sniffling still when I ask, "How'd you get into my apartment anyway?"

He licks his lip. "Uh, I have my ways." When I raise a brow, he puffs out a loud breath. "Fine. Turns out Frank has got an old Dodge he wants looked at. Besides, he knows my intentions were for the greater good." He winks and I laugh again, tears still leaking from my eyes. We're quiet for a beat.

"When you cry, I feel it here." He grabs my hand, placing it on his chest, and suddenly everything ceases to exist. It's only him and me and the words that shyly leave my lips next. "I love you."

His lips part, eyes blinking. "Say it again."

Laughing even more, I say, "I love you, Jared Williams."

"Fuck." He growls the word from somewhere deep inside his chest then dips his head and claims my mouth with his. We strip in record time for two people who refuse to stop kissing for more than a few seconds. Spreading my legs, he thrusts inside then takes my hands in his. My legs hook around his waist, my fingers linking with his while he stretches me and stares into my eyes. With his lips resting against mine, he starts to move in and out of me.

It's slow, but the intensity, everything about these mere moments in time, fires through every part of me. His body lowers until he's holding himself up on his elbows alone and bearing half of his weight on me. We don't talk, the only sounds are the ragged breaths we exhale into each other. Until we finally start to crest the sharp edge of pleasure, falling into it together and groaning as we stare into each other's eyes. Jared rolls to his side, hooking an arm over my stomach and pulling me to him until my head rests under his chin.

"Sleep, beauty."

Dousing the couch in some lighter fluid, I step back and take stock of my supplies.

Coffee. Fire extinguisher. Matches.

Feeling tired but more awake than I've felt in years, I bend down, grab the matches, and light one. The flame bobs on the end of the stick, its tiny bit of warmth struggling in the freezing temperature of the winter morning.

Jared had already removed the couch by the time I woke up, and I made him drag it down the side of the house to the backyard. He gave me a funny look but did what I requested without asking any questions.

The questions came when I asked him if he had any lighter fluid. I told him my plan and marched out the back door with my supplies in hand. After bringing out a small fire extinguisher, he retreated into the house to get his coffee.

I toss the match, watching as it meets the flammable fluid and fire races across the old fabric of the couch.

The guy from the shack next door sticks his head over the fence. He's missing three front teeth, has one speck of hair, and a beer can in hand. But he seems harmless. I remember him from the morning after I spent my first night here when he asked Jared for a cigarette as we were backing out of the driveway. It's hard to believe it's barely been a few months since that happened. The first of many times when Jared had crawled under my skin and left a confusing sting in his wake.

"Vera, isn't it?"

I nod, my brow rising.

"I'm Don. Top of the morning to ya." He gives me a toothless grin, his elbow slung over the fence. He must be standing on something on the other side, which is a little worrying. I make a mental note to make sure the windows are curtained off properly whenever I stay here from now on.

"Morning, Don."

"Say, why you burning that couch for?"

Taking a big sip from my coffee, I bring my gaze back to said rapidly burning couch. "It's contaminated." I shrug. "Best to be safe. Never can be too careful these days." My eyes lift from the flames to find Jared watching me as he leans over the railing of the back porch, a smile tugging at his lips and a cigarette and coffee mug in his hands.

"Ain't that the truth," Don mutters.

I turn back to Don, smiling.

"Well, cheers, Vera. Good to see you've decided to hang around." He raises his beer, and I lift my coffee in the air, too. He then drops back down to his side of the fence.

"Ready for me to come put it out now?" Jared asks.

I stare at the fire again, smoke billowing up and into the air. Lifting my coffee to my mouth, I mutter, "No. Not yet."

CHAPTER THIRTY

"**W**hat's all this shit for?" Jared asks me when I drop the crate of paint tins to the ground.

"What does it look like?" I head over to the garage, opening the door and switching on the light. He follows me. "Okay, what I probably should have asked is why the hell is there over five hundred dollars' worth of paint on the driveway?"

Tapping my bottom lip, I take a few steps to his workbench where a giant toolbox sits. "To paint the house. That should be obvious, no? Have you looked at it any time in the past ..." I tug open drawers, finding no sign of what I'm looking for. "Oh, I don't know. Decade?"

His hand closes the next drawer I open then he's spinning me around and crowding me back into the bench. "You want to paint? *You?*"

The question combined with his crooked smile makes me scowl. "Well, it needs to be done, doesn't it? Now, where are the paintbrushes?"

He just stares at me. That smirk still pulling at his mouth until it becomes a full-blown grin.

I blow out a loud breath. "What?"

He shakes his head then, cupping my cheeks, he leans forward to place a kiss on my forehead. "Nothing."

I watch as he pulls an old box out from under the bench. Paint trays, rollers, and brushes are tugged from it and placed on the concrete floor. He selects some and places them in the tray. "All right." He straightens. "If we're doing this, you should probably go grab something, um… else to wear." He winks and walks past me to the door.

"What?" I glance down at my dark blue sweater dress. It might be very last season, but there's nothing wrong with it other than that.

"Paint, Frost. You'll get paint on you. It's inevitable," he says over his shoulder before disappearing out the door.

Well, damn. He's probably right. I march back inside and tug on a pair of jeans and one of his work shirts. It smells like his garage even though it's supposedly clean, but it'll do.

I moved in a few weeks ago, right after the New Year holiday had ended, or rather, Jared moved me in. He'd been asking me every day since I burned his couch, and I kept telling him no. It was too soon. But Jared being well, Jared, doesn't believe in doing things by anyone else's timeline but his own. He knew he had me when I came over one night after work to find he'd filled Darren's old room with my bookshelves and was gently placing all the books in piles on the floor for me to put away how I like them. I couldn't believe he'd done it. But he bluntly stated that Darren wouldn't give a shit, and that a room is a room, and now this one is home for my books. Then he told me good luck with getting them out, and that he expects my ass in his bed every night from now on.

The lease on my apartment was up that week. So it was a choice between coughing up a hefty down payment for the new apartment I'd found, only to spend every night with Jared anyway, or admit defeat and do what I wanted to do. I had one condition, though. That he let me help pay half the bills, which in turn means he's not taking on any more side jobs like working at the Hedgington as a valet. And even though his house is a far cry from what I'm used to, I don't care. I just want the man who lives inside it. The man who lives inside my heart.

My future is unknown, wide open, and terrifying. But having Jared by my side only gives me more strength to take hold of what I want for myself and make it mine. To live my life my way, without fear and without apology.

Tugging my hair up into a ponytail, I head outside where we spend hours getting more paint on each other than the house. But by late afternoon, the front of the house is almost done.

I step back, looking at it. It's yellow. Canary yellow. The same color I suspect it was painted many years ago when the house was first built. I've got some white paint for the windows and doors.

"Huh." Jared wipes the back of his hand over his forehead. "Doesn't look half bad."

I snort. "Are you kidding? It already looks ten times better." I tilt my head, squinting at the roof. "I think we should fix the roof up, too." I hum. "I'm thinking gray."

He tilts his head too. "Well, fuck. I'm going to have to steal a ladder from work."

"It's not exactly stealing when it's your business."

He huffs out a laugh. "True."

I'm still staring at the house, smiling at Toulouse who's sitting on the windowsill and watching us from the living room when something wet hits my cheek. I squeal, stepping back so fast I almost trip.

Jared comes after me wearing a shit-eating grin on his face. "No, stay back. We're already covered in it." I glance down at all the yellow paint smudges on his shirt I'm wearing. Big mistake. He grabs me around the waist and swings me before lowering me to the grass then pins my arms to my sides with his legs. I laugh and scream, probably sounding totally deranged. His finger trails a wet line from my forehead right down the center of my face. He stops at my lips, and my eyes grow huge. He wouldn't.

He smiles evilly, lifting his finger and turning it to show no paint on the pad of it. "I licked it."

Narrowing my eyes to slits, I lift my hips, and it unbalances him enough for me to gain the upper hand, shoving him off and climbing on top of him. "You're an asshole." I drop my head, pressing my nose into his.

He crosses his eyes, making me laugh. "So you keep saying." He grabs the sides of my face and kisses me. "Yet you love me anyway."

Smiling, I admit, "Yeah, I kinda do."

Loving him doesn't mean I'll forget everything that's happened, but I'll also never forget what it felt like to allow him back in. Loving Jared is akin to stepping outside on an overcast, rainy day, only to be surrounded by warm sunshine.

Impossible.

Surreal.

Yet it's happened, and it's more real than anything I've ever known.

He squishes my cheeks in his hands. "Kinda?"

"Yeah, kinda," I mumble out.

He growls, rolling me onto my back and shoving his face into my neck to blow raspberries. I burst out laughing, slapping at his shoulder and grabbing the back of his head. "Stop. Okay, okay."

"Say it." The words are muffled into my skin.

Pulling his head up, I look him square in the eyes. "I kinda love you way more than I first implied."

He groans. "Devil woman."

He stands and starts walking back to the house. Scowling at his retreating back, I get up and run after him before jumping onto his back. His arms swing around to grab my legs, and I twist his head to the side to look at me. "I love you." He waits, and I relent some more. "It's insane and unhealthy how much I love you, you big—"

He lets go of my leg to shove his finger against my lips. "Let's not ruin it, Frosty pants."

He winces playfully when I nip his finger. "But I love you, too. So fucking much."

I place a kiss by the corner of his mouth. His tongue creeps out to lick me, and I laugh again. "Take me inside and feed me, already."

He marches inside, and we wash our hands. Jared prepares one of his famous sandwiches for us while I sit and admire everything he's doing with my chin in my palm.

"Enjoying the view, beauty?"

I nod a few times. "I am, but it'd be even better if you took your shirt off."

He pretends to be offended, his dark brows furrowing. "Your shamelessness knows no bounds."

"All because of you." I wink and take a sip from my glass of water.

"Ah, I've corrupted you. Good." He grabs the mustard from the fridge.

I chew on my lip for a moment then decide to just say it. "So my inheritance arrives next week."

He nods, squirting some mustard on his sandwich and a little on mine. He knows I don't like too much. I continue, "I think it's time you find them."

He puts the mustard down and looks at me. "What?"

"Maggie. I think you should hire a PI or something and find out where she is."

He sucks his bottom lip into his mouth, staring at me. "I've tried that. Took me months to save up a few grand and the shmuck spent it all at the casino and didn't find shit." He grins menacingly. "Well, he did find out what toilet water tasted like, as well as what it felt like to be on the receiving end of a good ass kicking."

I shake my head. "Jesus. No, I want to pay for it." I hold up a hand when he instantly throws a glower my way. "Please, let's hire someone decent and find her and the baby. They couldn't have gone too far. Not when she didn't have the money or support. She could be right here under our noses."

He leans a hip against the counter, sighing and turning his gaze to the ground. "That's why I ended up at the women's shelter, you know." He looks at me again. "I asked my probation officer to transfer me there. I was picking up trash on abandoned highways for a few months before the idea flew into my head. He agreed. I'd been behaving and doing everything right. Plus, I think he knew my motives behind the change. But ..." He shrugs half-heartedly. "I never saw her."

"So we'll find her. Together." My tone is firm.

He doesn't care, though. "No, I'll find her. I promised Felix I wouldn't stop looking. I've just been a little distracted of late." He smirks. "But I will find her. Keep your money, Frost. Your grandmother went to great lengths to make sure it was yours and yours alone."

He knows about the tenuous relationship of my family. I haven't seen my dad, nor have I spoken to him since that phone call weeks ago. I don't think I'll ever be able to find it in me to shut him out for good, but I need some time before I see him again.

"Think of it as a belated birthday present then," I suggest. He turned twenty-seven when we were apart.

He rubs a hand over the scruff on his jaw, giving me a soft smile. "You know I don't need anything else but you. I love that you care, that you want to help, but I'm not taking your money, beauty." He raises a brow at me when I go to argue again. "And that's final."

He goes back to making the sandwiches, and I try my best not to grumble too loudly. I can understand, I guess. I know a thing or two about pride. But it's still frustrating, especially when I know it troubles him. I don't want anything to trouble him. He's too good a man for other people's messes to weigh him down. While I'm not so much a bitch as to want any harm to come to Maggie or her baby, Jared is the main reason I want to do this, to try to find her.

Determination rises within me. I'll just have to work him around to the idea.

Challenge accepted.

I watch as he places the bread on top of the roast beef then brushes the crumbs off his hands. "Dinner is served, milady."

"Good, I'm starved." I go to yank the plate over to me with a sultry smile playing on my lips.

He catches my hand and leans over the counter, his

breath fanning across my lips. "Sick of roughing it yet, princess?"

Sometimes I wonder if that vulnerability he tries to hide will ever leave him. I know it's not because of me, but rather, a product of his past. But with every passing day we're together, I hope to stamp it out even more.

I lower my lips to his. "Never."

CHAPTER THIRTY-ONE

Epilogue
Seven Months Later

Jared

Vera closes the front door and locks it. Leaning against the front of my truck, I can't help but stare at her. Can't help but watch the way the sun bounces off her long black hair and the way the perfectly sculpted apples of her cheeks shift when she glances over her shoulder, giving me a small smile. If I try hard enough, I can still taste her on my tongue. I ate her after breakfast. She's my favorite snack. My cock agrees, hardening in my jeans as I remember the soft sounds of delight that escaped her perfect pink lips while she laid spread open on the kitchen counter not even twenty minutes ago. I silently tell him to stand down because we've got more important things to do. Fear tries to slither into my gut, and I do my best to extinguish that shit.

Thinking about what I'm about to do has me feeling like even more of a dipshit for all the crap that happened with Dahlia. Now that I know what it is to have someone become the only person you want to spend the rest of your life with.

No one can make me see the world differently quite like this woman can. Yeah, she's hurt me, she damn well almost destroyed me, and I'll always regret what I did as a result. But I'd let her hurt me over and over again now that I know her reasons for doing it in the first place. She loves me. *Me.* A lowly, smartass mechanic from the wrong side of the proverbial tracks.

I sometimes still have trouble believing it, but that doesn't mean I'm about to let her slip through my grease-stained fingers.

I would've proposed sooner, and I did, in an ass-backward kind of way. I've told her many times at random that she's going to marry me. She just has a way of making me speak every thought she elicits in my brain. Which is almost all of them. And every time I told her, she gave me that beautiful laugh of hers before saying she'd think about it when I actually got around to asking her properly.

It's taken six months, but I finally saved up enough to buy her a decent ring. It might not be full of diamonds or any kind of gold, but it's enough. At least, I hope it is. And I hope like hell she doesn't need to think about it for too long. This shit is scary enough. She can't leave a man in limbo like that.

"Wait up." I straighten from the truck and grab her hand. She spins around, raising a dark questioning brow at me.

Dropping to my knee beside the passenger door, I start my speech right away, for fear of choking if I pause long enough. "Vera Marie Bramston, I know you love your books, but you already know this isn't some fairy tale. I'm not some knight in shining armor. I'm going to fuck up, and I'm going to piss you off more times than I care to admit. But I will love you with every breath I'm lucky enough to take and make sure you know it every damn day. Because we don't need perfect when what we have is real. And I'll pick real over anything if it means I get you." I take a deep, much-needed breath. "Be my wife. Maybe not tomorrow or next month, but please tell me that you'll agree to be my wife someday in the not too distant future and make me the happiest son of a bitch in the whole damn world."

She just stares at me, her mouth slightly parted. Shit. Maybe I should've taken her to dinner instead of asking her on my driveway like the scumbag I am. But I picked up the ring yesterday and couldn't wait.

Fuck. I don't think my heart is even beating. I'd thump my chest, try to restart it, but I can't seem to move. Then she sniffs, wiping under her nose as tears start to stream from those beautiful, ice blue eyes. "That wasn't really a question, but I'm going to say yes anyway."

Shock and elation tear through me, and I almost drop the ring. "Y-yes?"

She laughs. "Yes. Hurry up and put that ring on my finger before I change my mind."

That snaps me back into action. I stand and grab her soft hand, sliding it on her finger. Lifting it to my lips, I kiss it. Then she jumps on me and starts kissing my face. I'd have probably dropped her if I wasn't so used to her sneak attacks by now. I grab the side of her face to bring her lips to mine, needing to see those eyes when I say, "I love you, Frost."

She exhales a shaky breath, and my heart starts beating double time. "I love you, Hero."

I kiss her hard then put her in the truck, and not gonna lie, I feel like skipping as I round it to the driver's side. She said yes. *Fuck me.* Just wait until old Graham hears about this. He still lives at the bookstore, but Vera's running it now, so she's there almost every day with him. I was shocked as fuck to learn he's her grandad, but looking at him after I found out, I don't know how I didn't see it sooner. The eyes. Not many sets of eyes in this world share that same light blue color.

The smile stays on my face until we're half an hour into our drive. I glance over at her, finding her amused eyes watching me. "Does this mean I can knock you up soon?" There my mouth goes again. Always betraying me.

She guffaws, choking and coughing. I frown, stubbing out my cigarette and reaching over to whack her on the back. "I'm fine," she breathes out in a wheeze.

"Really?" Wait a minute. "You don't want kids?"

She shakes her head. "Why would I? They cry, they stink, and they steal sleep from you." She then grumbles quietly, "I like my sleep."

I'm so outraged, I almost pull the truck over to the side of the old highway we're driving down. "No." It's all I can come up with.

"Yes."

"But …" I blink rapidly. "You never said you didn't like kids. Everyone likes kids."

"Not everyone and you never asked." She pauses, her voice tinged with fear. "Do you want your ring back? Maybe …"

"Shit, whoa. Stop right there. That ring is yours, and you are mine. Besides …" I reach for my cigarettes because I need another after this bombshell. She takes them from me and lights one, taking a drag before handing it over. "I'll change your mind."

She just laughs, which is fine. Because her reluctance to fight back on the subject tells me all I need to know.

She'll give me one.

Maybe two if I play my cards right.

I grab her hand and place it on my thigh. She squeezes it, and I try to ignore the blood shooting straight to my dick. This damn woman. I wonder if there'll ever come a day when I'm not sporting a semi whenever she's around. I tuck my cigarette between my teeth and adjust my dick in my jeans. She squeezes my thigh again, telling me without words that she's well aware of my suffering.

To stop my dick from hardening any more, I ask, "You gonna tell your dad?"

She laughs. "What do you think?"

"You're just gonna let him find out in his own time, then?" I grin.

"Probably." She shrugs, clearly not giving a damn.

Can't blame her. The guy's a straight up asswipe with severe anger issues.

I've only had the pleasure of meeting him once, five months ago at dinner. Where he grilled me about my job, tattoos, and lack of college degrees for thirty minutes before Vera said she'd had enough and that we were leaving. He apparently apologized. Not to me, but to her. And that's what matters. I don't need the guy to like me; that's not what's important. But seeing her happy is.

Stiff dick officially gone.

We pull into the parking lot of Penstville penitentiary just under an hour later. My stomach turns as I think about Felix stuck behind the electrical barbed-wire cage that surrounds the huge brick fortress. Three weeks. Just three weeks and he'll be out.

Vera has yet to meet him. Whenever I've asked, she's said she'd rather not walk into a den full of criminals that haven't been laid in God knows how long.

She's funny when she's scared.

But even though I know she's nervous—having never visited a jail before—she's here with me today. Which means more than I could ever possibly wrap my brain around.

I round the truck, grabbing her hand and helping her down. "You sure you want to come in?" It's really not that bad, but I need to remember that my version of not that bad is probably very different from hers.

She nods. "Yeah. Let's do this."

Pride fills my chest while I stare down at my raven-haired beauty. Christ, I'll never forget the day I first saw her, walking down the side of that highway as if she owned the damn thing. All dressed up and completely unaware of the effect she'd have on the unsuspecting drivers speeding by. I still have no idea what made me pull over, other than the fact I didn't want some woman's death on my conscience. That, and a bit of curiosity. I have moments when I just stare at her, feeling so damn glad that I did. I know that my paranoia and lack of trust in people almost fucked up the best damn thing I've ever had in my life, but I won't make that mistake again.

I lean forward, placing a gentle kiss on her full lips. She smiles, and my fucking heart inflates. "Let's, beauty."

We head inside through metal detectors and all sorts of invasive shit. After signing in, a meaty guard with a moustache that could rival Tom Selleck's takes us through to the visiting room.

Vera looks around at the few inmates sitting with their

families or friends, her shoulders dropping slightly. I wind my arm around her waist, tucking her into my side, and feel her relax even more.

Shouting starts somewhere nearby, and she tenses. My grip on her hip tightens, and she turns her face to mine. "Where is he?"

"He'll be out in a minute; they've gotta get him." I move us over to a table in the corner, and we take a seat. Vera still melded to my side.

The guard returns, bringing with him my best friend and my partner in crime. My brother.

People used to say we could pass as twins. But although I work out when I can, I'm nowhere near as big as Felix has gotten since he went to jail. He works out a lot. Told me that and reading is all he really has to do in this shithole. Plus, working out keeps his anxiety at bay. And he's got a fuck load of it, given his girl left him and he's never even met his own kid.

He's also got brown eyes instead of green. But I must say, my hair is much better than his. It would be, considering his is all shaved off into a crew cut.

Poor guy.

I go to get up, but hesitate when I look at Vera. She gives me a weak smile, telling me she's okay. So I stand and walk over to my brother, slapping him on the back and sighing with relief. He may have messed up and let me down in a huge way, but he's still my brother. The only family I have left besides the woman sitting behind me.

"Missed you, kid." He scruffs my hair, and I punch him in the arm. He's always called me kid, despite only being fourteen months older than I am.

"How's it hanging? Still keeping an eye out for creeps in the shower room?"

He laughs; the sound is gruff like he doesn't do it much, and I've shocked it out of him. "How's the shop?"

I nod. "Good." I gesture toward Vera. "Here she is."

Felix peers around me to look at a blank-faced Vera. "Well, shit. She came along this time."

We take a seat, and Felix holds out a hand to shake Vera's. She just stares at it then finally gives in and shakes his hand with a loose grip.

"Pleasure to finally meet you, Vera." He grins at me briefly when his eyes land on her ring.

She removes her hand and opens her bag. "Likewise. Bet you can't wait to get out of this hellhole." She squirts some hand sanitizer onto her hands and rubs, not giving two shits if she's offended my brother.

"Damn right, I can't." He tilts his head, watching her, and then glances at me again. I shrug, grinning like a man who won the moon and all the stars and got to keep them for himself.

Felix shakes his head, laughing behind his hand rubbing at the scruff on his jaw. He knows all about how awesome she is, so he knows what to expect. Sort of.

Vera puts her sanitizer away. "Are you going to tell him?"

Yeah, I swallowed my pride about a month ago and took her up on her offer to pay for a better PI. Kind of had to if I wanted to buy her that ring. Plus, time is running out. But it seems it was worth every penny. Dahlia ended up sending me the number of the guy her husband knows who then found her within a week of us contacting him.

Nodding, I fold my hand around Vera's on the plastic table. "We found them."

The End.

PLAYLIST

When Doves Cry—Prince

Every You Every Me—Placebo

The New Black—Every Time I die

Novocaine—Fall Out Boy

Dark Side—Kelly Clarkson

Blue and Yellow—The Used

Poison—Rita Ora

Tell It to My Heart—Taylor Dayne

ACKNOWLEDGEMENTS

My husband—Who, when asked to name a few tools a guy might use to remove stuff from his bike, decided to launch into a ten-minute-long speech about the ins and outs of Harley Davidson's. Thanks babe. <3

My children—The two reasons I'm still a functioning adult. You two can pull me out of the lowest of days, simply by asking an innocent question. <3 <3

My mum—For listening.

Billie—For beta reading this book like a boss, creating some badass teasers, talking me down from the ledge countless times, and for convincing me to set it free to the world.

Amanda—For not only beta reading, but for listening to my worries and being a friend.

Paige—As always, your commitment to my stories and your honesty is invaluable.

Michelle—My spreadsheet lover. There simply aren't enough words to describe how thankful I am for what you've done for me. But thank you. Not only for reading my work and believing in it, but for being one of the most beautiful friends a girl could ever have.

To all the lovely ladies in my Tea Room—Thank you for your enthusiasm and support of my books. But mostly, thanks for the wonderful friendship. I love you all tremendously!

Jenny from Editing4indies—I can't believe I'm writing these out again for the fourth time this year. And a huge part of why I'm able to do so is thanks to you. You're stuck with me!

Ena and Amanda from Enticing Journey—Thank you!!

Stacey from Champagne Book Design—Once again, I'm blown away by your professionalism and talent.

Sarah from Okay Creations—Thank you for creating a cover I want to stare at for the rest of my days.

And to the readers and bloggers who took a chance on me and are still doing so… you're amazing. It's indescribable, the way it feels to have that kind of support.

It's never forgotten and always, always appreciated.

ABOUT THE AUTHOR

Ella Fields lives in Australia with her husband, children and two cats. While her children are in school, you might find her talking about her characters and books to her two cats.

She's a notorious chocolate and notebook hoarder who enjoys creating hard-won happily ever afters.

Find Ella here:

Facebook:
facebook.com/authorellafields

Website
authorellafields.wixsite.com/ellafields

Instagram:
www.instagram.com/authorellafields

Goodreads:
www.goodreads.com/author/show/16851087.Ella_Fields

CPSIA information can be obtained
at www.ICGtesting.com
Printed in the USA
LVHW090754080122
708102LV00019B/394